# AGE OF CHIVALRY
## Book 3

# D.L. Narrol

# AGE OF CHIVALRY
## Book 3

DOUBLE DRAGON

# Chapter One

Late September 1910 Captain Colin Limmerick stood by the gunnel of his vessel. The ship's two steam pipes blew off excess as the one sail caught the chilled wind off the Irish Sea. He cranked away at the reel to bring in the latest catch. He put his bulging biceps to work as he pumped away at drawing the catch into the hold of the ship. The captain's first mate, Eddy, stood behind him as he watched the tall, robust captain put his muscles to work. The fish made it into the hold, while the captain stared at the sea.

"Captain?" Eddy asked.

The captain gazed at the sea, as if he were in a trance. He winced with panic when he saw several people splashing about in the water. He reached for his bottle of whiskey, which sat on the planked floor of the deck. He took a few swigs and continued to stare. People squirmed and gasped for air as they slowly sank below the captivating waves. Their screams became less and less until only a few remained afloat.

"Captain? Are yaz feelin' alright?" Eddy asked.

The last of the victims kept repeating the same phrase in Gaelic.

"Long live our Lord! And, long live Ireland."

The captain bit his lip with horror as he watched each one of them sink into the frigid sea.

"Captain! Captain Colin! Are yaz feelin' ill, or what?"

Colin turned to his first mate. "Oh, God!"

Eddy stepped closer to him. "What is it that ya see out there?"

Colin appeared horrified. "Oh, God! Sweet Christ!" He took the whiskey bottle and placed it against his lips. He started to drink profusely, while he focused on Eddy. He gazed at his first mate with penetrating eyes. Eddy noticed a tear run down his captain's cheek.

"Oh, sakes, Captain, yar cryin'? What's wrong?" Eddy pulled the whiskey bottle from his captain's hands. "Imagine a big strong man like yarself is cryin'. Ya got every wench chasin' after yaz. The crew goes on about how much they wished they had yar good looks and brains. Can't believe a man with so much to offer is cryin'."

Colin looked at Eddy with his lips parted. He unbuttoned his jacket. He pulled his tartan scarf from his broad neck and unbuttoned his shirt. Eddy could see his bare chest and stomach.

"Look at me."

Eddy noticed a deep scar on Colin's belly. "Oh, God! Captain, what happened?"

Colin examined his wound for the umpteenth time. He ran his large hands over bumpy aftermath of skin.

"What happened, ye ask, Ed? A sword did this to me."

"Oh, good Lord. What kinda mess did yaz get yarself into? Since when ya play with swords?"

"Since lately, I suppose."

"Are ya cryin' 'bout the wound, or are yaz in pain from it?"

"It does still cause me pain, so it does. Rosa stitched it up."

"Rosa? She's no medical doctor. Isn't she an archeologist?"

"That she is, but there wasn't a physician around. I'm not cryin' 'bout me wound, but tell me somethin', Ed? Are there people drowin' in the sea just now?"

Eddy slowly turned his head. He squinted his eyes as he scanned the water.

"I'm not seein' them, Captain."

Colin turned to his first mate. "What ye mean?"

Eddy sighed with frustration. "I'm confiscatin' yar whiskey. Ya really gotta cut down, don't ya think?"

Colin buttoned his shirt. "Cut down? So, ye think I'm a lush, do ye?"

"Think? I know. We's all gotta cut down, don't ya think?"

Timmy in the wheelhouse climbed down to the deck to where his captain was talking to the first mate.

"Howye, Captain?"

Colin tipped his tweed cap at his crewmember. "Timmy."

"Gotta message from me wench for ya, Captain."

"How is Deidre these days?" Colin asked.

"She says she's dyin' to see yaz again, Captain. I think she's in love with yaz."

Eddy placed his hand on Timmy's shoulder. "Be a good lad 'n leave us be for now. Yar captain has run into a problem, eh?"

Timmy sprinted to the galley. Eddy chuckled.

"Kids today."

Colin sat on the ledge of the deck. "I know ye don't know what me work is like at the university, but..."

"Ya never tell me anythin' 'bout yar research. Yaz always been very secretive 'bout it."

"I'm a fishin' captain and PhD candidate at the London University; strange combination, isn't it? But ye know, Ed, I was the one with the high grades in school. Here I am a simple man, a fisherman at that. Yet I always had that crave for research and higher education. But I've noticed the other PhD candidates like Rosa came from wealth. Did ye know her father was a professor? Same with Amoli's father."

"Of course, Captain, those that go to university don't come from workin' class people like us, eh?" Eddy nudged Colin's arm.

"So, why would I bore the first mate of me ship with me university bunk?"

"I've known yaz since ya was a wee lad on yar uncle's ship. Nothin' ya have ever said to me was ever borin'."

7

"Yer too kind, Ed. Can ye give me back me whiskey bottle now?"

Eddy handed it back to his captain.

Colin took a few swigs. "Don't want ye to repeat any of this."

"Captain, ya know ya have me word."

"I've been travelin' to past times in history, so I have."

Eddy grabbed Colin's whiskey bottle and took a large gulp. "Time travel?"

"Aye." Eddy took another gulp of whiskey. "Wanted to prove *Megaloceros giganteous* was sexually selected against 10,000 years ago, which led to its demise."

"The Irish elk yar speakin' of?"

"Deer, it was a deer."

"Deer, elk, what's the difference?"

"I was away from the ship earlier this year, remember?"

"Of course."

"I was in 840 AD helpin' the ancient Celts battle the Vikings."

"Oh, sweet Jesus," Eddy's eyes bounced around showing his nervous twitch. "Lord love ya, yar speakin' gibberish are yaz?"

"It's time travel, is what it is, if ye can believe what I'm tellin' yez?"

"Time travel?"

"I battled Viking warriors everyday. I even battled the head Chieftain of the Celts for Amoli."

"Amoli was there?"

"Aye. He wanted her for his own. Geez, I had to get her back, Ed."

"When did ya learn to use a sword?"

"Dr. Sasha Dimitrikov taught me in five feckin' minutes."

"Dr. Dimitrikov taught yaz? Sasha? He's an expert?"

"He learned in Russia, so he did. He's quite a skilled swordsman, I must say."

"Really? Yar pretty swift with a bow 'n arrow, though."

Colin took back his bottle of whiskey and drank it down to the last drop.

"Didn't notice a whole lot of archery when I was there, mate."

"Maybe archery wasn't invented yet."

"Donno, really. So, that's me story, Ed. Ye now know all of me secrets."

"Yer a wonder of the world, captain. Time travel, imagine that."

"I've traveled to prehistoric time periods as well. I've seen prehistoric mammals, even *Neanderthal.*"

"A cave man?"

"Sure, if ye wanna address 'im as that."

Eddy sat on the ledge by the gunnel beside his Captain.

"Captain, are you gonna time travel again?"

"I hope not. I'm plannin' a weddin'. I'm gettin' married on Christmas day."

"To Amoli, the little foreign lass from India? She's a beauty, that one. Nice ass on her, I must say." Colin grinned. "Glad to hear yar finally tyin' the knot. It's about time."

"Sunday, I've got to get back to London a tad earlier than usual. Get the boys workin' on the catch for Sunday night, okay?"

"Aye, Captain."

9

# Chapter Two

It was a brisk autumn day. Colin sat on the bench outside on the campus grounds of London University. He put on his glasses and began to read a book. Rosa walked by and noticed him.

"Good morning. What are you doing here so bright and early on a Monday?"

He placed the book on his lap and tipped his bowler hat to her.

"Howye, love? Yer lookin' as beautiful as ever."

She sat beside him. "Where's Sasha these days?"

"Received a letter from him the other day. He's not in Russia anymore, love."

Her eyebrows lowered close to her eyes. "Where is he?"

"He's in Geneva for a conference."

"Geneva? Conference? Is he that important?"

Colin chuckled. "Apparently, he is."

"For what?"

"He's teamed up with a group of Russian mathematicians 'n physicists, because they've been tryin' to develop a time machine, no doubt."

Rosa stood up to face Colin. "Time machine?"

"Aye, love."

"We closed the pathway through time. Our mission was accomplished. His time travel device led us to these unthinkable times in history. Why does he feel he has to create a time machine?"

"Donno. He's always callin' me the crazy one. Maybe he should look in a mirror."

"Do you need to venture back in time again?"

"I should hope not. I'm finished with all that. We're also hopin' we closed the pathway. Sasha did indicate that only time would tell."

"Well, I can't imagine with all that work we did that the pathway wasn't closed. Just can't imagine."

"Sasha should be back within the next few days. He's a busy man, apparently."

"Well, I suppose he is."

"Just by readin' his letters it didn't seem like he spent much time in Russia. Donno if his wife came with him to Geneva. Likely not, I assume."

"Oh, yes, his wife." She grimaced. "I almost forgot that he's married."

Colin took her hand. "A lovely wench like yerself should find yerself a nice gent, don't ye think? Don't waste yer time on Sasha."

"I'm not wasting my time on Sasha. I'm wasting my time on you."

He paused. "I see."

"I still think there's hope for us." Her eyebrows lifted.

He sighed with frustration. "Love, I'm marryin' Amoli on Christmas day. Me mind is made up."

"You've broken your engagement to her before, you can do it again."

"Ye don't want me, ye just think ye do."

Her delicate hands slid under his jacket and felt around for his chest.

"Yes, I do. I'd marry you right here and now."

"Ye wouldn't, ye can't seem to get past who I am."

"I know exactly who you are, Colin Limmerick."

"Ye don't. I'm a drunken fisherman whose only real experience with wenches is with whores. Ye have a hard time with that, I know. But now I have Amoli; she's changed everythin' for me, so she has."

"Yes, Amoli has brought you the happiness I could never give you."

"Ye can't deal with me past 'n Amoli can."

"My only problem is with Lorelei. I don't like her."

"She's always upon me ship, so she is. Ye'd have to get used to her if ye 'n me was a couple again, I mean."

11

Colin rubbed his large rough hands over his face. "Why are we even havin' this conversation? I'm gonna marry Amoli this Christmas."

"No, you're not."

He placed his hands on her shoulders. "Love, why ye doin' this?"

"You love me and I love you, so what's the problem?"

"Yer tolerance level of a drunken sea captain like me is very low, that's the problem."

"When you finally complete your PhD dissertation, will you remain in London?"

"Don't think I would. I've invested too many years in me ship."

"So, Amoli would live with you on the Atlantic Mermaid?"

"She may."

Rosa tore away from him with her hands in the air. "Rubbish!"

"Amoli accepts me, ye don't."

"She's a fool."

"That's obvious, because she's chosen me."

Rosa paced. "Sasha still hasn't mentioned his wife to me. Can you believe that?"

"Of course. I urged him to tell ye, but he must've backed down."

"What a swine he is."

She sat tightly beside him on the bench. He turned to her and ran his finger under her chin.

"Love, don't go chasin' rainbows."

She folded her arms. "He lied to me, Colin."

He pulled his watch from his vest pocket. "I've really got to keep an eye on the time. I've got to see Professor Cushing in a few."

"Is he finally going to sign off on your dissertation?"

"Likely, not."

"You've polished that paper with utter perfection. Is he refusing to sign off?"

12

"He left me a brief note. It didn't appear too positive. He never did fancy me research on *Megaloceros giganteous*."

"How absurd. I thought the chancellor was going to fix things between you and Dr. Cushing."

"She also left a note. Apparently, she's cross with me."

"Oh, my, Colin, I told you not to get mixed up with her. She's the chancellor of the university. She has the power."

He stared into Rosa's eyes and bit his lip. "I'll be seein' her later today in her office."

"It's always later, isn't it?" Rosa stood up. "If she has champagne ready I'd refuse it." He smiled. "Colin, if you want champagne so badly buy it yourself."

He stood up and bent over to kiss her on the lips. She blushed.

"Gotta run, so I do."

She grinned at him. He smiled back and walked off. Shortly Colin found himself at Professor Cushing's office door at the university. He gave a slight knock.

"Yes?"

"Sar, it's me."

"Ah, yes, Colin, do enter. I've been meaning to chat with you."

Colin took a deep breath and stepped inside his professor's office.

"There's nowhere to sit, sar."

"That's right. That old stool of mine finally gave out. Timothy Duncan was sitting on it at the time."

Professor Cushing hacked with laughter and then suddenly wore a serious expression on his face.

"Better him than me. I'm much bigger, which means I'd fall much harder."

"Did you know Timothy has a scheduled defense date for his dissertation?" Colin leaned against the wall and removed his hat and jacket. "If you think you are even close to your defense date you better think again." Colin turned to the wall to concentrate on a spider that tried to blend in with the chipping paint. "What do you think about that?"

Colin appeared startled as his concentration on the spider was interrupted.

"What, sar?"

"I am simply saying that you are not close at all to your oral examination."

*"Janey mac, well, well,"* Colin blurted, with a sigh.

Professor Cushing lifted his eyebrows. "Is that all you have to say?"

"Let me guess, yer unhappy 'cause I didn't include a chapter on yer horseshoe crab?"

"Yes! Colin, you are correct!"

"Well, at least I'm right 'bout somethin'."

"You see, the entire idea of gaining acceptance into the doctorate program basically means that you are to work under the direction of an academic advisor. You are supposed to do what your academic advisor, meaning me, tells you."

Colin sighed as he repositioned himself against the wall.

"Bollocks this is! Ye don't appear very well versed in evolution at all, sar. I was matched with yez 'cause ye was supposed to be an expert."

Dr. Cushing leered at Colin. "How dare you speak to me in that tone! I should have refused you from day one. You're nothing but an underclass Irish peasant."

Colin placed his hat on his head and recklessly put on his coat. He violently swooped his arm along Dr. Cushing's desk and pushed his belongings onto the floor with a crash. Dr. Cushing jumped up.

"This is so menacing of you! How dare you!"

Colin stood back from the mess on the floor.

"Yer lucky I didn't do this to ye."

Colin primped his coat and hat and stepped out of the office. Later that afternoon Colin sat in his university office going over student papers.

"So, Limmerick, I heard what you did to poor Dr. Cushing. This could cost you your doctorate," Timothy Duncan said, poking his head through the door.

Colin stared at him from behind a wood desk. "Good news travels fast, ye little wanker."

"You are definitely out of control. You're like a wild man."

"So I am," Colin said, placing his glasses on his face. "Would ye mind closin' the door? I've got loads to do just now."

"Only God could help you now." Colin removed his reading glasses and grinned. Timothy felt someone from behind push him into Colin's office. "I beg your pardon?"

"Get out of my way. You like fly on wall, you are pest, da?" Sasha Dimitrikov said, barging his way into Colin's office.

"Sasha! Good to see yez, mate!" Colin said, with a smile.

Sasha pulled up a chair and made himself comfortable.

"I come sooner than letter say, because I miss my Miss Rosa."

Colin stared at Timothy. Timothy stared back at Colin.

"Oh, I suppose I should be leaving," Timothy said, timidly.

Colin chuckled as Timothy exited. "Finally, the fool left."

"I not like him; he is stupid."

"How was Geneva?"

Sasha pulled out a cigarette from his jacket.

"I will say you; but first, I must smoke."

"I can't wait for ye to finish yer bloody fag. Just tell me about the conference."

"Mr. Limmerick, you so impatient. Are you ready?" Sasha searched his jacket for a match. He found one and lit the fresh cigarette in his mouth. "Ready?"

"What happened in Geneva?"

"Me with great Russian scientists created time machine."

"So, ye said in the letter."

"Oh. I say you already?" Colin grinned at him and scratched his head. "It will take you to past and maybe future. You want future next time?"

Colin laughed. "Me? Next time?"

"Da."

"What would I do with the future?"

"How far you want to go? You want 1914? You want 1939? You want 2014?"

"Nay, there's just nothin' I need with those years."

"You would meet your children's children, Mr. Limmerick."

"I just want Cushing out of me hair, is all."

"Dr. Cushing bad man. I will send him to year 2025, da?"

Colin chuckled. "Would ye stop, Sasha?"

"Mr. Limmerick, I will be most famous scientist in all world."

"What ye sayin' here, man? What ye meanin' by famous?"

"I will charge fee and take all people to chosen time in past. I will be rich!"

Colin shut his eyes. "Mate, ye wanna take passengers, is that what yer implyin'?"

Sasha grinned at him. "Passengers? Da, that is what I will do."

"Yer a fine feck, aren't yez? Ye can't bloody well be takin' passengers on this time machine of yers? Are ye mad? Yer time machine isn't a carousel ride at the fair."

Sasha grinned as if he had gone mad. "Better than carousel can ever be. I will do it. I will be most famous man in world. You will still be on your boat fishing for mackerel."

"Don't care if I get old 'n croak at sea, mate. Ye just can't be takin' people's money so ye can put them into life-threatenin' situations."

Sasha searched his jacket for another cigarette. "What is life-threatening?"

"Time travel is."

"It is only life-threatening if you get into fight with *Neanderthals*, head chieftain's of ancient Celtic clans, and try to irritate prehistoric monsters."

Colin rolled his eyes. "Oh, Mother of God, help this man."

"I am honest man and I will make honest money."

Colin stood up from his desk. "Nay, yer not."

Sasha's smile dissipated. "Not what?"

Colin walked around his desk and fondled his keys. "Yer not honest." Colin grabbed his coat off the coat rack. "Ye don't know the meanin' of the word."

"Where ye going?"

"I've got to see the chancellor, but I'll definitely make sure Rosa knows what yer intensions are. Sometimes ye can stoop low, mate, very low."

A muster of tobacco smoke filled the room. "You not tell Rosa. I not feel like her silly woman lecture."

"Get out of me office. I'll tell her 'n she'll definitely give ye one of her lectures. Yer such a shite sometimes," Colin said, as he slipped on his jacket.

Sasha casually smoked his cigarette. "You kick me out?"

Colin sighed. "I'm not. I've gotta be somewhere just now."

Sasha sprung up from his chair. "You jealous."

He strutted out of the office. Colin rolled his eyes back and blurted a faint chuckle. He scurried out of the building and crossed the street. He wrapped his tartan scarf around his neck.

"What's the hurry, big boy?" Colin turned his head to see Rosa there in a long blue coat wearing a hat with a blue feather. "Where are you rushing off to?"

"I think I need to see the chancellor."

"Oh, Colin, I told you to keep your distance from her. From what you told me she sounds dangerous."

Colin smiled and fiddled with his scarf. "Things aren't going well with Professor Cushing."

"When have things gone right with Professor Cushing?"

"Never."

"She hasn't done anything regarding your situation with your advisor, has she?"

"Ye meanin' Evelyn? She funded our last time travel expedition, did she not?"

Rosa shifted her eyes. "Yes, of course, but she hasn't made any attempt to place you with a different advisor."

"Well, I was just going to her office to demand a different advisor. I can no longer work with that shite." He took Rosa's hand and held it tightly. "Wish me luck."

As he stepped away from her, she tugged at his jacket sleeve.

"Do not accept anymore champagne or food from this woman. She's the chancellor of the university."

"Ye must think I'm a child?"

"Colin Limmerick, I know how you are when you're offered fine alcohol."

He grinned at her. "Love, I'll see ye later, hmm?"

He broke from her and walked off. He crossed several streets and made it to the chancellor's office. A receptionist sat at the front of a typewriter. Colin removed his bowler hat and gave a slight bow.

"Would Chancellor Evelyn Gordon be up to seein' me for a bit?" Colin asked with a forced smile.

"She's busy."

18

Colin's eyes scanned the room. He continuously put his weight on one foot, then changing to the next foot. "I have an appointment."

"I see you do have an appointment."

"Can ye tell her Colin is here to see her?"

"I don't know if I could interrupt her now. She's in a meeting with one of the deans."

"I see. Well, if ye get a chance, could ye try to let her know I'm here?"

"I'll see what I can do."

Colin stepped back and sat in the waiting room. The dean exited the office and Colin perked up in his seat. The receptionist entered the chancellor's office and then entered the waiting room.

"She says she will see you now."

Colin smiled as he sprung up from his seat to pace into the Chancellor's office.

"Evelyn, forgive me, I hope I'm not disturbin' ye."

She was watering her plants. "Enter, Colin. I wanted to have a chat with you." He entered her office with his hat in his hand and his jacket draped over his arm. "Please sit a bit. I was just minding my rhododendrons. They're not looking their best, I'm afraid."

"Shouldn't they be planted in yer garden outside?"

"Oh, yes, you could be correct about that. They really don't care for my office." Colin tapped his foot and she noticed. "Are you nervous about something? Shall I order some champagne?"

He stood up. "I don't need champagne at this hour, if ye don't mind me sayin'?"

"You? Refusing champagne? Something very serious must be on your mind."

"I can refuse a drink when offered to me," he said, as he loosened his tie.

"No, you can't."

He stared at the floor. "I can."

She peered at him. "What's bothering you?" she asked, as she continued to fuss over her plants.

"I initially came to ye with a complaint about me academic advisor. I spoke to the dean and he wasted me time. He suggested I bring this to yer attention."

She fluttered around her office and finally decided to sit at her desk.

"And, your point is?"

"Me point is he's still me academic advisor."

She placed the end of a pencil in her mouth. "A big strong handsome man like yourself can't deal with your pesky academic advisor? Boohoo, Colin."

"He strongly dislikes me for reasons that have nothin' to do with me research or me academic writin'."

"Oh, really? Well, allow me to elaborate. Dr. Cushing came to see me the other day. And he wanted to know if you and I are, you know, involved, if you can imagine?" She kept the pencil in her mouth and sucked on it. "What do you think, Colin?" She stood up and stepped very close to where he was sitting. "I know you want me right here and now. I'm all too sure that you would make whoopee with me right here in this office."

His eyes bounced around the room. "Evelyn, please. Don't do this."

She eased herself onto his lap and linked her arms tightly around his neck.

"Kiss me."

"I don't think we should do this anymore. It isn't right; yer the chancellor of the university. Dr. Cushing suspects us."

"I visualize you in my bed every night and I'm sure you do the same about me." She pressed her lips against his. "You used to thrust yourself into me, in and out, in and out. You are very creative in bed. I want to feel your big hard muscles again."

He tried to pry her off of him. "I wish ye the very best, but I wasn't attached to anyone when we had those few times together. Now, I am someone's suitor."

She slid off his lap. "Suitor? You're someone else's suitor? How dare you?"

"I'm sorry, Evelyn."

She stepped away from him. "Oh, my! How stupid of me to allow myself to get taken in by your manhood!"

His eyes widened. "Evelyn?"

"You are such a brute!"

"I thanked ye profusely for the fundin', but I'm goin' after payin' ye back. I should be able to have the money to ye by early next week."

"I don't want your Irish money!"

His lips parted as he took his time to respond. "Nothin' wrong with," his eyes shifted, "acceptin' Irish money, nothin' wrong with that. I think it's the least I can do, don't ye think?"

"You're somebody else's suitor? Who is she? You've been unfaithful to me."

"Unfaithful? "

"You believe your own lies. You're just awful. How dare you take advantage of me? You just wanted me for my body, you big brute!"

He sighed. "Oh, sweet Christ, that's not it at all." She sat behind her desk and pulled a pink hanky from her drawer so she could cry in it. "Evelyn, please don't cry. I never wanted to hurt ye. Forgive me."

"You robbed me of my true essence, you brute."

He stood on the other end of her desk with an awkward expression on his face.

"Can I do anythin' to make it up to ye?"

She stopped sobbing. "Yes, there is something you can do."

"Tell me 'n I'll do anythin'."

"Lets engage in some serious hanky-panky right here on my desk."

He stepped closer to her. "Evelyn, I can't do that, I'm sorry."

"I didn't tell you the despicable situation you put me in, did I?"

His eyebrows lifted. "Situation? How ye mean?"

She continued to cry in her handkerchief. "Oh, dear lord, what will I do? My life is ruined. Colin," she sniffled, and tried to catch her breath. "I think I'm expecting your child."

He stepped back and tried to sit down in the chair, but he missed it and fell to the floor. She sprung up from her chair and raced to his side. "Let me help you. You're the father of our child."

He tried to hoist his bulked physique up from the floor, but he failed every time. He looked at her.

"Evelyn, how do ye know yer expectin'?"

"I haven't received my monthlies in a few, now."

"Forgive me rudeness, but we do have to consider that yer 59 years old."

She stood up. "Oh, so it bothers you that I'm older than you?"

"It never bothered me. Yer a very attractive wench, but I think when a wench reaches her late fifties she would usually lose her monthlies, don't ye think?"

She had a stern expression on her face. "Are you calling me old?"

He was starting to sweat -- droplets of water fell from his forehead.

"Old? Not at all. But all wenches experience a biological change when they pass age 50, is all I'm sayin' to ye."

"Perhaps, but isn't it all too interesting to know that I have never missed my monthlies and now that you have stepped into my life I am now missing them. I should hope that you won't be a coward like some men and leave me alone to raise our child."

"I wouldn't do that."

"So, then, I suppose we have to wed."

His eyes followed her as she paced. He turned his body on his hands and knees and used a chair to prop himself up from the floor.

"Forgive me for this sudden upset."

"You and I would make a great team, Colin," she said, as she fiddled with her plants again.

He brushed some dust off his jacket. "Team?"

"Is that too strange of a thought?"

"Ye don't wanna team up with me. I'm Irish 'n that would surely become bothersome to ye."

She scurried over to him. "No, I didn't mean what I said before. I like it that you're Irish."

"Don't matter, really. I think I've got to be pushin' onward, don't ye think?"

She tugged onto his arm. "I know a quaint little place where we can go and have a bite."

He pulled away from her. "Please stop this! Dr. Cushing already suspects us. I'll be asked to leave this university before ye know it, 'n there goes me academic career." He recklessly got hold of the doorknob and flung the door open. "I really must run, now."

She watched him exit her office.

# Chapter Three

It was mid evening when Sasha and Rosa entered the popular university pub across the street. Several men made gestures at Rosa as she timidly trailed behind Sasha.

"I see Mr. Limmerick sitting at the bar," Sasha said as he took Rosa's hand to lead her to Colin.

"I knew he would be here," Rosa snorted.

Rosa and Sasha sat on each side of Colin. Colin glanced at Rosa.

"Love, what ye doin' in here? Yez a wench."

Rosa placed her hand on the bottle of whiskey that sat before Colin. "Oh, Colin, you're drunk again."

He buried his head in his arms. "I suppose I've had a few."

"Mr. Limmerick, time machine has been shipped to university lab from Geneva. You want to see it?" Sasha asked.

"Now?"

"I know you so drunk. Meet me at lab tomorrow morning at eight."

Colin's head hung low as he stared at his almost empty bottle of whiskey.

"If I live to see tomorrow, mate."

Rosa ran her hand along Colin's back. "You appear upset about something. Is everything alright?"

"Just wanted to drop by the pub 'n enjoy some fine Irish whiskey 'n a few pints. Nothin' wrong with that, is there?"

"Well, I think perhaps we should see you home," Rosa said, with concern in her voice.

"Nay, love. I'll be just grand, so I will. Ye 'n Sasha should run along 'n enjoy yerselves, uh?"

"Mr. Limmerick you not look so good. You too drunk."

"Just need to sit a bit."

Rosa tugged on his jacket sleeve. "You're much too big to carry, but I think we should call for a carriage and get you home."

"Not necessary, love."

Sasha stood up and tucked his shoulder under Colin's armpit.

"Help me with this; Mr. Limmerick you must go home."

Colin lifted his arms. "Mate, mate, what ye doin' here? I'll be just dany, so I will."

"I'll have you removed from this pub by force if you really want to push me?" Rosa threatened, in a stern tone.

Colin gave a slight chuckle. "Force, ye say? Then I bes' be on me way."

"Something happened with Chancellor Gordon, didn't it?"

Colin shut his eyes. "Don't want to recall me meetin' with that wench, so I don't."

"Oh, Colin. I told you to stay away from her."

"Ah, love, all is well, now, so it is."

Sasha helped Colin stand up. He pushed Sasha away.

"Mr. Limmerick, you fall over and I cannot pick you up."

Colin started to stumble but insisted he walk without facilitation. The three of them walked to Colin's flat. Rosa took Colin's keys to open the door to his flat.

"Colin, you need to get some sleep."

"Sleep?"

He staggered to his bedroom and began to remove his clothing. Rosa shut the door as she remained in the parlor with Sasha.

"I think its best I shut the door. We don't really need to see him naked."

Sasha laughed, as he pulled out a cigarette.

"I cannot wait until tomorrow morning. I want to see your face expression when you see my time machine."

"I don't think you want to see my facial expression. All this time travel malarkey should come to a close." Rosa perked her ears when she heard the water running in Colin's bathroom. "I'm glad he decided to wash up."

"Why put end to time travel? It is most great experience. In fact, I think all people should do it," Sasha said, looking for a match. "Like fair have rollercoaster, da?"

"Are you out of your mind? Have you forgot how life-threatening time travel can be? In almost all cases time travel goes wrong. The only instance it went well was when that meteor strike occurred in Siberia in 1908 and you had the energy from that to take us exactly to where Colin wanted to be."

"I not need meteor from 1908. I can do this with my own inventions. I am scientist!"

"Sasha Dimitrikov, I am actually embarrassed for you. Sometimes you can be such a fool."

Sasha sat on Colin's couch with ease as he ran an unlit cigarette under his nose.

"You will not say this when I am famous! I will be be rich man!"

Rosa shifted her eyes to the lavatory. "I haven't heard a peep from Colin since the bath water stopped running. Do you think he's alright?"

"He is big boy; he is fine."

"Colin!" she called, with no response. "Oh, my."

"You go see him in bathtub."

"I can't do that, Sasha."

"Why you can't? You afraid to see Mr. Limmerick with no clothes?"

"Of course not. How absurd. Alright, then, I will barge into a man's lavatory when he is bathing, if that suits you?"

"Go see Mr. Limmerick naked, you love him anyways. Go!"

She folded her arms. "Yes, I do love Colin and you apparently are married."

Sasha hacked on his cigarette. "Mr. Limmerick say you this?"

"What difference does it make who told me? How come you never told me about your wife in Russia?"

"You not ask."

She shook with anger as she clenched her hands and stormed off to the bathroom. She gave a faint knock on the bathroom door. "Colin, I'm coming in!"

He was immersed in sudsy water. "Love, ye want somethin' I'm supposin'?" She scanned his naked body and quickly placed her hand over her eyes. He chuckled. "I'd invite ye to join me, but don't think Amoli would fancy the idea."

Rosa removed her hands from her eyes. "Oh, I'm so sorry for barging in."

"You've seen me bare balls before; it shouldn't be such a shock now, should it?"

She backed up out of the lavatory. Sasha continued to sit and smoke.

"Why you look like you see ghost? You see Mr. Limmerick naked, da?"

Rosa sat beside Sasha. "Yes. It wasn't the first time. Tomorrow morning Colin and I will be in the laboratory to see your time machine. Maybe you should leave now."

"You mad at me because I have wife?"

"Well, I'm a little perturbed that you never informed me that you're married. I feel like a fool."

"I forget to say you."

Rosa stared at the floor. "What kind of a man are you? You were so determined to take me away from Colin. He could have killed you that night and now I find out you have a wife back in Russia. You're despicable."

"You so beautiful lady I can not resist."

"I don't know how you can live with yourself, Sasha."

27

"I live with myself, okay, I think," he said, blowing smoke rings with his cigarette.

She sighed. "Can you please leave, and we'll see you in morning at the laboratory."

He stood up to grab his jacket. "You not want to share vodka with me, even?"

"I don't think so."

Sasha slowly walked to the door. He put on his jacket and smiled at her as he left the flat. Colin entered the room with a towel wrapped around his bottom half.

"Sasha just leave, did he?"

"Yes. Tomorrow we'll meet him in the laboratory and see this time machine of his."

"Brilliant, so it is."

"I suppose. Are you expecting Amoli at any time?"

"She's at her aunt's house just now. She's expectin' me to turn up, no doubt."

"Well, I should be leaving."

Colin took a step toward Rosa. "Ye don't have to rush off, if ye don't want to."

"I've got work to do in the lab. I'm also teaching courses, just as you are."

"I understand."

She gave him a frozen smile and left.

# Chapter Four

Colin and Rosa met on the campus grounds early in the morning. Colin wore his glasses, his bowler hat, and a dark suit. Rosa was in a dark velvet blue dress with a long navy blue coat to match. They entered the Natural History building and walked up the dimly lit stairwell, which led to the laboratories. They entered the lab and found Sasha.

"Good morning, Sasha. We made it. Show us this mad invention of yours," said Colin, while removing his hat.

"Yes, Sasha, you definitely have us curious about this new invention," Rosa said, while she removed her gloves.

Sasha appeared anxious. "Not even kiss on cheek for my great accomplishment as scientist?"

"If you're asking me to give you a kiss, you're asking the wrong woman. Ask your wife."

He cackled as he walked closer to the time machine, which had a sheet draped over it.

"You ready?"

"Aye," Colin responded, as he leaned his body against the wall.

Sasha pulled the sheet off of the machine. "Here it is!"

Rosa's eyes widened. Colin flinched a few times as his eyes were fixed on the contraption. Rosa walked around it a few times. Her lips were parted. "This is a time machine?"

"The one and only!"

Colin grinned. "Well, it's definitely an interestin' piece of work, I must say."

Rosa continued to circle around it. She ran her hands along the wrought iron rails on each side. She stepped inside it and noticed the large dial that acted as a ceiling looking down. She stepped on the footstool and placed her hands on the handles.

"How many people can travel in this thing, Sasha?" she asked.

"Six. As you see, there is no place to sit. You must stand."

"The large dial resembles yer time travel device, only so much larger," Colin commented.

"So, Sasha, are you planning on charging admission?" Rosa asked.

"Why not?"

"All your patrons will either end up dead, or they will never return to 1910," Rosa said, with a serious expression on her face.

"This is time machine not time travel device."

"I see."

Colin stepped inside it. "So, ye can't sit down, eh? Me head is touchin' the dial. Ye didn't design it for taller gents like me."

"You must bend your knees," Sasha blurted.

"What if I don't want to? Does me head go right through the dial if we get a bumpy ride?"

"You must bend your knees, Mr. Limmerick."

"I won't do that. Don't want to."

Rosa tossed her hands in the air and sighed with frustration.

"Colin, just bend your knees."

"Mr. Limmerick, we close pathway through time. Why you want to go on time machine?"

"Dr. Cushing is insistin' I travel to prehistory and count the horseshoe crabs' legs. He's demandin' I include a chapter on that sort of junk."

"Are you really going to write a chapter on the horseshoe crab?" Rosa asked.

"I have to, or he'll never sign off for me defense date."

"That's just awful. I'm so sorry, Colin," Rosa said, clutching onto his arm.

"I'll do it to make 'im happy. I've never really taken his direction much on anythin', so I suppose I need to do this, unfortunately."

"Did you tell Chancellor Gordon this?" Rosa asked.

"She's more concerned about usin' me as a trophy, so she can look good in front of her friends."

Rosa glanced at Sasha, who appeared bored of the conversation.

"Well, Mr. Limmerick, when you want to travel back in time and what time period you want?"

"What difference does it make if I request a time period? We always end up somewhere completely different," Colin blurted.

"This is time machine. No more time travel device. This machine is accurate," Sasha responded, in a curt tone.

"Oh, well, then, I think it would be best if it could take me 10,000 years into the past."

"Same as first prehistoric journey?"

"Aye."

Rosa stepped in front of Sasha.

"Wait a minute, gentlemen, there hasn't been another meteor strike on earth since 1908; that's how you launched us back in time before by using the device. How will this time machine get the magnetic energy to do the same thing?" Rosa asked.

Sasha cackled. "Oh, my dear Rosa. I use steam now."

"Steam?" Rosa questioned.

"Da, steam work as good as meteor strike."

"There's no comparison. The meteor strike in Siberia is what got us to where we wanted to go with no errors, Sasha!"

Colin slid his arm around Rosa. "Love, perhaps steam works just as well. I fuel me ship with steam."

"Colin, your ship is not a time machine."

Sasha pursed his lips together. "So, don't come! I not want you to come anyway. You are bad lady and non-believer."

31

Colin took a few steps closer to Sasha and pushed him."Stop it, mate! Rosa needs to come; she's an archeologist. We need her expertise, don't ye think?"

"Nyet, I not think she is asset to our next time travel expedition."

Rosa clutched onto Colin's arm. "I would only go to accompany Colin, otherwise I wouldn't bother myself," Rosa said, in a partial whimper.

"You so in love with Mr. Limmerick. He will marry Miss Amoli Christmas day. You out of luck."

"I am aware of that." She turned to Colin with wet eyes. "I don't think I'm needed here today. I'll go to my office and prepare my lecture, if you don't mind."

Colin embraced her and kissed her on the head. She smiled and left the laboratory. Colin glared at Sasha.

"Are ye mad, man? Ye hurt her so much. Yer a fine feck if I ever saw one."

"Hurt her? Rosa is stronger than you and me together. I have no mercy for that lady."

"Obviously."

# Chapter Five

It was late Sunday night. Amoli was helping her mother and aunt prepare dinner in the kitchen. There was a knock at the door. Amoli's older sister answered it. "Hello, Colin, please come in."

Colin took her hand in his. "I hope I'm not too late. I just left the harbor."

"I know. Please sit and I will fetch Amolia."

Colin sat in the parlor and while the smell of curry filled the room. Amoli entered. She walked toward him and paused. "You're a little late," she said.

"I came straight here from me ship."

"You work too much. What will we do when we marry?"

"Ye can join me on the ship."

"Will you still partially reside in London?"

"Donno, really."

"Will you buy me a house?"

"If ye want me to."

"Can my sister live with us? She is already 24 and without a husband."

"Doesn't yer father have a stash of husbands somewhere in India?"

She chuckled. She stepped closer to him and eased onto his lap. "I am still not expecting your child. My menses unfortunately returned."

"Maybe yer nervous about the weddin'?"

"Excited is what I am. My mother is making my dress. We will have Indian cuisine."

Colin smiled. "Yer plannin' on burnin' a hole in me family 'n friend's guts, are ye?"

"If you wish to put it that way. Indian food has spices in it. Your food, I find, is very bland."

33

She cuddled in his arms and kissed him several times on the lips.

"Amoli, I've got to tell ye somethin'."

She immediately sprung up. "What?"

"I've gotta time travel again."

Her eyes widened. "Again?"

Colin fiddled with the buttons on his coat.

"Why?"

"Me arse professor is demandin' I provide a chapter on the alleged horseshoe crab's evolutionary process datin' back 10,000 years ago."

She smacked her hands over her face and started to cry. "Oh, Colin, when is this time travel nonsense ever going to stop?"

"I really don't fancy the idea, so I don't."

"So, then don't go."

"Dr. Dimitrikov has built this time machine, ye see. He says it's more effective than the device was."

She grimaced. "Time machine?"

"I think I'm gonna do this, lass."

"Then I'm coming with you. I'm sure Miss Emanuel is coming as well. It's so very obvious that she still loves you. I don't care, I have to come."

"Amoli, really wish ye wouldn't worry yerself over her."

"I don't like her. I find her to be very rude."

"Oh, Lord, please let's not do this, lass."

Amoli's mother and sister entered.

"Dinner is served," her mother announced.

They placed several large plates of Indian cuisine on the table. Colin stood up and took Amoli's hand.

"It all looks lovely," Colin said, smiling at her mother.

Dr. Sharma entered. "Good to see you, Colin."

Colin shook his hand. "I haven't seen ye at the university lately, sar."

"That is correct. I have taken some time off, because I must help my wife and daughter plan the wedding."

"Oh, I see. I didn't realize it takes so much time to plan a weddin'."

"Well, if we don't do it, it will not get done, now will it?"

Colin gave a frozen smile.

"Please, Colin, sit beside Amolia," Mrs. Sharma encouraged.

"Please, mother, do not give Colin such spicy food; he's European. He was very ill last time," Amoli cautioned.

Colin smiled. "It looks brilliant, so it does."

Dr. Sharma had the first taste and everyone else followed. Amoli poured the wine.

"Father, mother, I would like to inform you that I will be helping Colin with his next field work assignment for his academic advisor."

Dr. Sharma sat back in his chair. "Is it time travel again?"

"Aye, sar. I'm sorry for that, but Amoli insists on coming along."

"Well, of course, she will soon be your wife." Colin smiled, as he watched Amoli's kid brother enter the room and grimace. "Time travel is risky. I am not keen on my Amolia accompanying you on such an adventure," Dr. Sharma blurted.

Amoli stared at her food. "Father, I will do it, despite your wishes."

Dr. Sharma chuckled. "Of course, my Amolia has a mind of her own. We can no longer hold this girl down."

"I'll do me best to keep her safe. She'll soon be me wife 'n I love her to bits."

Amoli grinned with explosive happiness. "Oh, Colin, why do we have to wait until Christmas day? I want to be your wife right now!"

"Oh, well, lass, if yer comin' with me on the next prehistoric expedition, then it'll surely take some time."

She sighed with frustration and stared at the plate in front of her. Dr. Sharma and his wife made sure Colin had ample food on his plate. Amoli's brother stood beside where Colin sat at the table and watched Colin eat. Colin had become used to being stared at when eating, so he ignored him. Dr. Sharma bent over the table and tried to pile more food onto Colin's plate. Colin put his hand in front of his plate.

"Please, I think there's enough, thank-ye."

"Are you refusing my wife and daughter's fine cuisine?" Dr. Sharma asked with his eyes bulging out of his head.

Colin smiled at him and watched Mrs. Sharma shovel more food onto his plate. He finally took notice of Amoli's brother standing beside him. They continued to eat. Everyone was silent. Amoli put down her fork.

"Colin."

"Aye, lass?" he responded, with food stuffed in his mouth.

"I am so afraid of another time travel expedition."

Mr. and Mrs. Sharma stopped eating and stared at Amoli and Colin.

"Lass, I caution ye not to come. I would definitely do me very best to protect ye, but as ye already know with time travel there's no guarantees."

Amoli nestled up to Colin's arm. "I have to come with you. I will soon be your wife."

He took her hand and held it tightly in his. Dr. Sharma slowly stood up from his chair and pointed his finger at Colin.

"You are to see to it that my Amolia is safe at all times."

"There's no question," Colin responded, as he noticed Amoli's brother reveal his slingshot.

36

# Chapter Six

Some hours later, Sasha entered the laboratory. He noticed that he was the only one there. He walked to the back of the room where his time machine was locked up behind a barrier. He pulled out a large key to unlock the lock when he felt somebody standing behind him.

"Why are you so secretive?" asked Rosa.

Sasha turned to her. "It is only you."

"Only me?"

"I am busy man. Go! Leave me."

"I think you're taking this time machine idea too far, Sasha."

"Mr. Limmerick, he need it."

"Colin is not handling his academic advisor very well, either."

"What is he to do?"

"He could have dealt with Dr. Cushing a year ago, when there was still time. He needed to work on changing his Irish brogue a bit. His mannerisms are too working-class, if you know what I mean. Anyway. I would dismantle that time machine and forget all about it."

Sasha laughed. "I do no such thing. I will be rich and famous some day."

"Sasha, you are absolutely mad."

"Go, I must do work."

"Fine, I'll leave. I suppose you have some finishing touches that you feel so compelled to work on. Why don't you ever send for your wife?"

Sasha's smile dissipated. "My wife? Why you ask about her?"

"We all know so very little about her. Is she pretty?"

"Not as pretty as you," he said, as he ran his index finger under her chin.

She stepped back from him. "What's her name?"

"You not need this information."

"What are you trying to hide, Sasha?"

"You ask too many questions. Lady is not supposed to ask so much, especially if she ask so much to man, da?"

Rosa crossed her arms. "Oh, Sasha, please. Yes, I will leave now."

She turned away from him and walked to the exit. Sasha was bent over his time machine as he watched her leave the room. Some minutes passed and Colin entered the laboratory.

"Howye, mate. Still workin' on the time machine?"

"I am very busy. You want to travel with it?"

"Only if it takes me 10,000 years into the past. This last Celtic excursion was not in the cards, so it wasn't."

Sasha smiled. "You make effective Celtic warrior, Mr. Limmerick."

"Me swordsmanship just doesn't have the expertise that ye have, mate."

"This machine will get you to 10,000 years ago."

"Well, then, when do we leave?"

"Who is coming?"

"Rosa, Amoli, ye and me. That makes four."

"We have room for two more, if you want?"

"Who else? Just us four is dany with me."

"Us four, it will be us four again. We leave Monday morning when you come back from your ship, da?"

"Sounds good. I'll inform the wenches 'n we'll be off."

Sasha's eyes widened. "Wenches? Oh, da, you mean ladies. You talk like sailor."

Colin chuckled. "It's what I am, mate."

# Chapter Seven

It was Monday morning. Colin had just returned from his ship. He was wearing rugged fisherman attire. Rosa and Amoli stood in the laboratory, while Sasha went over last minute calculations for their excursion. Colin firmed up his tweed cap on his head.

"Mate, I'm hopin' this time machine will surely get us 10,000 years in the past. Wouldn't want to be launched somewhere that we're not prepared for. We had a rollickin' time on the last time travel expedition, don't ye think?"

Sasha was bent low behind the control box of his time machine.

"Steam should get us to desired destination, Mr. Limmerick."

Rosa shook her head. "I have a bad feeling about steam power."

Sasha stood. "Why you say?"

"I just don't think steam will get us to where we want to go. Steam doesn't employ magnetic energy as it did the first time we time traveled to the prehistoric past," Rosa said.

Amoli nestled into Colin's bicep. "I'm scared."

"I'll be with ye at all times, lass, no need to be scared," Colin reassured her.

Rosa paced around the machine. "I think Amoli is correct. She should be scared. Only God knows where this thing is going to take us."

Sasha took a handkerchief and wiped his sweaty forehead. "Step into machine. We go now." The four of them stepped into the machine. Colin had to keep his knees bent. Sasha had a grin on his face. "Are we ready?" he asked, as he set the huge dial above their heads. A heavy pounding sound like a hammer meant that the machine was in motion. Amoli crept her hands over her ears to null the sound. "Keep hands on handles, Miss Amoli!" Sasha cautioned.

Amoli's eyes bulged as she frantically placed her hands back on the handles. The machine began to spin. Rosa glanced at Colin with a nervous expression on her face. The machine spun at a faster pace with the rate of acceleration increasing with each second. Colin's grip on the handles was so tight, sweat poured from his hands. The machine spun into the vortex of time – faster and faster. They could feel the pressure against their bodies. The sound of the moving dial above their heads spun loudly making a hard crisp propeller sound. Amoli's heart beat so hard she was afraid she was going to have a heart attack. Sasha grinned with excitement as his golden hair blew in the mist of the moving dial. Colin tried to keep his eyes on Amoli and Rosa, but the debris that lifted from the fast moving machine blinded his vision.

They spun with the machine past the speed of light, through the vortex of time. The spinning acceleration pressed against them, where their faces felt stretched. The sounds were loud and crashing. The four time travelers were standing, their knees almost buckled. The pressure intensified.

They finally landed with a turbulent crash. Rosa's head had fallen over the handlebars. She opened one eye to notice that they had landed. Her hair was mussed over her face. She slowly lifted her head as she tried to focus. "Good God, where are we?" she asked.

Amoli lifted her head to acknowledge Rosa and started to cry. "I don't know where we are. I'm so afraid. That was a dreadful ride."

Sasha had fallen to the floor of the machine. He heard the females' voices and opened his eyes. He wiped the blood from his nose.

"We land somewhere now. It look like prehistoric times, da?"

40

Rosa remained standing in the machine. She scanned their surroundings. "Prehistoric? The plant life doesn't look prehistoric to me, Sasha."

"You are only woman. You not know."

"I'm an archeologist. I would be able to recognize if we were set back into prehistoric times."

Colin had fallen. His head lay back where blood dripped off his forehead. Amoli knelt beside him to wipe his head.

"Oh, Colin, please answer me. Open your eyes."

His eyes slowly opened. "Oh, God, help me. I don't time travel too well, so I don't. I feel so ill, so I do."

Rosa knelt on the other side of him. "Don't try to move. Stay still. I can fetch you some water, maybe."

"Don't want any, love. This is typical for me. I just don't time travel well at all."

Sasha noticed the numbers on the dial. "What is this?" he mumbled.

The two women tried to help Colin up. Sasha joined them to give him a hand.

"Mr. Limmerick, we are in year 1487 AD," Sasha said, with a sigh of frustration.

Colin's eyes widened. "We's in the year 1487? Oh, feck to that!"

Rosa rushed to Sasha. "We're in 1487? I told you steam power would not get us to where we wanted to go!"

He stepped back from her. "You not know anything. This has nothing to do with steam power."

"Then, tell us why we're in 1487?"

He glanced at the time machine. "Something go wrong, I not know why."

"None of us wants to be in 1487. We're going to get killed in this time period," Rosa blurted.

"Why you say?"

Colin stepped toward Rosa. "Yeah, why, love?"

"King Henry the 7th is why. This is the time just after *The War of the Roses*. It's a turbulent time and I don't think any of us want to be subjected to any of the torture methods that were used."

"Torture!" Amoli squealed.

"Love, that doesn't mean any of it would happen to us, so it wouldn't."

"Yes, Colin, it certainly would."

Sasha raised his hands. "I not know what to do. Who I pray to now?"

Rosa stepped closer to him. "Are you religious, Sasha?"

"Religion? Some religion, maybe. I live under Czar's rule where there is some."

"The year 1487 was a time where the Catholic Church ruled the government as well."

Colin placed his hand on Sasha's shoulder. "Don't worry, mate. Ye just gotta get us outta here, is all."

"I must try to find why we land in this time."

He bent low behind the machine and started to take it apart. Amoli flinched when she heard the sound of horse hooves hit the ground. She turned her head to find three men dressed in partial armor and chainmail on horses.

"You!" one of the men shouted, as he pointed at Colin.

Colin stepped back. "Aye?"

"You, stand beside such a strange work of God. Who are you?"

Colin stepped toward the man, who remained on his horse.

"Colin Limmerick, so I am."

"I have not seen you at court. You do not serve the king."

"I'm a, um, simple countryman. A fisherman is what I am," Colin answered.

"Fisherman?"

Colin's eyes shifted from side to side. "I serve the king by sellin' his kingdom me catch, uh, so I do."

He glanced at Rosa and she glanced back at him.

42

"I've not seen you. Not at all. You lie!"

"I'm givin' ye me word."

The man swung his leg over and came down from the horse. He walked in front of Colin to examine him.

"You are not part of the king's nobility. I have never cast my eyes upon a man of your large stature. Who are you?"

"Colin Limmerick, so I've already said."

"I don't believe you. You will be burned at the stake for this. What a size you are and yet you exclaim yourself as one of the king's men?"

"Yer judgin' me by me size? Why?"

"Someone of your size would have served the king. You would have led the king's knights to serve the House of Lancaster to return with victory."

"A simple fisherman, so I am. Mean no harm to yez." Rosa and Amoli remained still as Sasha fiddled with the control box of the time machine. Colin glanced at Sasha. "Mate, stop what yer doin' 'n join me here."

Sasha slowly stood up to stand beside Colin. Colin smiled at the three men.

"You are not. How dare you exclaim this?"

Colin tried to breathe, but couldn't. "I'm a fishin' merchant, so I am.

"You're a witch! The king will be notified at once of your presence on these lands."

Colin's eyes widened as he turned to Rosa. His lips were parted as he tried to gather the words to respond.

"Witch? Surely, yer mistaken, man! A fisherman, so I am, but not a witch."

"Lies. You do not resemble the merchants of these lands. The king will be informed and you will be found."

The three men rode off on their horses. Colin gazed at Rosa.

"What a bleedin' shite he is. Where does he gather that I'm a witch?"

Rosa took a breath and placed her hands on Colin's arms.

"You have to think before you speak."

"He wants to cease me, what for?"

"You're built different than them, you speak different. You carry yourself different."

Amoli stepped toward Colin and took his hand in hers.

"How about me? I look different. What will they do to me?"

Colin ran his hand along her cheek. "Oh, God, don't have an answer for ye, lass."

Rosa stepped beside Amoli. "I wouldn't worry. Trade was quite solid with India in 1487."

Amoli looked at Colin. "How does she know so much?"

Colin smiled. "Rosa's a brilliant wench, so she is. What doesn't she know?"

Sasha glanced at the forested area that surrounded them. "I hear voices. Primitive people want my time machine."

Rosa laughed. "Yes, they probably do. I suppose that's what makes us witches."

"I think we bes' leave. We should get the time machine outta sight, wouldn't ye think?" Colin said, with a panicked expression on his face.

"Da, I will help," Sasha sighed, as he squatted down to help move the machine.

"Maybe, we can push it behind a bush or somethin'." The two men moved the machine when a sudden school of arrows whizzed past their shoulders. Colin flicked his head back. "Duck!"

Rosa and Amoli hid behind a large tree. Sasha and Colin lay flat on the ground. Two archers rummaged around looking for anything out of the ordinary.

"Come out! Show yourselves! I know the witches are hiding!" called out one of the archers. Colin could feel a sharp pointed object at his back. "Get up, witch!"

Colin slowly stood up with the arrow still pointed at his back.

"I haven't done anythin' to yez," Colin said, with his arms in the air.

"Turn around and face us! Tell us why you do not serve the king?"

Colin tried to smile at the men. "I serve the king as a fishin' merchant to his kingdom. If ye want me to lead yer knights to the Yorkists, then surely I'll serve the king that way. But haven't the House of Lancaster defeated the Yorkists already?"

"Do not question me. Then we will take you to the king."

The other archer found Amoli and Rosa behind the tree. He grabbed Amoli's arm and shook her violently.

"A foreigner!" shouted the archer.

Colin jumped on the man from behind and punched him to the ground. The other archer pulled out his bow. Colin grabbed it and snapped it over his knee. He grabbed the man by the throat and thrashed him to the ground.

"Get out of me sight!" Colin shouted. "I swear I'll finish yez both right here!" The two crawled on the ground and stood up with their eyes fixed on Colin. "Leave us! We're not witches! Go!" Colin shouted.

The four time travelers watched the two archers run into the brush. Sasha placed his hand on Colin's arm. "Next time, I blow off their heads. I bring gun."

"They was an easy fight," Colin said. "They left their horses as well."

Sasha grinned. "Lucky for us."

"Colin, you don't want to get in trouble in this time period. They used horrible torture methods. Just calm yourself. Sasha needs to get us out of here. This is not the time period we asked for," Rosa pleaded.

Sasha stepped in front of her. "Problem is I not know why we come to this time. All should have gone as planned. I am very upset."

"I know, Sasha. It must be very frustrating for you," Rosa said sarcastically.

Amoli nestled under Colin's arm. "I love you, Colin. You always protect me."

He smiled at her and kissed her head. Rosa gathered some of their belongings.

"Well, maybe we need to camp somewhere away from any towns. The people here appear to be quite horrible. I really wish we didn't land here, Sasha."

Rosa turned her head abruptly when she heard the hard thumping sounds of several horsemen. Colin glanced at Sasha.

"Maybe yer gun should be on-guard, mate."

"I can't believe this. They keep coming to bother us," whispered Rosa.

"I'm so scared!" Amoli blurted, as she stayed close to Colin.

"These are the king's knights; they have very bad attitude. I hate them already," Sasha blurted.

The head knight stopped his horse in front of his band of men.

"I am Sir Williams. I have an order from the king to cease you four. You are suspected of witchcraft."

Colin remained still. "There is no evidence here of witchcraft."

"We have been informed," said Sir Williams.

Colin squinted his eyes where the creases around his eyes became evident. "Informed? By who?"

"By Sir Gallen who was almost killed by the giant."

Colin's eyes widened. "Giant? Who's the giant?"

"You are! You will now be taken to the king. He is curious to see you before you are sent to the dungeon."

Rosa squeezed Colin's arm. "Dungeon? Oh, my God! Sasha get us out of here!"

46

Several knights slid off their horses. They held their swords and pointed them at the four time travelers. They tied up their hands with rope and took them to the king's castle.

When they arrived, the king sat at his throne with his wife beside him. The four time travelers were brought forth, while the rest of the king's court stood back as spectators. Sir Williams stood before the king and bowed to the floor.

"M' lord, I have brought you your request."

The king and his queen examined the time travelers. The queen stared at Colin profusely. Rosa noticed. The king stood up from his throne.

"Do they speak?" he asked Sir Williams.

"Yes, they do, m' lord." Sir Williams looked at Colin. "Speak to the king. Speak!"

Colin stepped forward and bowed to the floor.

"Yer majesty," Colin said, with angst and hesitation.

The king stepped closer to Colin. "Who are you?"

"Colin Limmerick, yer majesty," Colin answered, with his head low to the floor.

"Stand up," ordered the king. Colin stood up and stared at the king with a blank expression on his face. "A man with your build would be very useful in battle, no?"

Colin kept his head low.

"Prove to me that you are not a witch."

"I'm not, yer majesty."

The king stood directly in front of Colin and continued to stare at him. He looked at Sir Williams.

"Take these four to the dungeon."

# Chapter Eight

Colin had spent the night with Amoli in his arms curled up on the damp dungeon floor. Rosa lifted her head, as she noticed a glimmer of sunlight beam through the tiny window high up on the wall. She stood up and brushed the dust off her dress. Sasha was in a deep sleep. She knelt beside him and ran her fingers along the side of his face.

"What? Something wrong?" He snorted as he awoke.

"Wrong? What could be wrong? We're in the year 1487 under King Henry VII. He will probably order all of us to die in the ever so coy and renowned fifteenth-century fashion."

Sasha chuckled. "You read too many history books. Let me sleep some more."

"Sasha, we're in a fifteenth-century dungeon!"

Colin perked his head as Amoli also awoke from the chatter.

"Didn't sleep well, so I didn't," Colin grunted.

Rosa threw her arms in the air. "Of course, you didn't! I'm sure this *trés beau décor* has definitely enchanted you."

Colin stood up and helped up Amoli. She nestled herself in his arm. Two guards arrived; they opened the cell and stepped in. They poked their swords at Colin.

"The queen wishes to see you," one of the gaurds blurted.

"What for?" Colin asked.

One of the guards jabbed the point of his sword into Colin's thigh until he drew blood. Amoli squealed.

"The queen wishes to see you!" the guard commanded.

Colin glanced at Rosa. He slowly kissed Amoli on the lips, and left.

"Miss Emanuel, why do you think the queen wants to see Colin?" Amoli asked, as she tried to take deep breaths.

Rosa shook her head. "Who knows?"

"I must get back to time machine and figure out what go wrong, but I cannot. We are trapped in this terrible place," groaned Sasha.

Rosa paced around the cell. "We can't stay in here. This isn't even fit for rats. I have to think of a way to get us out."

"How about Colin?" Amoli asked, with panic in her voice.

"If I think about what they may have in store for Colin, then I won't be able to find a way to get the three of us out of here," Rosa said, as she tried to refrain from crying.

"Why do everybody always pick on Mr. Limmerick?" Sasha asked, while trying to straighten his shirt.

"He's very noticeable. He towers over everyone; immense muscles, and he has a kind handsome face," Rosa said.

"Well, I don't like it. My poor Colin is always the target for everything," Amoli said.

Rosa ignored Amoli. "I'll come up with an idea to get us out of here."

Colin was brought to the queen. Sir Williams announced his arrival. The queen sat at her throne without any expression on her face. Colin bowed as low as he could to the floor with his head hung low.

"Stand up, Colin Limmerick. I want to see your face. My husband, the king, has business to settle in the north. He will not be present for a some days."

Colin stood straight to face the queen.

"I can see that you are a well-built man. We can use you in battle, but first you must be knighted."

Colin's eyes widened. "Knighted?"

"Agreed?"

Colin stared at the floor, bewildered and silent.

49

"Yes, tomorrow you will be in tournament. The blacksmiths will make armor that could fit a man of your size."

"Tournament, m' queen?"

"Yes, jousting tournament. How is your archery?"

"Fine, I suppose, m' queen."

"Good. This afternoon, you will be going on a royal hunt for venison. You will be suited with a proper sized bow 'n arrow."

Colin remained with his head tilted toward the floor.

"When you pass your way into knighthood, you will be known as Sir Limmerick. Your strength will be an asset to us."

Colin bowed as low as he could go. Sir Williams pointed his sword into Colin's back.

"Will that be all, m' queen?"

"Yes, take him to the blacksmith's quarters."

*** 

Rosa banged on the heavy steel door of the dungeon cell. She called out several times until one of the royal guards entered.

"What's all the noise?" the guard asked.

Rosa stepped close to him and took his hand.

"We haven't been fed yet, my dear man."

"Food, you need food? Of course, I'll fetch you food."

Rosa smiled at him. "Thank-you."

Sasha chuckled. "I understand your plan."

"Good. Just go with it," Rosa said.

"Your beauty can conquer any man," Sasha said, as he undressed Rosa with his eyes.

The guard returned with a tray of food. He placed it on the floor.

"I was able to snatch a flask of wine for you, as well."

50

"Wine? How wonderful," Rosa gasped, as she clung to the guard's arm.

"A fair maiden like you deserves the best," he said.

"Well, then, I don't think it's appropriate for me to be locked up in this cell. I did nothing to wrong the king," she said, as she kissed him on the cheek.

"I will see what I can do." He grinned at her and left.

Amoli sat beside the tray of food. "For dungeon life, this food looks very good."

"We even got wine," Rosa snickered. "Do we have anything to celebrate?"

Amoli's smile dissipated. "I just want to cry."

"Vodka would be better. I would like to smoke, but I cannot."

"Smoke? Are you crazy? They would definitely think we're witches if they saw you smoking a cigarette."

"This is difficult life for me."

"Well, stop dreaming up time machines that can't get it right, Sasha."

"So, beautiful lady with so big mouth. I love you so much."

"No, you don't," she said, as she paced around the dungeon floor. "You never did and you never will."

\*\*\*

Some hours passed where Colin spent some time with the blacksmiths.

"We will make several swords. All of them will fit your size," said the experienced blacksmith. "And all of them will suit your several needs if you are to be knighted. Since you have a jousting tournament coming up this jousting sword should suit you."

Colin smiled and tilted his head to the man as a gesture of thanks. Sir Williams entered the blacksmith quarters.

"The queen wants to see you," he ordered, with the point of his sword in Colin's back.

"Now what?" Colin expressed.

The queen sat at her throne and watched Colin enter.

"Colin Limmerick, how was your day with the blacksmith?" she asked as she stood from her throne.

Colin remained low to the floor. "Very well, m' queen."

"Stand up. I want to see you." He rose. "Sir Williams, make sure Colin is fitted with the correct attire. If he is to be knighted and belong to my court then he must dress accordingly. Take him to the seamstress." Sir Williams glared at Colin. "Sir Williams, get Colin prepared for this afternoon's hunt. Suit him with a proper bow 'n arrow."

"Yes, m' queen."

Later that afternoon Colin was on horseback dressed in woolen hose with velvet doublets, made to fit his body closely. He followed the other knights with his horse as they rode into the dense brush of the English forest. Colin stopped his horse to wait for any traces of deer. He pulled out his bow 'n arrow and targeted the first deer that made its appearance. The knights were impressed at his skill.

"You let it get away on purpose," Sir Williams commented.

Colin lowered his arrow. "Did I?"

"Her majesty and her court need to feast on venison tonight."

"I see. I won't let it get away again."

"You will be knighted before you know it," one of the knights said to him.

"I still have a tournament to pass tomorrow," Colin said grudgingly.

"I don't think you will have a problem with that. You have the physical strength."

\*\*\*

Rosa, Sasha, and Amoli finished eating when the guard returned to their cell.

"I have returned," he said.

"Rosa stood up to face him. "Yes, I can see that. I think there's still some wine left. Would you care for some?"

"Yes, thank-you." She took his hand and brought it to her lips. He sat on the floor by the tray of food. "I must say, I have never come across a maiden as fair as you."

She smiled as she poured him some wine. "Of course, you haven't."

"Who is this man?" he asked, pointing at Sasha.

"Oh, he's my brother. Please, don't mind him. This other maiden is my sister."

He appeared somewhat confused. Amoli paced a bit at the other end of the cell. She turned to stare at the cell guard. She noticed how he stared back at her.

"I will get you out of this dungeon tonight, because I want to see you in my bed chamber," he said.

"Well, in that case, you first must bathe."

"Bathe? Whatever for?"

"Trust me, it will do a world of good for you."

"Where can I bathe?"

She chuckled. "Where? Well, I really don't know where you can actually bathe."

He laughed. "It sounds so different to me. Do you bathe?"

"Well, unfortunately, I haven't lately. But, yes, I normally bathe. Everyday." He shifted closer to her. She smiled as he slid his arm around her back. He looked at Sasha.

"How did you allow your fair sister to end up in a dungeon cell?"

Sasha glanced at him with little interest. "I not know. It just happen. King not like our clothes."

The cell guard took a double take, when he realized Sasha's foreign accent.

53

"Were you born someplace else?"

Sasha lifted one eyebrow while he tasted the wine. "Da. I live under Russian queen for ten years."

Amoli stood away from them and tried to keep a distance from the cell guard. The guard looked at Rosa.

"I want to see you in my chamber tonight. I will come after tea, and you and your siblings shall be released. If the king were to discover this I would be sentenced to death."

Rosa hugged him. "Thank-you. I don't even know your name."

"I am James. What is your name, fair maiden?"

"Rosa."

He stood up and smiled at her as he made his way to the door.

"I think I will love you."

"I feel the same."

He left. Rosa looked at Sasha and took a deep breath. Sasha wrapped his arms around her and kissed her lips.

"I love you. You so beautiful lady."

She pushed him away. "Keep your distance. Remember, you're my brother, so act like one."

\*\*\*

Colin spent the afternoon practicing his archery on whatever small game he could find in the forest. Later, he rode back to the young city of London to park his horse. He walked through the town passing by merchants who had something to sell. He noticed a poorly constructed thatched roofed building, which may have been a pub. He entered, and sat at a long wooden table. A large flask of ale was placed in front of him and he started to drink. Sir Williams sat beside him with a large flask of ale in his hand.

"Tomorrow, first thing, be prepared for your armor fitting." Sir Williams stared at Colin. "Something is bothering you?"

"Aye. Me three friends in that dungeon, is what's botherin' me."

"Oh, yes, well they escaped."

Colin's eyes widened. "They did?"

Colin abruptly exited the pub; he walked briskly through the city where he scanned every inch of scenery for his friends.

"Where would they go?" he muttered, as several young peasant women passed by him with flirtatious grins on their faces. He dashed from the city and entered the outer-forested area. The bushes were dense, as he called out, "Amoli! Rosa! Sasha!"

He plunged through the trees, where he continuously called their names.

"Colin!" Amoli answered back.

"Lass? Where 'bouts are yez, lass?"

"Over here!" she called out, from behind dense brush as she waved her arm.

"Can't really see yez!" She dashed into his arms and they embraced.

"Lass! I found ye! Oh, dear God!"

He gripped her and tightened his arms around her. He kissed her several times on the head, then scooped her up in his arms as he kissed her mouth several times. She smiled with tears of joy running down her face.

"Colin, I was so worried."

He placed her on the ground, as he looked around.

"Where's Rosa 'n Sasha at?"

"I don't know." Tears poured out of her eyes. "I don't know."

His eyebrows lowered close to his eyes with concern. "What ye mean?"

"Last I saw of them is when we all realized the time machine was gone."

"Oh, God."

"I'm so sorry, my love. Dr. Dimitrikov went crazy. I never saw him so upset. Miss Emanuel was crying and screaming. It is so terrible I had to get away. I'm very sorry."

He clutched onto her. "We have to find them."

She was silent as she stared into his eyes with a serious expression. "Tomorrow, I'm in a joustin' tournament."

"What's that?"

"Ye don't wanna know, so I'm tellin' ye."

"I don't want you to keep risking your life to suit the culture of these silly time periods. I want you to stop doing this."

"Now that the time machine is gone I really have no choice but to joust."

"Have you ever done this before?"

"Joust? I run me own fishin' boat, lass. Never really found the time or the need to joust in our year 1910."

# Chapter Nine

Later that evening Colin found some garments to dress Amoli.

"Her majesty the queen has provided me with a small cottage to lodge in. It's quite nice. I want ye with me tonight. Oh, how I've wanted ye these past few nights."

He led her to a thatched-roof cottage. It had a cozy bed in the corner with several warm sheepskin blankets.

"This is lovely, Colin, for the fifteenth-century," Amoli said, embraced in Colin's arms. "I haven't found a bathtub yet."

"Now, lass, we need to find Rosa 'n Sasha. Don't think I could sleep knowin' they's aren't here with us, if ye know what I mean."

"I'm oh, so very worried as well."

He took her hand and kissed it. "Come, lass, I'll lead ye to the horse the queen provided for me. Don't know why she's bein' so kind to a stranger like me."

"Maybe she's just a very nice queen."

Colin looked at her. "Don't think so. I think she fancies me size 'n strength. He hoisted Amoli up upon the horse and then hoisted himself. They rode through the dense dark forest. "Rosa!" Colin called out. "Sasha!"

There was no response. Amoli sat behind Colin on the horse. She kept her eyes wide for any signs of their friends.

"Colin, there was the time machine!" Amoli blurted, as she pointed. Colin reined in the horse and swung himself and Amoli onto the ground. He knelt down to touch the matted brush the machine was on.

"It seemed so heavy. How could they move it?" Colin glanced at her. "Yer right, lass! I don't think they dragged it away or anythin' like that. I just found some pieces of it on the ground. They disassembled it alright."

"Oh. Dr. Dimitrikov wouldn't like that."

Colin stood up. "Sasha! Do ye hear me, man?" Colin called out again.

They heard the brush rustle a few times.

"Da!"

Colin turned around to see Sasha standing behind him.

"So good to see yez, mate! Where's Rosa?"

"She is here with me," Sasha said, expressionless.

Rosa stepped from behind Sasha as Colin pulled her toward him and he wrapped his arms around her.

"Oh, I'm so glad to see yez both."

Rosa buried herself in Colin's arms as a tear trickled down her face.

"Thank God you're alright, Colin. I was so worried when I didn't see you for days. Where did you go?"

"The queen had me practice me archery with other knights 'n squires. Tomorrow she's got me in a joustin' tournament, 'n if I survive that I'll be knighted, if ye can believe it?"

Rosa pulled away from him with Amoli staring at every move she made. "Jousting tournament? Since when you know how to joust?"

"They've already fitted me with armor."

"Armor won't protect you. Colin, you don't know how to joust, or do you?"

"I'm so much bigger than these gents here in this time. What could go wrong?"

"You're such a target because you are so much bigger. You're actually calm about this, aren't you?"

"What else can I do? The queen's men have dismantled the time machine, haven't they?"

Sasha rubbed his hands over his face. "Da," he said, with a sigh of frustration. "I find many pieces scattered everywhere. Why they want pieces of my time machine?"

Colin threw his hands in the air. "The feck I know what these people want!"

Rosa pulled on Colin's arm. "I see you're dressed like a knight. I must say you look very dapper. So, tell me, where's the king these days?"

"He's north."

"How nice," Rosa said, with a serious expression on her face.

"What am I to do? I have to follow the queen's request. Our time machine is no more. I think we's all fecked, so I do."

Amoli burst into tears. Sasha shoved Colin.

"Now you make Miss Amoli cry. You are brute. If I have to I will build another."

"How? With what, Sasha?" Rosa demanded. "Sticks and stones?"

Sasha grabbed Rosa's shoulders. "You not know how I feel about this. If anyone get into my way I will kill them. I will make sure we leave this time period on time machine or even with time travel device."

"Yes, but your time travel device is capable of taking us to the time before the dinosaur extinction. It has no rhyme nor reason behind it!" she shouted, so loud her voice cracked.

"I like to see you do better. My time travel device may be our only hope."

"Dear God!" Rosa said, turning away from him.

"You afraid Mr. Limmerick will die in joust. I will bring my gun and shoot opponent."

"Then we'll all die. Jousting is completely different than the Viking battles of 840 AD. Everyone in this century would see that you have gunpowder. They would claim us as witches and burn us to the stake. We're doomed, thanks to your stupid inventions!" Sasha walked a few meters away from Rosa and lit a cigarette. Colin placed his arm around Amoli, and tried to dry her tears.

"Colin, you have to focus on that tournament and win tomorrow. If the queen has you knighted, then that's as good as it's going to get for us. I'm just wondering when the king returns, will he agree that a total stranger is being knighted?"

"Why wouldn't he?" Colin asked.

"Because you are strikingly handsome and the king is not, that's why. You're this towering mountain of muscle and he is not, that's why. The queen is obviously attracted to your beauty, something the king will never have, that's why!"

Colin tightened his arms around Amoli. "I'll have to win that tournament."

"You must win that tournament, but when you become one of the queen's knights, then what?" Rosa asked.

Sasha flicked his cigarette butt on the ground. "Then what? I say you what: I will find us way out of this time and back to 1910."

"Oh, really, Sasha? You're so conceited over these ridiculous inventions of yours. I have lost faith in you as a scientist," Rosa blurted.

His eyes widened at Colin. "I always say you she is not to be invited on expeditions. She is not worth it."

Colin placed his hand on Sasha's shoulder. "Ye know what, mate? The queen has provided me with a cozy little cottage. Why don't we all slumber there tonight 'n get ourselves some rest?"

"Rest? I cannot at time like this," Sasha snorted.

Colin glanced at Rosa who scowled back at him.

"Well, like it or not, I'm in a joustin' tournament tomorrow 'n we all should get some rest."

Amoli forced a smile. "Colin is right. We should stop fighting. It's hurting my ears."

They made their way to the cottage. Colin smiled as he passed Rosa and Sasha a pile of cotton blankets.

"Ye see how hospitable her majesty can be."

Rosa grimaced. "Hospitable? She obviously wants you to be her secret suitor. Just don't let the king find out."

"Suitor?" Amoli questioned. "Maybe she's just a generous queen."

"Don't be foolish, Amoli. All Colin has to do is practice his archery and have one jousting tournament and suddenly he's knighted? How absurd. You must go through a series of rankings before you are knight, Colin Limmerick!"

Colin sat on the bed and rubbed his face. "So, what am I to do?"

Rosa walked over to him. "Win that tournament tomorrow."

"Understand that, so I do."

Amoli faced them. "Can Colin and I sleep in the bed tonight? After all, Colin and I will soon be married."

Rosa gave a sarcastic smile. "Go ahead."

Colin took Amoli's hand and brought her close to him.

"Rosa, love, don't know why yer spillin' out so much negativity."

"I don't like what I'm seeing here!" she shouted, in a panic as she and Sasha spread blankets onto the floor.

Amoli fell into bed exhausted. Colin smiled at her as he removed his knight attire. He was naked. He slid his hand over Amoli's breasts. Sasha blew out the candle. Rosa spooled herself into an array of blankets with her back to Colin and Amoli. Sasha lay beside Rosa and placed his hand on her shoulder.

The temperature that night dropped considerably, as they heard the howling wind whistle through the cottage. Rosa had finally fallen asleep until the sound of Colin's groans and Amoli's squeals filled the room. Sasha snored in a deep trance. Rosa opened one eye taken by the vibration of the fifteenth-century bed, which swayed back and forth, hitting against the wall. Rosa sighed and tried shutting her eyes again, but the bed continued to smack up against the wall over and over. Colin's groans became louder and Amoli shrilled.

61

Rosa abruptly sat up. "Can't you two stop for just a minute?"

Colin propped himself on one elbow. "Are we keepin' yez up, love?"

Rosa pushed her hair away from her face. "What do you think?"

Amoli peered at Rosa from under the blanket.

# Chapter Ten

The morning was brisk. Sir Williams knocked on the cottage door. "How now, knight-to be?" he asked, as he pushed open the heavy door. He was surprised to see others with Colin in the cottage. "Oh, I see you have kin with you?"

"Kin? Aye, so I do," Colin responded, as he tried to pry himself out of bed.

Rosa lifted her head and stared at the knight. The knight smiled at Rosa.

"And who is this pretty maiden? Your wife?"

Rosa smiled as the knight helped her up. Colin grinned as Amoli stared at him.

"She's not." Colin tried to wrap some cloth around his lower half. "She's a good friend. Almost like family, one could say."

Sasha lifted his head and sat up. Amoli pulled the covers over her head to stay out of sight. The knight looked at Amoli.

"Is this your maiden?"

"Aye. We are to marry soon."

"Marry? Oh, I didn't know," the knight said. "Is she foreign?"

"Aye."

"She's from our far away trading partner I see. Do not allow the queen to know of this marriage."

Rosa glanced at Colin, then at the knight.

"Why? Are knights not allowed to marry?" Colin asked, poking fun at the idea.

Sir Williams appeared serious. "The queen has plans for you to belong to her and a selected lady in waiting."

Colin's lips parted. "But there's a king?" Colin asked.

"Of course, there is the king."

Colin looked at Amoli. "Doesn't the queen realize it's dangerous to have a lover?"

"The queen is very enchanted with you and she wants very badly for you to be her head knight."

Colin sat on the bed as Amoli started to cry. Sir Williams bowed his head to Rosa and left. Colin held Amoli close to him.

"It's a curse," he said, with Amoli crying in his arms.

"What's a curse?" Rosa asked.

"The way I look gets me into trouble."

Rosa placed her hand on Colin's shoulder. "You need to be more aware of things. You lived on that ship of yours for so long that you no longer understand how people operate. The only women you were in contact with were your mother, your sister-in law, and those disgusting whores. You are completely oblivious to women."

"Aye, aye, you've said this to me countless times, love, but right now I've gotta a problem, so I do."

"Just win that joust today, that's all I can say to you. Use that mighty strength of yours and knock your opponent off his horse," Rosa said to him.

Later that morning Colin was fitted with his armor and was brought to his horse. He had ridden this horse before; therefore he tried to achieve some contact with it before his armored headgear went on. Rosa, Sasha and Amoli wore fifteenth-century attire, as they sat amongst the queen's court in the arena.

"Pardon me, but you three are not part of the queen's court. I don't recognize any of you," a young squire said.

Sasha glanced at him. "You are right, but we are friends with one of jousters."

Amoli's face was wrapped in nylon scarves. She tried not to look at the squire.

"What are your names? I will see if you're on the queen's guest list."

"You not need to know."

Sasha stood up and plunged a dagger in the squire's s shoulder. The three of them ran out of the stadium.

"Sasha, you fool!" Rosa shouted, as they ran into the town and tried to blend with the population.

"Fool? He ask many questions. I not like. He deserve it."

"Are you insane? You can't be jabbing your dagger into innocent people."

Amoli was nervous. "Lets not try to fake our way in. I'm too afraid. I know Colin will win this tournament," Amoli said.

Colin sat on his horse dressed head to toe in plated armor with his lance in hand. He took a few deep breaths, as he noticed the crowd that awaited him. The sound of the trumpet blared, which indicated the joust had begun.

Colin rushed out in front of the spectators on his horse. His opponent galloped toward him with a protruding lance. As the opponent got near, Colin recklessly knocked him off his horse. Colin took a deep breath, as he turned around to face the opponent who was being helped back onto his horse. Colin re-positioned himself on the horse, where he found the armor to be uncomfortable.

His lance was ready for the next charge, when he noticed something on his opponent's armor. As he got closer, Colin's eyes widened when he noticed the time machine lever was wrapped around his opponent's neck. The opponent charged with his protruding lance and knocked Colin off his horse. The crowd roared.

Colin lay flat hindered by his armor when two squires came to help him up. He stood up, towering over the squires as he hoisted himself onto his horse. He took a deep breath, which hurt his chest due to the restricting armor. He sweated profusely, as he repositioned himself on his horse and charged at his opponent.

Colin rode faster than he had ever ridden a horse, and charged relentlessly at the knight and threw him off his horse roughly into a crash landing. Astonished, the crowd stood up and roared. They didn't know who this giant stranger was in the armor, but they expressed their admiration for him with their roaring applause. The knight lay on the ground wearing bashed armor. His two squires tried to help him up, but he was knocked out.

The queen cheered as her eyes were fixed on Colin. Colin rode his horse toward the queen. Still on his horse, he remained a few meters from her and removed his armored headgear. His long, crimson hair blew in the wind, and his handsome smile took over the queen. He gleamed at her. She stood up along with roaring applause. Colin bowed his head to her. He circled around with his horse, as he noticed the crowd shouting something. He glanced at the queen and then at the crowd. What were they yelling about? The queen's advisor ran down to the floor of the stadium.

"The rose! Where's the rose?" the advisor shouted at Colin.

Colin was confused. "Rose? Where am I gonna get meself a rose? I donno!"

Her majesty's advisor ran to Colin, who was sitting high upon his horse.

"One of the squires was supposed to pass you the queen's rose! What did you do with it?"

"Squire? There wasn't a squire who gave me a rose. I'm sorry. I only have one squire 'n he didn't hold a rose."

"You were supposed to give the queen a rose to woo her with your victory."

"I was?"

The queen continued to stand gazing at Colin with the roaring crowd behind her. She glanced at her advisor, who ran back to be by his queen's side. He bowed to her.

"I'm sorry, m' queen, he is without rose."

"What happened to the squire who was supposed to give it to him?" she pressed, pretending to smile at her royal subjects.

66

"He said no squire approached him with a rose."

"I want you to find that squire and send him to me. He will be thoroughly punished, if not executed for this."

"I will find the squire, m' queen."

He bowed to her several times, as he walked backwards and away from her.

# Chapter Eleven

Colin lay on the bed of the cottage, where he tried to sleep off his immense exhaustion. Sir Williams pushed the door opened. Colin sat up.

"I thought maybe it was me friends who stepped in. I'm worried. I haven't seen them for a while. Have ye seen them?"

"No, I haven't."

"I'm very tired. The jousting tournament took the wind right outta me, I'm afraid."

"Your knighting ceremony is starting shortly."

"Oh, yes, I'm to be knighted, so I am," Colin said, placing his head back down.

"The queen was expecting her rose."

"I'll have to go fetch some roses, then. I wasn't approached by a squire."

"You can get her roses, but it will do you no good. The point of winning the jousting tournament was to woo her majesty with a rose. I found the squire."

"Oh, was he sleepin' on the job?" Colin asked, with a chuckle.

"He was stabbed in the shoulder."

Colin sat up. "What?"

"He was stabbed with a dagger. He managed to stop the bleeding. He had the rose to give you, but he was stabbed by someone who claimed to know you."

Colin slid off the bed. "Who?"

"He said it was a man with a foreign accent with a foreign woman and a local woman. You know this man?"

"Ah, um, shall I change me clothes for the knightin' ceremony?"

"Yes, two servants are to be expected any time now, and they will fit you with the proper attire."

Sir Williams made his way to the door and exited. A few moments after Sir Williams left the cottage Sasha, Rosa, and Amoli entered. Amoli ran into Colin's arms.

"Colin! Oh, how I've missed you!"

He stared at Sasha. "Mate, have ye gone mad? Why'd ye bother to stab a squire with a dagger?"

"The king's men will burn Sasha at the stake for this one," Rosa said, folding her arms in front of her.

"Yer damn lucky the squire lived," Colin said, as Amoli buried herself in his arms.

"He ask so many questions. I am tired of this."

"A few servants will be here shortly. They're gonna fit me with me knightin' clothes."

"Oh, yes, you obviously won the joust. We missed it, because Sasha was too busy stabbing young kids," Rosa said, with fury in her voice.

Sasha turned to Rosa. "I do what I have to do. You not understand, because you only a woman."

Rosa looked at Colin. "Shall I smack him in the face, or would you like the honors?"

"Enough of this. We're livin' in a dangerous time period, that we are. I'm to be knighted shortly. I want Amoli with me for this event, but don't think mixed marriages was too common in 1487."

"They are not that common in 1910 either," Rosa blurted.

"I've seen Englishmen with Indian wives, that's not true, love," Colin responded.

"Colin, I'm so frightened," Amoli whimpered.

"What concerns me more is when I was in the joustin' tournament I noticed me opponent was wearing a piece of the time machine around his neck; kinda like jewelry, ye know."

Sasha's eyes widened. "Why you not say me earlier?"

"Ye was too busy scufflin'."

"What part of time machine you see?" Sasha asked.

"It was the time machine's lever, if ye can believe it?"

69

Rosa tore Amoli away from Colin and took her spot.

"Oh, God! Colin, this is serious. How are we going to gather pieces of the time machine if the king's people are using its parts as jewelry?" Rosa asked, in a panic.

Amoli stood back in silence. Her lips were parted as she watched every move Rosa made.

"Stay calm, love. We have to leave this time period, right Sasha?" Colin asked, with Rosa in his arms.

"I will try to mingle with people and learn how to find all time machine parts, but if worse is worse, we go with time travel device and leave machine here."

"I like the sound of that," Rosa said.

"No guarantees where we go."

"It's worked before for us. It has always taken us home, hasn't it?" Rosa indicated.

"Da, but it give last reading I not like."

Colin took Amoli's hand and clutched it in his. "What readin' did it give ye?"

"It say 1970 AD."

"The future?" Rosa yelped.

Amoli smiled. "I think the future would be better than the past."

Rosa glanced at her. "It could be worse for all we know."

"My father always says that things get better with time," Amoli instilled.

"Amoli, think about it. What does the year 1970 mean to you?" Rosa asked.

"It's not that far in the future from our year. It's only 60 years."

Rosa crossed her arms. "Sasha, it has to be 1910. It can't be any earlier or any later."

"Da, day, I understand."

"I think yez all should stay away from the king's nobles 'n such. The less they see of yez the better," Colin said, as he led Amoli and Rosa to the door.

70

"I go find pieces of time machine now. We will miss knight ceremony. Sorry."

"No worries. I'm not a knight, but a fisherman, rather."

Rosa smiled at Colin. "And you're a PhD candidate, don't forget."

"That's what's got us into this mess, don't ye think?"

Amoli grabbed onto Colin's beard and pulled his lips in front of hers. She kissed him several times.

"I hope I can spend the night with you."

"Can yez return here just after dark?" Colin asked.

"Of course, my love," Amoli said.

"Lass, I was just kiddin'. Don't really want ye roamin' 'bout these lands alone. It's quite dangerous."

The three of them left the cottage. Colin slumped onto the bed to rest. Sir Williams stormed in raging.

"The knighting ceremony has begun. You now will be addressed as Sir Limmerick." Colin pushed himself off the bed and followed the knight to the occasion. "By the way, Sir Limmerick, the king has returned from the north."

Colin stared at the ground. "I see."

"He will see you knighted today."

"Me concern is if it's dany with him."

"Yes, he would definitely approve. He is attending with his wife, the queen."

They scurried to the main hall located in the central part of the castle. Colin lifted his head and noticed the large clusters of nobles and ladies all in honor of the new knight. He turned his head to get a glimpse of the king and queen who sat at their royal thrones at the other end of the hall. The queen stared at him. He bowed his head and smiled at her.

Sir Williams placed a rose in Colin's hand. "Give this to the queen."

Colin felt awkward, but fumbled his way to the queen. Two nobles had crossed their swords on the floor where Colin was meant to kneel down. Colin knelt to his majesties with his head bowed low. The horns sounded in the background as the king rose. All spectators bowed low to the ground to their king. The king looked at Colin.

"Rise," the king said to Colin. Colin stood up to face the king. King Henry Vll stepped closer to him. "The queen insists you are to be knighted. I don't really know who you are. You are a stranger to me. Where are you from?"

"Ireland, yer majesty," Colin responded.

"Hmm, you are an Englishman. Well, that is suitable to me, but I never knew you as a squire. Were you ever a squire?"

Colin focused on the floor. "Squire?" Colin took time to respond. "Aye, so I was."

The king looked at his queen. "Who is this man?"

"He will be useful to keep our kingdom from any uprisings. Look at the size of him."

"Fine, we will knight him. Proceed with this occasion."

The nobles appeared more at ease as the trumpets sounded throughout the hall. Colin was knighted.

# Chapter Twelve

Later that evening Sasha and Rosa rummaged through the forest looking for the parts of the time machine. Rosa held a large basket in her arms, which carried a few of the time machine pieces that they had already found.

"Sasha, I'm exhausted. Can't we stop to rest?" asked Rosa.

"Miss Amoli not wish to help, she only want to be with Mr. Limmerick, so it leaves you and me."

"I'm over-wrought from all this. We're only finding a few pieces. It's obvious the king's people have possessed these pieces."

Sasha stopped what he was doing. "You are right. We must go to village and look for them there."

"The only thing is, we could get captured."

"I use gun."

Colin returned to the cottage after eating a feast with the nobles. Just as he shut the door there was a knock. Sir Williams pushed his way in.

"Her majesty, the queen, has requested to see you."

Colin followed Sir Williams. The queen waited just outside her bedchamber.

"Sir Limmerick," the queen said, with a smile on her face.

Colin bowed to the floor. "Yer majesty."

"Do enter my bedchamber." Colin stepped into her room. He scanned the royal bedroom in awe. "Sir Limmerick, I think you will do a fine job keeping our kingdom safe from any uprisings, yes I do. The king may even want to send you to explore the new world."

"New world?"

"Yes, there could be many useful findings there for England. It is something we must further explore. Also, I wanted you to know the king is not at the castle tonight."

She stepped closer to him where her hands ran along his chest.

He stepped back. "I'm sorry."

She stepped toward him. "Sorry? Sorry?"

He took a few steps back. "I must respect the king as well as yerself, yer majesty."

"The king is always away, and I must admit that I am very fond of you, Sir Limmerick."

"Thank-ye, but it's best I leave."

"Are you choosing not to be with me?"

"I think it's best if I leave. The king is in the castle. It would be best that I leave."

He fumbled for the door and made his exit. When he arrived back at the cottage Amoli was standing in front of the door wearing a fifteenth-century dress. Colin smiled.

"Lass, I'm so glad to see you."

She jumped into his arms. "I want to go home."

He entered the cottage carrying Amoli in his arms. He lowered her onto the bed and began to remove his clothes.

"I was just with the queen of England, if ye can believe it?"

Amoli sat on the bed and struggled to remove her centuries old attire.

"Why? What does she want?"

"Me, I think. Rosa was right once again. I've made me way up to knighthood so much faster than the others, 'cause she wants me. One of the knights mentioned to me that she fancies me."

"Did you tell her you're with me?"

"I didn't. I think it's best that yer not brought into the picture. Where are Sasha 'n Rosa?"

"They're trying to find the pieces of the time machine."

"Surely, they will come here tonight?"

"I suppose they will."

Colin stood before her. She sprawled on the bed naked. He slipped into bed and cupped her ample breasts in his hands. He squeezed her breasts together to create plunging cleavage and kissed them several times. She could feel his overwhelming erect penis plunge into her – in and out. He penetrated her. He was so aroused; his groans became louder.

"I love ye, Amoli," he panted, in a deep breath.

She yelped with a high shrill, where his penetration touched her with heightened orgasm.

"Colin!" she screamed. He pulled out of her when he realized that she was crying. "I have never known love like this. I love you so very much and I want to be your wife so very much."

He lay beside her on the bed. "Then, why the tears?"

"The queen is married to the king. She may likely get her way with you, because she is the queen and this is 1487."

"Lass, I would never let that happen."

"She's the queen. I'm sure she is used to getting what she wants."

Rosa and Sasha walked into the cottage to find Colin and Amoli lying in bed naked together.

"Oh, I suppose we're interrupting something," said Rosa, who tried to focus on something else in the room.

Sasha looked at the lovers and chuckled. "Mr. Limmerick maybe just make baby, da?" Rosa shoved Sasha. "It not so horrible. Look at Miss Amoli's face. She has big smile. She want very much, da?"

Amoli giggled as she buried herself in the blankets and nestled against Colin. Colin sat up to push his long forelock from his face.

"Any luck puttin' the time machine back together?" Colin asked.

"No at all. We're going to have to intermingle with the villagers more I suppose," said Rosa, with a sigh. "Colin, get dressed."

75

There was a bold knock at the door. Sir Williams let himself in. Amoli was startled.

"Excuse me, Sir Limmerick," the knight said. "Forgive me for barging in, but the queen continues to request you."

"Where's the king now?" Colin asked, with concern.

"He's not far. He could be at the stables."

"If the king is near, why is she askin' for me?"

"If I were you, I'd get dressed and get to her highness as soon as you can." Amoli gasped. Sir Williams looked at her. "Don't let the queen see this woman. She will likely have her executed."

Rosa jumped into Sasha's arms. "Oh, God!"

Amoli let out a frantic scream. Colin wrapped his arms around her.

"Lass, don't leave this cottage. I'll just see what the queen wants 'n be right back, so I will."

Rosa's eyes widened. "Colin, if this isn't the first request tonight by the queen, I'd be very careful."

He stood up naked and slammed his fist on the wooden table.

"Feck! What the hell am I to do? If she wants me to feck her tonight 'n I refuse she'll more than likely have me executed. If I agree to feck her tonight the king will likely have me executed. What am I to do?"

Sir Williams stared at the floor. "I'm sorry. I don't really know you. You're a newcomer. The king is wary of that. The queen, however, is very attracted to you. She wants you in her bed chamber at this moment."

Sasha stepped close to Sir Williams. "Can you say her that Mr. Limmerick is on his way, but he has to hunt some deer, or something like that?"

"At this time? I'll just tell her that he's on his way."

Sir Williams left. Amoli wept as she remained in bed. Rosa stepped beside Colin.

"Get dressed and go see the queen."

76

"Can't we just leave this time period?" Colin asked, looking terrified.

"Go sleep with queen. Miss Rosa and me will go to pub and look for time machine parts. Miss Amoli stop crying. I will fix problem."

Colin got dressed. He kissed Amoli and left. Amoli sat and cried in a continuous mourn.

"You have to accept what's happening. Colin is a time traveler," Rosa instilled.

"How can I sleep tonight knowing he will have to give in to the queen?"

Rosa sat beside Amoli. "Accept it. If you don't you'll go out of your mind."

"How come you're accepting it?" Amoli asked, with her eyes swollen with tears.

"I've had to accept a lot of things when it comes to Colin. He's marrying you, not me. So, if he gives in to the queen, and I think he may have to, then you have to accept it. He hasn't the choice."

Sasha paced around the room. "Come, Rosa, we not stop at all tonight until we find all pieces of time machine."

Rosa stood up. "And what if we have to risk our lives in order to get those pieces back?"

Sasha handed her the time travel device. "Take it. If I not successful, you take Miss Amoli and go back to 1910. If you go to other time, then you must keep trying. You know how device works, da?"

Rosa and Sasha embraced.

"Sasha, I'm coming with you."

Amoli dried her tears. "I'll come too. I don't want to be alone here. I'm so worried for Colin."

"We're all worried for Colin, the poor man. He always gets the short end of the stick," Rosa commented.

"Miss Amoli, get dressed. We all will go. I will keep dagger and gun handy. If I have to I will use," Sasha said.

# Chapter Thirteen

Colin appeared at the queen's door. Sir Williams stood behind him. He stared at the door. He took a few seconds to think about what to do next. He slowly turned his head to face the knight standing behind him.

"Something wrong, Sir Limmerick?"

Colin took a deep breath. "I don't want to do this."

"This is the queen's request. You are part of her nobility, therefore you must adhere to her request."

Colin cleared his throat and knocked on the door. He stood so close to the door his lips almost touched the wood. He heard footsteps approach and the door swung opened. The queen's lady answered to the faint knock.

"Ah, yes, Sir Limmerick. Her majesty has been expecting you. Do come in."

Colin bowed as he entered and the door was shut tight with a dead bolt. He remained in a bowing position until the queen approached him.

"What took you so long, Sir Limmerick?"

"Forgive me," he said, with his head hung low to the ground.

"Rise. I want to see your eyes." He stood up to face her. "Why are you silent?"

"Forgive me."

She stepped close against him. "Yes, I wanted to see those eyes of yours. Green like a forest." She rubbed his chest. "Kiss me."

He bent his knees and tilted his body toward her to kiss her cheek.

The Queen giggled. "Are you ever tall."

He tried to smile at her. "The king is near. I don't think this is a good idea."

He tried to push her hands away from him.

"Then, when the king is away, it is a good idea, yes?"

78

He stepped back from her. "This is never a good idea." He glanced at her facial expression. "Forgive me, yer majesty."

"Am I not desirable to you?"

He stared at the floor. "No question, yer majesty, but I cannot betray the king."

"You are a very loyal subject, Sir Limmerick; strange for a Celt." She whisked about the room dressed in her white flowing nightgown. "Fine, have it your way. We will wait until the king leaves the castle, which will be tomorrow after court."

Colin's eyes widened. "Then I expect to see you sometime after. I will be wearing this again."

Colin bowed to the floor. "Until tomorrow, yer majesty."

"You must stop pushing me away. Your behavior does not look well on you."

He nodded, as if he agreed with her. She bowed along with him, so her eyes could meet with his. She brought her lips to his and kissed him. He jolted, but tried to refrain from pulling away. She kissed him several times. He tried to reciprocate. He helped her up and kissed her cheek.

"This is all I get from you? A kiss on the cheek?"

He stood straight. "You will get more, later, my queen. Forgive me."

"How very interesting it is that you feel it can be done your way. Are you not from this time period, knight? Why do you shy from me?"

"You and the king were just married one year ago, my queen. I don't think I should be anywhere near your bed chamber."

"You don't think? You are telling me, the queen of England, what you think?"

"Forgive me."

"I can't forgive you. No man has every behaved this way with me. Tell me, knight, what is wrong with you?"

"Nothing is wrong with me. You are newly married to the king."

"That is none of your concern."

"It will be me concern when the king finds out."

"You are afraid of the king?"

He was silent.

"A true knight and noble should fear nothing."

"A true knight 'n noble is what I am, but I must respect the king."

"You abide by the Catholic church, don't you? A true Catholic Celt is what you are, aren't you? Be gone. I will see you after court tomorrow at my bedchamber. Do not be late, knight!"

Colin bowed to the floor and walked backwards to make his exit. Sir Williams was waiting outside the door.

"That was quick."

Colin sighed. "Aye."

Sir Williams escorted Colin back to the cottage. He entered to find Amoli crying on the bed. He lit a candle and walked with it to her side. She threw her arms around his neck and kissed him several times.

"I was so worried."

"I managed to postpone things for a bit. Where is Sasha 'n Rosa at?"

"They're visiting the pubs to see if they can find any of the time machine pieces."

"I hope Sasha plays things out a bit."

"I don't know if Dr. Dimitrikov can do that. He seemed reliant on using his weapons."

"In this time period, one has to use them, surely that's true."

She kissed his lips several times. He removed her clothes and smothered her naked body with kisses.

\*\*\*

Sasha and Rosa walked into one of the pubs. Rosa noticed the men staring at her. She tugged on Sasha's sleeve.

"I don't think I'm supposed to be in here, Sasha."

Sasha pressed his body against hers and plunged his tongue down her throat. She gasped with her arms flapping in the air. The other men observed and continued to drink their ale. Rosa pushed him back.

"Are you out of your mind?"

"Remember, you are my woman. It is 1487. I do what I want to my woman, da?"

She wiped her mouth with her sleeve. "Good, God, help me."

Sasha pulled out a chair for himself and yanked Rosa onto his knee. He pulled her blouse down to just cover her breasts. He recklessly kissed her neck.

"Could you please calm down? What has got into you?" she asked.

"Men are comfortable with us in this place now. You not see this?"

"I suppose you're right, but you could've warned me."

"Nyet, it is better to make you surprised, da?"

The barmaid approached Sasha. He looked at her, and said, "Vodka."

The barmaid stepped closer. "Vodka?"

Rosa's eyes widened. "He meant to say ale. He has a cold, don't mind him."

The barmaid smiled. "One drink? Just for you?"

"Da. I am the man."

"Can we stop this child's play and look for the time machine pieces? You're just doing this for your own enjoyment."

He brought his lips to hers and kissed her. "Of course, you are beautiful woman. I cannot help myself."

"Sasha." She sat beside him and watched him drink his ale. "Are all Russian men as horrible as you?"

"Worse!" Sasha said, taking a drink. "I hate this drink. Mr. Limmerick love it. I not know why."

"I don't believe you. I have met some Russian men before at the university. They were very cordial."

Two of the king's nobility walked in and sat at the wood table across from Rosa and Sasha.

"They look like the king's knights, what do you think?" Rosa asked.

"I not know who belongs to king. They dress better than merchants and peasants. I not know this."

"Big help you are. I wonder if they would have any of the parts on them."

"I will go talk to them."

"About what? You have a foreign accent. They could react negatively toward you."

"Russian people could be in England in this time, nyet?"

"I don't really know much about Russian history."

"You are archeologist, you should know this."

"I know that *Mammoth* roamed Siberia during *Megaloceros Giganteus'* time, but I don't know about human settlement in historic Russia." She rolled her eyes back. "I wish Colin were here to bail me out from your hysteric behavior."

"Even if Mr. Limmerick here he would be with Miss Amoli. He love her and will marry her. She has bigger breasts than you. Mr. LImmerick like that very much."

"Can you please behave like a grown up?" she said, as she peered down at her tiny breasts.

The two knights conversed with each other and drank large flasks of ale. Sasha stood up to roam around the pub. Rosa sat by herself staring at her uncomfortable shoes. One of the knights from the adjacent table walked over to her.

"Excuse me, but are you alone here?"

Rosa looked at him as he knelt beside her.

"Alone? No, I'm here with a friend who's standing over there," she said, and pointed at Sasha in the distance.

"He can't really be a friend if he's not beside you, can he?" the knight asked, as he gently caressed her shoulders.

"Can you not do that?" she said, trying to push his hands away.

"Do what? Oh, you don't like this?"

"Well, I'm very sore from all the gardening I do every day."

"Gardening? I need a gardener. Would you like to help me garden my vegetables?"

"I would love to," she said, with a nervous twitch.

Sasha returned to the table. He sat beside Rosa and gave the knight a dirty look.

"Sorry, if she is yours," the knight said.

Sasha glared at him and drank his ale. The knight walked away.

"Sasha, we're not getting anywhere with this. I'm afraid of these people. They're dangerous."

"Then we leave machine here and we use device and hope we not go to 1970."

"I think maybe that's what we should do. We can take our chances, I suppose. The future can be very frightening, though."

"Time travel is frightening. What you think?" Sasha said, as he slid his arm around her and gave her a sloppy kiss on the lips.

She pushed him away. "The thing is Colin needs to see the time of Megaloceros again. It's what Dr. Cushing requested."

"Only way is to go to 1910, then go to 10,000 years in past. We cannot do it from 1487."

She sighed with frustration. "Fine, then we'll do it that way. Hopefully, we won't go to the future. I'm so afraid for Colin."

"You always think of Mr. Limmerick, but you not think of me, why is this?"

83

"You have a wife in Russia, Colin does not."

"Mr. Limmerick, he have Miss Amoli."

"They're not married yet."

"You want to break up Miss Amoli with Mr. Limmerick?"

"Goodness, I'm not that kind of a woman. I would never dream of such a thing."

***

The brightness of the new day beamed through the cottage. Colin rolled over in bed to caress Amoli, who layed beside him.

"Lass, I need to be at the king's court now," Colin said.

"You're a knight, I can't believe this. I wish Dr. Dimitrikov would get us out of here."

Colin kissed her several times. "It's not so easy, so it's not. I've gambled with not just me own life, but with yers 'n Rosa's. I'm sorry."

"Don't be. I love you for who you are."

He slid out of bed with a sheet wrapped around his lower half and fumbled to put his nobility attire on. Sasha and Rosa lay asleep on a bed of cotton and blankets.

"Colin?" Rosa called out, as she lifted her head.

"I'm expected at court now, love. Just ye sleep, alright?"

He tried to fit into a pair of hoes.

"Will the king be there?" she asked.

"Likely."

Colin finished dressing. He made sure his sword and dagger were secured on his body. He kissed Amoli and left. Amoli sat up in bed with blankets up to her neck. She looked at Sasha.

"So, Dr. Dimitrikov, did you find any of the time machine pieces?"

Sasha sat up and rubbed his face. "Nyet."

84

"What do we do now?" Amoli asked.

"We go with device and risk 1970."

"The future scares me," Amoli said, with a quiver in her voice.

"It's that or Colin gets executed. Take your pick," Rosa said, as she tried to get dressed under her blanket. "That queen is playing Russian roulette with Colin's life."

"You're acting as if Colin will be executed for sure. Nobody has said anything that he would be killed, have they?" Amoli asked, raising her voice.

"The queen of England wants Colin to sleep with her. If he doesn't he'll likely be executed. If he does, he'll likely be killed when the king finds out. I think 1970 is looking better and better."

Rosa struggled to lace up her fifteenth-century dress. Amoli started to cry as she threw her arms around Sasha.

"Dr. Dimitrkov, do something. Please save Colin."

"I cannot help that women find Mr. Limmerick so irresistible. I not know why."

Rosa helped Amoli get dressed by holding a sheet up for privacy.

"So, as soon as Colin returns from court let's get the device and go," Rosa said.

"Not so fast. Not so easy. I have problem with energy. I need energy for this to happen," Sasha said.

"So, how can we create energy?" Rosa asked, in a panic.

"I not know. We are in fifteenth-century. I not know."

***

Colin sat at the king's court. Sir Williams sat beside him. The king and queen entered the large room filled with north renaissance moldings along the walls and ceiling, accented with great northern renaissance paintings. The king watched his royal subjects bow to him until he gestured for them to sit.

"We have had our last defeat over the Yorks. Richard lll has admitted his defeat and the throne is ruled by us, a Lancastrian throne, in deed," the king said, with a grin, as his wife gleamed with happiness at Colin. The king stood up. "Where is our new knight? Ah, yes, Sir Limmerick, you came to us too late. You would have been great help during *The War of the Roses*." Colin bowed his head. "A man of your size and stature will definitely work to our advantage."

The queen smiled at Colin. He scanned the great room. He noted the knights who made up most of the royal's nobility. He focused on each man. The king continued to discuss the church and intertwine it with their latest victory. Colin noticed how exhausted he was as he sat in this piece of history. He was quite aware of the queen, who was so fixated on him. His eyes felt heavy; he tried not to fall asleep with boredom. A knight who sat across the room fiddled with something in his hands. Colin's eyebrows lowered as he realized what this man was playing with. It looked familiar. It was one of the time machine dials. Colin's eyes widened and he started to cough. The king and his queen felt interrupted by Colin's hacking.

"Do you need to leave, Sir Limmerick?" asked the king.

"I'm fine, yer majesty," Colin said, with his head bowed low.

Another long hour had passed when Colin realized how uncomfortable he was sitting for so long in a chair that was more suited for a smaller man. He tried several times to reposition his body, but he knew he would be noticed so he remained still and suffered through the long-winded court session.

As his eyes bounced around the intricate room, he noticed another knight was holding another piece of the time machine. Colin squinted to see which piece it was, but the knight was sitting too far away. Finally, the court session ended. The king and his queen rose from their thrones to make their exit. Colin glanced at Sir Williams, who was already standing.

"Limmerick, what's wrong? You couldn't seem to sit still. I'm sure the king noticed," he said, as the nobility slowly stood to leave.

Colin hoisted himself up from the small chair.

"Ye need to understand: I'm just not yer size 'n all this isn't fittin' for me. I'm sorry."

"Oh, yes, of course. I suppose the seating isn't comfortable for you." Colin smiled. "Oh, by the way, some of the queen's ladies have shown great interest in you."

Colin focused on something else. "I see."

"A gathering will be at the castle in honor of the king's victory over the thrown. You are expected to attend."

"I don't understand something: if the queen's ladies are interested in me 'n the queen is interested in me, what am I to do?"

"If the queen wants you, you cannot refuse her." Colin took a deep breath. "If the queen's ladies want you, you should show some interest. The queen would expect that and it would make her look loyal to the king."

"I see. You've met me fiancé."

"Yes, she must be completely out of the picture if you want her to live." Colin stared at the knight. "Come now, we must go riding through the forest. There could still be some enemy attackers around. Our mission is to finish them."

"The queen asked me to her chamber," Colin said.

"Do you fear the queen?"

Colin smiled. "Well, ye see I was plannin' on marryin' me fiancé 'n now I'm expected to be with the queen."

"Set your fiancé free. Let her go. She can no longer be with you. You're now part of the king's court."

"You shouldn't keep the queen waiting."

"Where's the king at?"

"He's either riding or fencing."

"He's near. I don't think I should go to the queen."

Sir Williams gave Colin a slight shove. "Go to her. She's expecting you."

Colin sighed with frustration. He tilted his head to the knight and walked off. Colin arrived at the queen's chamber. He knocked on the door. Her lady answered.

"Enter, Sir Limmerick," the young woman said.

Colin walked in to find the queen lying in bed naked. Her lady left. Colin licked his dry lips. He knelt to the floor. "Yer majesty."

"Why are you standing before me all dressed?" she said, sipping wine in a gold goblet. Colin stepped toward her. He wanted to smile, but couldn't. He began to undress. He kept his eyes on the door. "Are you afraid the king will enter?"

"Aye."

"He's going about his daily routine just now. He won't enter. That, I know." Colin stood beside the bed naked. "I've never seen a man who even resembles you. You're magnificent." She gestured for him to join her in bed. He slid in beside her. "Kiss me!"

He grudgingly lay beside her. He kissed her neck several times and rubbed her almost non-existent breasts. He lay on top of her tiny body and entered. She screamed and groaned, panting and shrilling with each thrust in and out. She entangled her fingers in his hair, as his huge pectoral muscles expanded with every heavy breath he took. She felt some pain from his size; something she was not used to. When he finally pulled out, she tried to catch her breath.

"You're absolutely enormous. I think I'm bleeding," she said, wiping her inner thigh with a cloth.

He sat up. "I'm sorry."

She sat up and stared into his eyes. "Who are you? Even your complexion is different than any man I have ever seen."

He was confused. "Complexion? It's the same as you, isn't it, yer majesty?"

"You have such color in your face. Color I have not ever seen. I have not seen a man as you, not ever."

"Not sure what ye mean, yer majesty."

"Do you see specialists of medicine to make you this way?"

"Special doctors?"

She smiled at him. "I will call my ladies to dress me. Do you need help as well?"

"Help to get dressed? I can do that for meself, I think."

He sat at the edge of the bed and hurried himself to get dressed. Her ladies entered to help their queen dress. Colin watched as he knelt to the floor to the queen.

"Enough, Sir Limmerick, you can go now. I will call for you tomorrow," she said, as the ladies gleamed at him.

Colin walked backwards to the door and left. He walked to his horse outside the castle and rode to the cottage. Amoli was crying in Sasha's arms. Rosa walked to Colin and hugged him.

"How are you?" she asked.

Colin removed his sword and dagger. "How am I?" He looked at Sasha. "I'm not doin' well at all. Mate, get us outta here!"

"Colin, what happened?" Rosa asked.

"I don't wanna be here anymore. Just don't wanna be a feckin' knight 'n part of the king's nobility. I saw a few of the nobility with the time machine parts when I was at court this mornin'."

Sasha brought Amoli to Colin. "So, they have all pieces. They must die for this."

"Ye try it, mate, 'n ye'll surely be executed. We can't stay here. Sir Williams informed me that I'm not to be seen with Amoli, or Amoli's life could be in danger. The three of yez gotta settle somewheres else."

"Oh, God!" Rosa yelped, as she started to pace.

Amoli fell into Colin's arms to whimper. He looked at Rosa and Sasha.

"The longer we's stay in this time period, the worse things are gonna get, no doubt." Colin tapped Amoli's cheek. "Lass, yer gonna be fine. I love ye to bits, so I do. We's gonna be married soon enough."

Rosa gathered their belongings. "Where should we go?"

"Just try 'n offer yer services to some family or somethin'. Just blend in with the peasant crowd," Colin said, as he held Amoli in his arms.

He placed one hand against the wall.

"Colin?" Rosa said, as she stepped closer to him. "Are you alright?"

He leaned against the wall. "I just can't do this anymore. What's wrong with me? Why am I like this?"

Rosa placed her hand on his arm as she glanced at Amoli, who appeared frightened.

"Like what, Colin?" Rosa responded.

"Why do so many wenches act so strangely when they see me?"

Rosa caressed his arm. "It must be your manly magnetism."

He chuckled. "Ah, me magnetism. You've often told me I'm disgustin'." Rosa smiled and rubbed her hand up and down his shoulder. Colin flicked his forelock from his face. "When I was a younger man, I rather fancied this kind of attention from wenches, but now it's gettin' bothersome. I'm always in some kinda deep shite about it."

"I don't like it, Colin," Amoli said, as she held his hand in hers.

Colin kissed Rosa on the cheek then he kissed Amoli on the lips.

"Yez three best be off. I'll give ye the horse I have, surely, I can get another somehow. Just go away from here for yer own safety."

"Mr. Limmerick, we must get those time machine pieces at once," Sasha said.

"I'll try 'n get them back from the nobility. Don't know how I'll do it without a fight, though," Colin said.

Rosa stood in front of Colin. "I'm so worried about you. Please play their game and stay alive."

He stood tall and looked at her. "Play their game? That means I've got to mount the queen on demand."

Amoli yelped. "What do you mean?"

He glanced at Sasha. "Believe me, lass, it's not me pleasure. If the king catches us, that'll be it, no doubt." He trembled as Amoli cuddled in his arms. He looked at Sasha. "Just don't know how much of this I can take."

Rosa stomped her feet. "Can't you do something, Sasha?"

He looked at her. "I can only do what I can do. I'm not magician."

"Just be off, now 'n I'll get to work 'n retrieve those time machine pieces," Colin said, as he kissed Amoli on the forehead.

Rosa tugged on his arm. "I love you, Colin, please stay well," she said, with a sniffle of sorrow.

Colin tightened her hand in his. The three of them left. Colin took a deep breath. He made his way to the pub the nobility usually would go to drink ale. He entered, and noticed Sir Williams sitting with a group of young knights.

"Ah, Sir Limmerick!" Sir Williams shouted. "Come join us!" Colin smiled at them and pulled up a stool. They passed a frothy flask of ale in front of him. "Drink up, knight!"

Colin noticed two of the knights sitting at the table had time machine parts sitting in front of them. Colin guzzled the ale with his eyes fixed on the two knights. The knights cheered. Colin smiled.

"Yez didn't know how much I fancy a fine ale, eh?"

They knights chuckled as they managed to send another large flask of ale to Colin. He smiled as he noticed the white froth bubble over the glass.

"Bet you can't drink another at the speed you drank the first?" Sir Williams said.

Colin smiled and tilted his head to them. He placed the flask to his lips and drank up. The knights looked at each other. One of the knights who was fiddling with the time travel piece glared at Colin.

"Who are you?"

"Irish, so I am," Colin replied. "Me Christian name is Colin."

"You come riding out of nowhere and you're suddenly her majesty's favorite. Who are you?"

"Surely, I'll answer yer question if ye could let me see that piece in yer hands just now," Colin said, drinking his third large flask of ale.

"I think its gold and I won't let you even come near it. I'll soon have all the riches a man could want."

Colin sighed. "It's not gold, I can assure ye that. "

"How do you know?"

"Just look at it; it most certainly don't shine like gold. Gold it's not. It's some other type of metal like brass. That's not gold, yer surely mistaken."

The knight tightened the piece under his armpit. "Brass? Never heard of it."

"It's a mixture of different metals that looks like gold, but it's not. That piece in yer hand is of no value to yez."

"You lie!"

Colin sighed. "Call me what ye wish. I assure ye, it won't bring ye riches."

"How can you tell where you're sitting?"

Colin chuckled. "Yer a stupid man, anyone can tell it's not gold."

The knight stood up and drew his dagger. "You dare disrespect me? Who are you, anyway?"

Colin stood up and pulled out his dagger. Sir Williams stood up.

"Where is our honor? How are we displaying our honor of chivalry? We're the king's nobility and this is how we act during our time of play?" Sir Williams reasoned.

Colin kept his eyes on the other knight. "He's got himself a chunk of brass 'n he's too stupid to admit it isn't gold."

The other knight glanced at the piece and then glared at Colin. He examined it again and again. Sir Williams picked it up and held it.

"It doesn't seem to weigh what gold would weigh. I think Sir Limmerick is right."

The knight took the piece and tossed it on the table.

"Here, whoever wants it? I have no use for it."

Colin's eyes were fixed on the piece as it sat on the table. Sir Williams smiled.

"Knights, there is a celebration ball tomorrow night at the castle. The king is very pleased about having a Tudor throne and we all must act as knights should act. No more of this nonsense about gold and brass."

Colin picked up the piece and held it in his hands.

"I wouldn't mind this, if it's dany with ye?" Colin asked, the angry knight with a smile.

"Do with it as you wish. I have no use for it," the knight said, as he staggered off into the crowd.

That evening Sasha, Rosa, and Amoli walked through several villages and forested areas.

"Sasha, this isn't going anywhere, we really need to rest," Rosa said, as she found a log to sit on.

"You not want to find place to sleep tonight? Fine, we will walk all night," Sasha said, throwing his hands in the air.

"Would it be possible for you to build us some shelter?" Rosa asked.

"Da, I can do. Let us gather branches, twigs, wood, all we can find and I will make some kind of shelter. I will begin to make tools now."

Amoli yawned. "I'm so exhausted, and I'm so very sad I'm not with Colin."

"You don't want to be anywhere near Colin in this time period. Do what he said and stay away," Rosa cautioned.

Amoli's voice quivered. "It's very difficult for me to accept that he has to sleep with the queen."

She began to cry. Sasha slid his arm around her.

"Miss Amoli, please understand if queen wants, she gets. No one is to ask questions, da? It is the way of this century."

"What a terrible time to live," Amoli whimpered.

"Da, it is not nice time, I agree."

The early morning mist surrounded the wet English countryside as Colin and Sir Williams rode their horses for their enemy patrol routine.

"So, Sir Limmerick, tonight the king is giving an evening of much festivities in order to celebrate his winning of the throne," Sir Williams said, as his horse trotted gallantly through the forest.

Colin smiled. "It was two years ago, wasn't it?"

Sir Williams chuckled. "We have experienced no further attacks in two years. It has been a clear Tudor throne. We must celebrate."

"Fine."

Sir Williams' eyes widened. "Is that all you can say?" the knight asked, as he leaned over his horse to get a better glimpse of Colin.

"What else should I say? Good?" Colin said, more interested in the scenery.

"The queen expects us all to be there, but especially you. You are her favorite." The two men continued to trot on their horses. "Tell me, Sir Limmerick. Everyone is wondering who you really are. Where are you from?"

"Ireland is where I'm from. Don't know what else I can tell yez.

"It's not just your appearance. It's the way your demeanor. You're just different from all of us."

Colin glanced and forced a smile. "I assure ye, I'm just like everyone else."

They continued to ride. About five or six men on horses approached them. They encircled them with spears and swords extended. Sir Williams glanced at Colin.

"Get ready. These men are Yorkists." Colin pulled out his sword and positioned his sack of arrows in front of him. "You're not allowed on this land! Leave!" shouted Sir Williams.

The men did not withdraw their swords. One of them positioned his horse beside Colin. He pierced the point of his sword into Colin's shoulder. Colin glanced at him.

"Remove yer sword," Colin demanded.

The man pierced his sword even deeper into Colin. Sir Williams extended his sword at the enemy.

"Remove your sword or we will fight you to the death."

The enemy withdrew his sword from Colin and slid off his horse. He waved his dagger in the air.

"Come! Fight me, giant knight!"

Colin glanced at Sir Williams as he slid off his horse. He pulled out his dagger and held it in front of him. His opponent stepped closer to him with his dagger in hand.

"Fight me! Lancaster!"

Colin grimaced. "Lancaster?"

"You! Henry Tudor managed to get himself a giant knight to fight his battles, didn't he?"

Colin shoved the man and tripped him to the ground. He forced his weight on top of the man and held his dagger to the opponent's neck.

"Shut up, ye feck!" Colin blurted, holding his dagger to the man's throat. Sir Williams appeared surprised with a smile on his face. "Get yer men 'n feck off! This isn't yer territory!" Colin snorted to the man as he released him. The man stood up, but kept his focus on Colin. "If I see yez in these lands again, you'll surely get arrows in yer guts!" Colin shouted, as he watched the men jump onto their horses and ride off.

Sir Williams watched them vanish into the forest. He chuckled and smiled. "Wait until I tell the king about your bravery. He will definitely be pleased."

"Don't tell the king anythin'. I was just actin' in self-defense."

"You're part of the nobility. It's your job to protect the throne."

"Aye," Colin responded, with a sigh.

He hoisted his bulked physique onto his horse. Later that afternoon, Colin trotted through the forest on his horse alone.

"Sasha!" he called. "Rosa! Amoli!" He spotted one of Amoli's veils. He stopped and slid off his horse. He picked it up and searched the ground for other clues. "Amoli!"

He heard the bushes rustle in the distance. Amoli poked her head from behind the dense trees. She waved her arm.

"Colin! Over here!" He pulled his horse toward her. She fell into his arms. "I miss you so much. I'm very worried."

He held her against his body and stroked her head with his hand.

"Lass, I can't tell ye how much I miss ye." He kissed her lips several times. "Where's Sasha 'n Rosa at?"

"They're coming. Dr. Dimitrikov built a small shelter for us. He's very handy, you know."

Colin smiled. "Glad to hear it."

Sasha and Rosa rummaged through the forest to make their way to their friends. Rosa leaped into Colin's arms, pushing Amoli away. Colin kissed Rosa on the head.

"Love, yer lookin' lovely."

She touched her hair. "I could use a bath."

Colin looked at Sasha. "Well, mate? I've given ye a piece of the time machine. When can we be off?"

Sasha lit a cigarette. "My last one." He spit a few times as he chewed some of the tobacco that came lose. "You not give me time clock dial. Where is it?"

Rosa took the cigarette from Sasha. "You can be so foolish sometimes. If someone saw you smoking a cigarette, we'd all be burned to a stake."

Sasha took it back. "It is all I have. I must smoke it."

Rosa scanned the surrounding area. "Then, hurry up!"

Colin took Amoli's hands and held them. "Clock dial?"

"Da. It is most important."

Colin stared at the ground. "Shite. I don't know if I can do much more, mate. I think yer gonna have to find this clock dial. Barely remember what it even looked like. I'm expected to be at the king 'n queen's ball tonight at the palace. Just raged with this, so I am."

Amoli buried herself in Colin's arms. "I wish we could go back to our time."

Colin brought her delicate hand to his lips. "I'm with ye, lass."

Sasha smoked his cigarette to its butt and took a few more puffs. "Da, I will do. You go to your royal ball, Mr. Limmerick, and drink your royal wine. We are starving and sick."

Rosa shoved Sasha. "Don't be an idiot. We're holding our own. If you're part of the king's nobility, then you must attend this ball."

Colin smiled. "I don't think I should stick 'round here much longer. I'm not to be found with Amoli."

Rosa hugged Colin. "You need to leave; get going."

Colin kissed Rosa on the cheek and then he kissed Amoli on the lips several times. He climbed up on his horse and trotted off. Amoli wept in Sasha's arm, as she watched Colin ride off.

# Chapter Fourteen

Colin entered the palace dressed as a dashing knight. Sir Williams met him at the entrance as two of the king's musicians played their lutes at the far end of the palace. Sir Williams gestured to him.

"You're late, Sir Limmerick." Colin focused on the musicians but remained silent. "The queen has been asking for you."

"Me? Why is she askin' for me? She should be askin' for the king."

"She wants to see you. She's sitting on her throne beside the king. She's expecting a dance."

"I can't dance, unless perhaps she's willin' to accompany me with a fine Jig or reel."

"You need to see her right away."

Colin nodded his head. "Aye, I'll go to her."

As Colin started to walk away, Sir Williams tugged on his arm. Colin turned to him with surprise.

"Knight, you're walking right into danger if you keep this up."

Colin glanced at the queen sitting on her throne at the other end of the palace.

"How ye mean?"

"You appear so unaware," Sir Williams said, gently.

"Of course, I'm unaware. Not from here, so I'm not."

"Ireland is not so different, is it?"

Colin stared at the floor. "It is."

"I've been there several times. It doesn't appear so different. The Irish have to obey our English king. How is that so different?"

Colin sighed. "What am I doin' that will put me in danger?"

"You're not responding to her majesty's requests, of course."

Colin bowed his head and made a Catholic gesture of the cross in front of himself.

"Forgive me, I'll go to her now."

Sir Williams watched Colin make his way through the crowd on route to the queen. Her face brightened when she saw Colin coming her way. She sat more comfortably on her throne as the towering, handsome knight stood in front of her and bowed to the floor. The king gleamed at Colin and the queen fluttered her eyelashes as her fan covered her blushing complexion.

"Sir Limmerick, you have finally arrived. You are looking so well, I must say," she said.

He lifted his head to face her. "And I see you're lookin' as fair as ever, yer majesty."

She giggled. Sir Williams knelt beside Colin.

"Ask her for a dance," he whispered.

Colin lifted his head entirely. "Yer majesty, I would like to ask ye a favor, if I may?" He forced a smile. She grinned. "Would ye be so kind in havin' the next dance with me?"

She giggled. "Of course."

She extended her hand to him. He kissed her hand several times. The king didn't notice for he was busy speaking to Sir Williams. A different song began. She gestured for Colin to stand up from his bow. He took her hand and gently helped her off her throne. The king was engrossed in a planned conversation with Sir Williams. Colin took her hands and observed how couples in the fifteenth-century danced. He smiled at the queen.

"Forgive me, but I can't dance."

"You can't dance? Of course you can, you're part of my nobility."

Colin focused on the other couples. "Almost like an Irish reel, wouldn't ye think?"

She smiled. "Then this should be easy for you."

He tried to concentrate, and performed an Irish reel with the queen at his hands. She giggled and smiled.

Several ladies in waiting gawked at the handsome knight, as a few of them snickered at his awkward dancing. When the dance ended, Colin bowed to the queen and kissed her hand several times. He escorted her back to her throne.

"Thank-ye, m' queen," he said, as he held her hand in his.

"Several ladies-in-waiting are expecting a dance from you," said the queen.

He shifted his weight from one leg to the next. "I feel so popular."

"Which one will be your bride?" the queen asked, glancing at the young women.

Colin's fake smile dissipated.

"What's the matter? Are they not fair enough for you?"

Colin's eyes widened. "Aye, they's all beautiful, but not as fair as ye, of course."

She snickered. "Of course. Choose one now."

"Can I think about this a bit?"

She shoved him. "Definitely not. You are part of the nobility, our king's court. You must choose your bride."

He swallowed to clear his throat. He focused on the young women. They stood in a line wearing their best dresses. Colin tried to place one foot in front of the other. He noticed the young woman at the end of the line who didn't appear as anxious. He stood in front of her. The other maidens' eyes sunk when they realized who Colin's pick was. The young woman was rather thin with long dark hair pulled back in a scarf. Her dress was plain compared to the other women. Colin extended his hand. She was surprised.

"Can I ask yer name?"

She smiled. "Beatrice."

"Would ye like to join me for a dance?"

"Thank-you," she said, bowing her head to him.

She took his hand and he brought her to the floor to join the other couples. The lutes continued to play with one flutist who had joined them.

"You are new to the king's court, no?" she asked, as they danced. "I hear you're from Ireland?"

"Aye."

"I also hear that you are a fearless knight and the king holds much promise for you."

Colin's eyes shifted a bit. "Donno 'bout that, really."

"Everyone knows the queen has eyes for you."

Colin stumbled and tried not to knock the young woman over.

"Everyone knows? She's the queen, though. She's married to the king."

"She has eyes for you."

"Does the king know this?"

"He's always here and there. He's too interested in other things. After all, he is the king of England."

Colin stopped dancing. He kissed the young woman's hand.

"Beatrice, thank-ye for this dance, but can ye excuse me? Suddenly I'm not feelin' me best."

She smiled. "Of course."

He vanished into the crowd. He walked with his knees bent, so the queen wouldn't see him. He remained at the other end of the palace ballroom, where he could drink some fine wine. He guzzled the flask of wine he was given. Someone poked him on the shoulder. He turned to see who it was.

"Beatrice?"

"Sir Limmerick, you dropped this piece of gold," she said, handing him a piece of the time machine. "What is it? I've never come across anything like it."

"Not gold, so it isn't. It's brass, if ye can believe it?"

"Brass?"

"It's the hand that goes onto a dial like a clock, ye see."

"Did your clock break?"

His eyes scanned over the guests where he noticed the queen was in deep discussion with the king. He smiled.

"Aye, me clock did break."

"Oh, my father is a clock maker. Would you like me to take it to him?"

He pulled it away from her. "Not necessary; I'm sure I can fix it meself."

She stepped closer to him. "Why do you shy from me?"

"I'm not. Forgive me for bein' rude 'n such."

She stepped even closer. "Am I not beautiful enough for you?" She pulled away from him and buried her head in her scarf. "Forgive me. I'm being too forward."

He sighed. "Oh, feck."

She looked up at him. "Forgive me, what did you say?"

He nervously took her hand. "Feck, I said feck." She looked at him with a confused expression. "Tell me somethin', Beatrice, if the queen is interested in me 'n everybody knows, why she wants me to choose a lady-in-waitin', I don't know."

"Because, Sir Limmerick, it's the way things are done. I'm surprised you are unaware of this."

"Well, I suppose I'm a Catholic. Do ye, do ye fancy me at all?"

"Of course I do, you're of the king's court."

Colin's eyebrows lifted. "But do yez fancy me at all? Me?"

"Of course. All the ladies-in-waiting would like to be chosen by you. You are of great discussion around the kingdom. You're very handsome."

"That's not brilliant that I'm a big discussion. In fact, it's not at all brilliant."

"Well, I'm glad you chose me. I feel very lucky. The more I speak with you the more I am enchanted with you. It's as if you're from another time."

Colin bit his tongue. She noticed he was experiencing some pain by the expression on his face. Two of the king's guards stood beside Beatrice and tilted their heads at her. Colin was confused.

"What? What's goin' on? Who are they?"

"They are here to escort us to one of the king's chambers. I'm surprised you are so unaware."

"Oh, feck."

The two guards carried their spears as Beatrice and Colin followed them to the chamber. They entered a large room with servants waiting around a bed with an awning. Fine linens draped from the awning over the bed. Colin stared at the servants, oblivious to why they were present. Beatrice stood close to Colin.

"It's time. We are to engage on this bed. The servants are waiting."

Colin's eyes widened. "What the feck are they doin' in here if we's supposed to *engage?* Why aren't they leavin'?"

She giggled. "They'll be near by if we need anything. You chose me. I'm now your lady-in-waiting."

Colin pulled the linens off the awning and flopped on the bed. "Oh, Christ, help me." The servants stood at the end of the room. Colin kept his eyes on them. "We's expected to do somethin' here tonight?"

She giggled again. "Of course. You chose me, Sir Limmerick."

He took a deep breath and rubbed his hands over his face. She glanced at the servants and asked them to leave the chamber.

"We will marry and have a child or two or three, or four?"

He didn't reply.

"We need to undress. That's why the servants were here."

"Don't really need someone I don't even know to help me take off me bleedin' clothes, don't ye think?"

"You speak very funny to me."

He sighed a few times. "I can't sleep with ye tonight. I'm sorry."

"You must! You chose me! We must plan our wedding day!" Her voice grew louder. She pulled away from him. "Why did you choose me?"

"I had to choose someone, now didn't I?"

"What did you expect was going to happen in this chamber tonight?"

"Didn't know we was gonna be escorted to a chamber at all. Thought all we had to do was dance."

"And what a terrible dancer you are."

His eyebrows lifted with surprise at her comment. He turned away from her.

"Ye just hurt me feelings."

"You dance too much like an Irishman."

"So, that's what I am."

She gazed at him as if she was in a trance. "Is there someone else?"

He hesitated to reveal the truth. "Aye, so there is."

"Would I know her?"

"Not at all."

"She's a peasant?"

"She's an Indian princess."

"A foreigner?"

"Aye."

"Does she pray to Christ?"

"Don't think so."

"Why are you with her?"

"I've said to much already, now haven't I?"

"I will have to tell the queen that you're promised to a peasant girl. She won't be in favor of it."

"How does all this affect the queen?"

"The queen has great admiration for you. I'm one of her chosen ladies-in-waiting; therefore, you chose me and I am supposed to be the mother of your children. We were to start tonight."

He ran his large square hands through his hair. He sighed in order to catch his breath. "Okay, I'll, um," he paced, "yeah, surely we can sleep together tonight 'n soon enough you'll be expectin' me child."

She smiled at him. He started to remove his clothes. He helped her with hers. She slowly laid on the bed naked. His large naked physique hovered on top of her. He panicked when he noticed his penis had difficulty keeping an erection.

"What's wrong with you?" She placed her hands on his semi-erect penis. "What's wrong with you? Am I not fair enough?"

He closed his eyes and tried to imagine Amoli. He gasped and groaned with the thought of Amoli lying before him. He couldn't open his eyes for his erotic dream would end. Then he heard an even louder scream from Beatrice. He opened his eyes, where he realized his true bride wasn't lying before him, but rather a thin teenage girl who knew very little about anything. She grinned at him.

"I am no longer a virgin. We will have to wait and see if I am with child." Colin lay beside the young woman in wretched silence.

"Where is your tongue?" she asked. She reached for a cloth and wiped the blood from her inner thighs.

He stared at the vaulted ceiling and said nothing.

# Chapter Fifteen

Sasha knelt by the time machine with Rosa by his side.

"I think all is back in place now. Only missing few parts. It should still work," Sasha said, as he glanced at Rosa with a smile.

She grinned at him. "Then we need to find Colin and off we go."

"He is deep within kingdom. Remember, he is part of king's court," he said, as he sat back in the bushes.

"You know, he really does stick out in a crowd. He's always at the wrong place, at the wrong time. Poor Colin."

Sasha let out a loud cackle. "Poor Mr. Limmerick? How about me? I must do all for everyone."

"I'm not going to respond to that. We really need to find him."

"Da, and we must keep Miss Amoli from crying. She so sad without him."

"All she does is mope. I don't really blame her."

Sasha ran his finger along Rosa's cheek. "You know, you more beautiful each day."

She rolled her eyes back. "Oh, please, Sasha. Don't make me laugh."

"I not try to make you laugh. We do so much together," he said, as he nestled himself beside her.

"You have a wife in Russia."

Sasha pulled back. "Alright, if I not have wife, would you be with me?"

She tried to focus on something else. "I really don't know. I'd be afraid of infidelity. Colin, on the other hand, would never cheat on his wife."

"How you know?"

"He's Catholic. Colin just wouldn't do it. He's such an honest man."

"What if circumstances make him do it?"

"Circumstances? What circumstances?"

"Maybe more beautiful woman than Miss Amoli come along."

Rosa abruptly stood up. "I'm the more beautiful woman and he does not cheat behind her back. He knows I still love him."

"He sleeps with Queen of England, that to me is cheating, da?"

"Well, there are life-threatening circumstances tied in with that."

"Why you love him so much? He not so great."

"What do you mean?"

Sasha slowly stood up. "He too big like bull. He is drunk always, and works too much."

"Works too much? Whose going to pay his bills?"

Sasha stepped closer and slid his arms around her waist.

"What are you doing?"

"It is time you stop it with Mr. Limmerick. He marry Miss Amoli, not you. I am here and he is not. I find you irresistible." He brought his lips to hers and kissed her several times.

She pulled back. "You have a wife."

He stepped back. "I will leave her. My marriage not good, ever."

"Stop this. I don't think this is a good idea."

He stepped close to her again and ran his finger along her lips.

"You so beautiful lady."

"You don't even like me. What are you saying?"

"I love you is what I say you."

Her eyes widened. "Oh, God. Sasha, I can't be with a married man."

He slid his arms around her waist again.

"It's against my beliefs," she insisted as she tried to pull away.

He brought his lips to hers and started to kiss her. She slowly reciprocated as he pressed his body against hers. They kissed without any resistance.

They heard the bushes rustle loudly and the hard sound of horse hooves. Sasha turned his head to see Colin sitting on a horse.

"Colin!" Rosa shouted.

He slid off his horse. "Don't come too close to me, love. Where's Amoli at?"

"I think she's around the shelter Sasha built. She's yearning for you," Rosa said.

"Tell her not to. I think I'm in big trouble with the kingdom now."

Rosa stepped closer to Colin. "Oh?"

"I'm somehow promised to this lady-in-waitin'. I so stupidly told her I had someone else in me life. She wanted to know what kingdom. I so stupidly said there wasn't a kingdom attached to me fiancé 'n this lass lost her mind, so I gave into her."

"Tell her she not adequate and to bug off," Sasha said.

"Not that easy, mate. We was supposed to feck with servants in the room right with us. This is all set up as part of the king's court."

Rosa tried to swallow. "How awful. Is she at least pretty?"

"Not at all. The queen isn't a ravin' beauty, either. Gaunt, twiggy girls is what they both are." Colin stared at the ground. "I had to mount her. She said Amoli would be killed if I didn't. I'm supposed to marry her 'n have loads of children with her. She's all fecked up over it 'cause I'm engaged to marry a peasant girl. The queen won't fancy this one bit, no she won't. Amoli's not part of any king's court, ye know it."

"Colin, are you even allowed to be out of the castle?" Rosa asked, in a panic.

109

"I'm not. I think they's lookin' for me. It won't be pretty what they have in store for me. I did comply to this lady-in-waitin', but she was quite put off by me preferrin' to marry someone else, especially someone who isn't part of their bleedin' court."

Rosa took Colin's arm, but he pushed her away. "Ye can't be doin' this, love! If they come 'round lookin' for me, they will surely think yer me fiancé 'n kill ye. Ye 'n Amoli need to stay away from me."

Sasha tugged on Colin's arm. "I not have all time machine parts, but I think machine can go. We must find Miss Amoli and go now."

The hard thumping sound of horse hooves hit the ground as the king's knights held their swords in front of themselves.

"Sir Limmerick!" shouted Sir Williams. "The queen demands you at her throne at once!"

Colin tried not to glance at Rosa. He glanced at Sasha as several knights swarmed him and poked their swords at his back. "Sir Limmerick, you are expected at the queen's throne immediately!" Sir Williams shouted. "At once!"

They chained Colin's ankles in order to tug him back to the castle.

Sasha discreetly raised his gun.

*"Sasha! No!"* Rosa whispered in a fluster.

Sir Williams and his band of men take Colin and vanish into the English countryside.

Amoli suddenly appeared. "What's going on here?"

Sasha took Amoli's hand and brought it to his lips. "Miss Amoli, we have problem."

"Is the time machine broken?"

"It is not time machine this time. Mr. Limmerick was just seized by queen's guards. He is in trouble. You must stay away from him or you will be in danger."

Amoli watched Rosa cry, curled up on the ground rocking herself back and forth.

"Why? Why is he in trouble?" Amoli blurted, in distress.

Sasha searched his jacket. "I not know." He paused, as he continued to search for a cigarette. "I not have any more."

Rosa stopped crying. She slowly stood up to face Amoli. "Don't try to see Colin; you'll be in danger. I knew it was a big mistake coming to this time period."

"We have to get Colin back and leave this time period," Amoli blurted with panic.

Rosa started to pace. "We have to find him in the castle." She looked at Sasha. "Do you think this queen will ease up on Colin?"

"Nyet. I not think she would. He make plans to marry common girl, not king's court. Not good. Maybe queen wants Mr. Limmerick for herself. Who knows?"

Rosa threw her arms in the air. "We can't let him die here. We have no choice, but to save him. He's our Colin and we love him."

"How we get inside castle?" Sasha asked.

"I have to think, but the clock is ticking. They might even kill him tonight."

Amoli howled, "No!"

"If we get into castle, I will bring gun and shoot them all," Sasha blurted.

"You want to assassinate King Henry Vll? You want to completely change history?"

"It is better than watching Mr. Limmerick die."

"I agree with Dr. Dimitrikov. Who cares about history?" Amoli squealed.

***

Colin bowed before the queen. She focused on her new royal subject.

"Rise, Sir Limmerick. I want to see your face," she said. He stood before her and kept his eyes to the floor.

"So, Sir Limmerick, you are planning a wedding? A wedding to a peasant girl?"

"Not a peasant, yer majesty."

The queen rose from her thrown and her royal subjects took a step back.

"If she's not a peasant, then who is she?"

"She's from another kingdom in a far away land."

"What other kingdom? I am familiar with all the kingdoms. Where?"

He continued to stare at the floor. "Not Europe."

Her eyebrows furrowed. A small puddle of sweat formed on the floor surrounding Colin.

"Who is she? I would know of her most definitely."

"I'd rather keep it to meself, if ye don't mind me sayin', yer majesty."

Her eyes widened. "You're withholding information from me?"

"Forgive me."

"Did you share a bed with Beatrice last night?"

"I did, yer majesty."

"Good."

Beads of sweat poured off his face and onto the wood-planked floor. "Tell me, Sir Limmerick, do you expect to marry Beatrice and have children with her?"

He kept his posture in a bowing position.

The queen lowered her eyebrows. "You shared a bed with her last night, did you not? She could be with your child this minute for all you know. You must plan your wedding to her right away. You must be with her always. I thought she wasn't fair enough for you, but if you agreed to share a bed with her, then she must be suitable to your liking."

"Aye." Colin noticed the tiny, gaunt young queen pace the room in fury.

"I brought you into our kingdom and convinced the king to keep you as part of our nobility. You cannot disappoint me, or I will be forced to have you undergo

112

great methods of torture. Do you understand, Sir Limmerick?"

"I understand, yer majesty."

"Now, I want to see you at my chamber in less than an hour. Do not disappoint me, knight."

"Aye, yer majesty."

The guards indicated that it was time to have Colin escorted out of the queen's quarters. Colin found himself in one of the several castle courtyards. He walked around aimlessly, where he focused on the several marketers who were selling woven garments and jewelry. Beatrice was standing by the guild workers at the other end of the courtyard.

She walked to Colin and curtsied. "Good afternoon, Sir Limmerick. You're looking dashing today."

He was startled by her welcome. "Dashin' ye say? I don't feel dashin', so I don't. Can't really speak to yez for too long. Gotta see the queen in a bit."

"Have you seen the queen yet today?"

"I have."

"And how was that meeting with her?"

"Rather *shite*, I must say."

Her smile dissipated. "I sometimes feel troubled by how you speak. I'm never sure what you're saying to me."

"Well, I'm supposin' that's 'cause I'm Irish."

"Yes, people from Ireland are known to speak quite strangely."

"Tell me somethin', Beatrice, are ye gonna be plannin' our weddin'?"

"You are also supposed to partake in this affair."

"Don't really know the first thin' 'bout plannin' a weddin' in the fifteenth century, so I don't."

She snickered at him. "Then I will help you."

"Good to hear it."

"I wanted you to know that I feel different today. I think I'm with child. Other maidens can tell right away. We better plan the wedding very soon."

He lowered himself to her ear. "Did ye know the queen wants to see me in a few minutes at her bed chamber?"

Beatrice smiled. "Oh, yes?"

"Aye. Don't ye find that odd?"

Beatrice shrugged her shoulders. "She's the queen. She can do as she wishes."

"It doesn't bother ye?"

Beatrice laughed. "I don't feel it's my place to say."

Colin sighed and stood straight towering over the crowd of marketers. He noticed a small elderly man pull a crate of wine along the yard. Colin stepped forward to grab a jug of wine.

"How much for this?" Colin asked.

"It'll cost ya a half schilling," the elderly man answered.

Colin fondled with his ancient currency and gave the money. He glanced at Beatrice and smiled.

"Ye want some?"

She gestured *no* to him. He pulled out the plug and placed the jug to his lips. He began to drink profusely. Beatrice watched him drink almost half of it without any breaks. He placed the jug in his knapsack.

"Needed that, so I did."

She laughed as she stood beside him in the midst of the busy marketers.

"I am learning to like you, Sir Limmerick," she said.

"I'm learnin' to really hate meself, fancy the fact that yer feelin' the opposite, so I do," he responded, with a slight drunken slur.

He pulled the jug out of his knapsack and finished it off in front of her. He embraced Beatrice and left the courtyard. He approached the queen's chamber. A guard stood in front of the door holding a spear. Colin gave a slight bow.

"The queen is expectin' me. I'm Sir Limmerick."

114

The guard grimaced at him. "Wait here. I will check if she is expecting you." The guard returned. "Go in, she awaits your arrival."

Colin pushed the door opened. He bowed to the floor. She approached him and watched him bow. She was dressed in her full royal attire.

"Rise," she said. He stood up to face her. "Finally, we are together, knight." He tried to smile back at her. "There is my bed. Quickly, this shouldn't take too long."

He stepped closer to her. She ran her hands along the inside of his thigh. She grinned. Two young female servants entered the room to help the queen remove her royal garments. The queen pranced to her bed naked and watched the two servants undress Colin. He felt awkward having such young girls help him remove his tights. The two servants stood to the side of the room to wait. Colin stood before the queen without his clothes.

"Come to me," the queen said, as she lay sprawled on the bed. The cold stone floor made Colin shiver as he walked to the bed. He lay beside her, noticing the two servants in the background.

The queen gazed at him. "Kiss me."

Colin appeared less rigid as other times for he was too intoxicated to care. He kissed her when she asked for it. She howled with lust as she felt his body next to hers.

"Oh, what a good knight you are."

He lifted his eyebrows not really knowing how to respond. He lay on top of the queen and tried to fit his erect penis inside her. He kept a strong image in his head of Amoli and thrust himself inside her. The queen groaned and panted as he penetrated her.

"Can't believe I'm feckin' the queen of England," he blurted, in a drunken stupor.

The two servants stood still with no expression on their faces. When Colin finally pulled out he lay beside her.

*"Amoli,"* he sighed.

"Pardon? Knight?" the queen responded, confused. She fondled his lengthy hair. "How are the wedding plans with Beatrice?"

Colin's eyes widened. "She aims on gettin' on with them immediately."

"Do you know if she's carrying your child?"

"She seems to think so."

"Good. The king will be pleased to hear this."

"Speakin' of the king, yer majesty, where's he at just now?"

"He's back in the north again. He's always here and there. He's the most powerful king in Europe."

"He won't walk in on us then, will he?"

The queen snickered. "Well, if he did, he would want your head more than mine."

Colin jumped out of her bed. "Where's me clothes at?" He demanded, to the servants. "I'm thinkin' he'd want yer head just as much, wouldn't ye think?" They rushed his clothes to him. He sat on the bed and struggled to get his hose on. "I don't want any more of this shite."

The queen's mouth opened with surprise. "Excuse me, knight? Are you drunk?"

"I don't want to feck ye or the other bitch as well. Ye both don't even know how to be with a man. Yer both lousy in the sack."

She sat up in bed and demanded her servants bring her clothes.

"Have you lost your mind? Where is your sense of chivalry? You're a knight. You're not supposed to be drunk when the queen asks to see you. That is not chivalry!"

"Don't want any of this. I'm not even from this stinkin' century. I'm from yer future."

"So, you are a witch?"

"Yer more of witch than I could ever be, ye witch. I'm from the twentieth century. That doesn't make me a witch." He tied his sash around his waist and picked up his sword from the floor.

"What a waste this is; such a strong, handsome knight and you will have to die for this. What a shame."

"Yer fecked up! I'll be off in me time machine before ye can even appoint yer next headsman!"

She turned to her two servants. "Fetch my guards!"

"Not afraid of yer meek little fifteenth-century guards. Don't scare me, so they don't."

She clutched a cushion as she sat at the far end of the bed.

"You're going to die for this. You were always so defiant. How could you carry on with your knighthood if this is the kind of man you are?"

"Don't want yer feckin' idea of knighthood. I carry on with me own idea of chivalry, not yer made-up disjointed version, ye bitch!"

Several guards stormed into the room. They bowed to their queen as they waited for her instructions.

"Take him to the smallest dungeon in the castle. Chain him up and let him rot until further instructions. I must plan something for him."

They poked the points of their swords at his back. He turned to one of the guards and kicked his sword out of his hand. Colin thrashed the man to the floor and smacked him several times in the face until he drew blood. Another guard slashed Colin's shoulder with his sword. Colin stood up and kicked the man in the stomach. Another guard slashed Colin's thigh where he punched him to the floor knocking out several teeth. The queen sprung up from the bed and into the corner of the room. She screamed for more security, where several more of the knights stormed in.

"Take Limmerick to the dungeon! Chain him up! He's very strong! Don't let him get away!" the queen shouted, with hoarseness in her voice.

117

Rosa, Sasha, and Amoli paced around the time machine.

"Sasha, maybe it's best we enter the castle with you shooting your gun at everyone," Rosa blurted in despair.

"I bring enough bullets; we can shoot all!"

Rosa paced around him. "How many bullets did you bring?"

"Enough."

Amoli paced around the time machine.

"But you know Mr. Limmerick, he not like this. I know," Sasha added.

"Who cares what Colin likes? We have to get him out of that place," Rosa whined.

Amoli stopped pacing. "We have to get him away from that castle. We don't have a choice. Yes, Dr. Dimitrikov said the time machine can get us out of this terrible time period, but we're not going anywhere without Colin."

Rosa also stopped pacing. "Alright, how do we enter the castle?"

"I make proposal to see queen. I say her she is beautiful, when we all know she is not. I propose to sing to her, da, sing. I will sing song about queen, da?"

Rosa rolled her eyes. "Okay, mister music man, start writing your song. This is the most ridiculous idea that has ever come out of your mouth."

"Why you say ridiculous? You not know. She is queen, ugly queen at that, I will make her feel beautiful."

"You're such an idiot!"

Sasha looked at Rosa. "Why you say this? I will get us in castle."

Rosa folded her arms. "Oh, yes, Sasha, you will definitely find us a way into the castle. You will also buy us a way back into that disgusting dungeon."

Amoli snickered softly where she tried not to let Sasha hear her laugh.

"You not believe, so I not care. I will get us safely into castle. We will get Mr. Limmerick and bring him to time machine, da?"

"Maybe we can break into the castle at night when everyone is asleep?" Amoli suggested.

"The castle is guarded all night, as well as all day," Rosa responded.

"All I can think of is posing as someone else, but we won't get through the drawbridge, even. I'm Indian and this is the fifteenth century."

Sasha stepped closer to Amoli. "They not used to people of your looks in fifteenth century. *Jungle Book* not created yet, da?"

Rosa sighed. "We have to get Colin. I say we plunge our way through the castle using Sasha's gun," she said, with a quiver in her voice. "It's drastic, but we haven't the choice."

Amoli's eyes widened. "You're suggesting we shoot people?"

"Whatever it takes to get Colin back with us, I don't really care about changing history at this point. We need Colin back here with us."

"I like idea. It is what these people need, da?" Sasha commented, with a grin.

\*\*\*

Colin opened his eyes to find himself chained to musty cinder blocks in a tiny, dark cell. He lay flat on his back on the cold, damp floor as he noticed two rats sniff around his leg and scamper off.

"Oh, God, help me," he said. "How did I ever get meself in this kinda mess? Oh, Christ, please help."

The chains around his wrists were bolted to one of the cinder blocks behind him. As he pulled his arm forward,

119

the block would shift. He tried to sit up, but the chain was too short. He looked behind his shoulder and pulled his arm forward again and noticed the block shifted even further. The door swung opened and one of the dungeon guards entered the cell.

"Here is your food. It's not much, but it's something." He laid a tray of soup, bread and water on the floor beside Colin. "So, you're here for violating her majesty?"

Colin tried to look anywhere, but at the guard.

"I heard them talking about you outside. You're going to be sentenced to hard labor before your execution."

Colin focused on one of the rats in the corner of the cell. "Don't be too happy. Once you see what they've got in store for you, you'd prefer to get burned at the stake."

"I don't care, really," Colin spewed. "Go, feck yerself."

The guard stepped toward Colin. "What did you say?"

Colin tried to sit up. "I said, go feck yerself."

"That'll cost you 30 lashes," the guard said, as he pulled out his whip from his side pouch.

He pulled out a large key and unchained Colin from the wall. As he did so, Colin punched him to the ground, leaped over the guard, and wrapped his hands around his throat. The guard turned several shades of red. Colin released his hands and stood up. He kicked the man in the head and knocked him out. He took the key and dragged the guard outside the cell behind a stone pillar.

Colin scanned the narrow, stone aisle-ways to realize he was alone. He caught his breath and moved through the dungeon to the closest exit. He found himself in a courtyard cluttered with bushes, trees and flowers. He flopped behind a bush and closed his eyes. A few hours had passed. Colin opened his eyes to see a man dressed in red cloak kneeling beside him with a bucket and cloth. He gently rubbed Colin's face with the warm cloth.

"Ah, you finally woke. I thought you were going to sleep forever. You must adore the sweet smell of lilac," the man said.

Colin sat up. "How long was I asleep?"

The man handed Colin a clean towel. "Long enough. Are you the king's prisoner, or are you the king's nobility?"

"Both."

"Come, follow me to the cathedral. I will get you into clean clothes and get some decent food in you."

Colin stood up. "How'ye gonna get me outta this castle?"

The priest chuckled. "Oh, yes, you are a giant of a man, aren't you? I have this cloak. Put it over you and bend down as low as you can. Do not show your face." Colin threw the cloak over him and bent his body low. "Whatever you do, don't say a word. Someone is bound to recognize your dialect."

Colin took the man's arm. "How should I call ye?"

The man smiled. "Father Abbott."

"How is yer rapport with the king, Father Abbott?"

"Not so good, but he tolerates me. He has no choice. The Vatican has placed me here."

Colin smiled. "I have a confession, Father."

"Not now. First, lets get you outside the castle."

The priest pushed opened the door that exited the courtyard. He looked down the narrow hallways of the castle and tugged on Colin's arm. Several castle guards walked past them. They noticed Colin hunched over with a brown cloak over him. They continued with their duties, trying not to pay much attention to the priest and the man with the cloak draped over him.

121

# Chapter Sixteen

Rosa poked around the town streets, noticing how the common people lived. She saw a family selling freshly baked bread, where she stood before a young woman, who took money for the bread.

"How much for a loaf of bread?" Rosa asked.

The young merchant smiled. "A half schilling."

Rosa paid her for the bread." She turned from the young woman and then stepped toward her again. "Excuse me, do you sell clothes?"

"No, I'm sorry. You'll have to walk to the other end of the town for that."

"Well, um, could I buy what you're wearing right now?"

"My garment? It's not for sale. I'm wearing it."

"So?" Rosa's eyes shifted. "Who's that other woman over there? I want her dress as well. How much?"

"She's my sister, but neither is for sale. I already told you."

"Who's that man with you?"

The young woman smiled. "He is my fiancé."

"I think he would be the right fit for my fiancé," Rosa said.

"Oh, you're soon to marry, as well as I?"

"I need your clothes, your sister's, and your fiancé's"

"I'm sorry, that's just not possible. Go to the other end of the town and you will find it. Now please leave."

Rosa grabbed her arm. "What are you doing?"

Rosa punched the woman in the face and she fell to the ground. Amoli hid behind a horse shelter.

"Miss Emanuel, where did you learn how to punch people?" Amoli squealed.

"No time for chatter. Let's hurry and get these clothes off this woman. I've got to go after her sister. I have no idea how I'm going to get my way with the fiancé."

"Where's Dr. Dimitrikov?"

"Don't even bother to get him; he'll just shoot everyone. I think we can do this without bullets," Rosa said, kneeling on the ground furiously trying to get the woman's dress off her body.

The sister noticed what Rosa was doing. "What did you do to my sister?"

Rosa punched her in the face and watched her fall to the ground.

Amoli yelped.

*"Shhh.* Don't draw attention to us. Fetch Sasha, so we can finish the job".

"Did Colin teach you how to do this?"

Rosa grinned. "Look, we're in a trying situation. Do you have any other suggestions?"

Amoli scampered off into the crowds to find Sasha. Rosa feverishly pulled the clothes off the other woman as well. Amoli returned with Sasha by her side.

"Who you want me to get, Miss Amoli?" Sasha asked, as he noticed Rosa pulling the women's garments over her head.

Amoli pointed. "That man over there. Can you get his clothes without shooting him?"

"Nyet. Bullets is all we have, da?" Sasha walked in front of the man.

"Pardon me, but are you with these two maidens?" asked the young man.

"Da."

"Well, they just harmed my loved ones."

"Give me clothes, your clothes. Give them, now!"

"Have you gone mad?"

Sasha punched the man in the head.

Rosa glanced at the knocked-out man lying on the ground. "Sasha, you weren't supposed to make his mouth

123

bleed. I hope you didn't loosen any of his teeth. Try and find a dentist around this time period."

"I not even like dentist in our time period. They always make pain, da?"

Amoli struggled to get the dress on. "It doesn't quite fit me. What do I do now?"

Amoli tried to stuff her ample breasts inside the dress.

Rosa stepped closer to her. "You're breasts are enormous. I don't think any dress could ever fit them."

Sasha grinned at Rosa. "Why you think Mr. Limmerick like Miss Amoli so much?"

"I'll have to let the dress out, somehow. I hope there's enough material for me to do so," Rosa said. "By the way, Colin is not as shallow-minded as you. I'm sure the size of Amoli's breasts are not the reason he has agreed to marry her."

Amoli giggled. "He says I'm beautiful and that he loves me."

"You could definitely lose a stone," Rosa said, under her breath.

"Are you calling me fat?"

Sasha dressed himself in the other man's clothes. "No time or place to fight. Act like grown ladies. Still, how we get into castle?"

"I'm going to take this bread and pretend as if the king ordered it," Rosa said.

"They have more bread here, Miss Emanuel, we should take it all and propose it to the king," Amoli suggested.

The three time travelers took the remaining loaves of bread and headed for the castle. Four knights sat on their horses before the drawbridge. Rosa stepped forward. She gave a slight curtsy with a nervous twitch.

"Greetings, fine gents. The king has ordered bread and we are only too happy to deliver it ourselves."

Sir Williams glanced at the other three knights.

124

"Bread? Does anyone know if his majesty is expecting bread from peasant bakers?" The knights nodded their heads. "We will have to find out before you enter the castle," Sir Williams said.

Rosa's eyes bounced around. "Well, then, please do so."

"We are on guard duty. We are not to disturb his majesty," Sir Williams grunted.

"Oh, well, then, what shall we do? The king was adamant about receiving his bread today," Rosa insisted, as she glanced at Sasha and Amoli.

Sir Williams slid off his horse. "Very well, I will go. Wait here." Before Sir Williams entered the castle, he took a long look at the three time travelers. "I've seen the three of you before with another one of our nobility."

One of the other knights stared at Amoli. "Who is this moor?"

Amoli stepped forward. "I am an Indian princess, not a moor."

"You're not my princess, you're a moor."

Rosa tugged on Amoli's arm. "Uh, she is an Indian princess. She has been doing business with the queen. Keep in mind England does a great deal of trade with India. I wouldn't be so dismissive, if I were you," Rosa said, as she dried her sweaty hands on her merchant's dress.

"Oh, yes, trade is quite active with India, you are correct," the knight said.

"Yes, do keep your line of Chivalry at hand. This is what a good knight should do, yes?" Rosa assured.

Sir Williams returned. "His majesty does not recall ordering bread, but his queen has decided to allow you three into the castle. She is curious to see you and sample the bread."

Rosa grinned at Sasha. "Oh, well, thank-you."

She and Amoli gave a sloppy curtsey and Sasha bowed at the four knights.

\*\*\*

Colin knelt before a large crucifix in the cathedral and prayed with rosary beads in his hands. Father Abbott stood at the side by a large painting of Christ. He observed Colin pray. Colin knelt with his head down as he recited his prayers in a whisper.

"Well, I can see you are a good Catholic," the priest said. Colin expressed the sign of the cross in front of himself as he rose with a slight bow to the statue of Christ. "You said you have a confession to make?" asked the priest.

"Aye. I'm engaged to marry, but since I've arrived here the queen insisted I sleep with her. Surely, I didn't want to obey her wishes. She's married to the king and I'm promised to another lass. She also encouraged me to plan a weddin' with this lady-in-waitin', who I have no interest in ever seein' again, so it may be."

The priest's eyes widened. "Oh, my, such complications. So, you caught the queen's fancy?"

"So, I did, somehow. Doesn't even know who I am, so she doesn't. Suddenly I'm knighted 'n well, they put me in the dungeon, 'cause I called the queen a bleedin' bitch."

The priest's eyes widened even more. "Oh, so you cussed at the queen? Well, that should get you into a great deal of trouble, don't you think?"

"Supposin' so."

"You can't cuss at royalty. You will definitely be impaled for that one."

"Don't fancy the queen or the lady-in-waitin'. They're bitches, for sure they is."

The priest sighed and focused on the large statue of Christ that sat behind the pulpit of the cathedral.

"Where are you from?"

"Irish, so I am, Father."

"Irish, oh, yes, of course you are. Well, if you've got yourself in this kind of trouble then I'd have to say you are in some kind of trouble. Oh, yes, unfortunately. Everyone knows, even how wrong our king or queen can be, they are never wrong. Why on earth would you do such a silly thing as cuss at them?"

"'Cause, Father, this is me confession to yez. Not from this century, so I'm not." The priest sat down on one of the benches. "A time traveler is what I am. Not really accustomed to fifteenth-century ideas of what yez call chivalry, if ye know what I mean."

"No, I don't know what you mean."

"Well, this whole knighthood thing has got me down, so to put it. Me own ideas of chivalry just aren't fifteenth-century ideas of chivalry."

The priest lifted his eyebrows. "Alright then, if you are not a fifteenth-century man, what kind of man are you?"

"Twentieth, Father."

"The future? So you're from the future?" The priest snorted with laughter. "Tell me, how the twentieth century is different than the fifteenth century?"

Colin paused to think. "Automobiles, but not everyone has one. I had one, but I sold it. Me academic advisor has one, so he does. Me ship, I own me own ship. A man of the sea is what I am. Me ship runs not just with sails, but with steam power, so it does. We travel the country by rail. Ye know a locomotive. It's rather fast, so it is. The Americas always use locomotives, so they do. Never been there, though. Hope to sail there some day. That would be the new world to yez."

The priests' lips parted. "Automobiles? Locomotives? The Americas?"

"Aye. The Americas has established cities 'n such. We even have communication like telegraphs. We listen to music on phonographs. People are built bigger in me century. Can't fit into yer armor even if I tried."

127

The priest responded, "Forgive me for saying, but please tell me the truth. Are you a witch?"

"Anythin' ye don't understand has to be witchcraft. Do I look like a witch to yez?"

"You look like a giant, that's for sure."

"Okay, won't lie to yez, so I won't. I'm rather huge even for me own time. Me own Uncle Kevin was almost as big as me."

"I'm sorry, I didn't get your name."

"Colin, or Sir Limmerick, so I'm known around here."

"How did you travel from the future to this time?"

"Sasha's time machine, no doubt. He left Russia 'n fled to England, if ye can believe it?"

"This story you're telling me is extremely difficult to believe. So, Sasha built the time machine? This is all an act of God."

"Sasha claims he built it in Switzerland with a team of others similar to him. But I've gotta tell yez, Father, his time travel device don't work as it should."

"Time travel device?"

"Aye. I fought eye to eye with *Neanderthals*, so I did; took on great Vikin' warriors, so I did; found me jewel in the wild, so I did, *Megaloceros Giganteus.*"

The priest rubbed his tired eyes. "I don't know what you're speaking of. I have never heard these names before. Are they terms of sorcery?"

"Sorcery? I'm no witch, so I told ye. A time traveler, so I am."

"What do I do, now?"

"Easy. Ye don't do a thing. Ye just remember me, don't tell anyone. It's supposed to be a secret, but since yer a man of the cloth, ye can take it."

"No, I don't think I can take it. I don't really believe what you're saying to me. I think, perhaps, you have gone mad. It's the only answer I can come up with."

128

Colin sat on the same bench as the priest. "A simple man is what I am. Mad? Not me, Father."

"Simple man? You slept with the queen and your lady-in-waiting, and yet you're engaged to marry someone else? You are not a simple man."

"But that's who I am. The queen did it by force. She must fancy something about me, don't know what. Don't really fancy her. She's a bitch, so she is."

"The queen's guards will be looking for you. What shall I do to save you?"

"Don't burden yerself. It's me feck-up 'n I gotta get meself back with me friends so we can return to our time."

"Your friends?"

"Aye. Me wife-to-be, for one. Rosa, me former wench, 'n Sasha. I haven't seen me fiancé in a few days now. Miss her, so I do."

"If you run into the countryside they'll find you and bring you back to the dungeon."

Colin stared at the floor. "It's me fault for tryin' to play God. It's what I deserve."

"Don't say such a thing. For some reason, I'm growing very fond of you. We are all God's children and this is what God had in store for you."

Colin smiled. "People, on first impressions, either love me or hate me bleedin' guts. When I was sixteen, used to blame it on the freckles on me nose 'n me crimson hair."

The priest placed his hand on Colin's shoulder. "I believe your story."

"Blame it on science, Father. Science has come a long way. We study our planet the way it was thousands of years ago."

"Perhaps, I can bring you to my sister's home. She lives with her daughter, my niece. They have a small farm on the fife. Maybe, the queen's guards wouldn't think to look for you there."

129

"Don't wanna impose, so I don't. I can pay ye back, if ye want?"

"Pay me back? With what?"

"Ye wanna see the twentieth century?"

The priest's eyes widened. "Are you asking me if I want to see the future?"

"Surely, yer curious, no doubt. Ye can continue yer priesthood in the twentieth century, if that's dany with yez?"

"Good God, no! I am quite content here in my time, thank-you."

Colin stood up. "Sorry 'bout that, if I offended yez."

The priest took Colin's arm. "We should get you to my sister's home at once."

*** 

Rosa, Amoli, and Sasha stood before the queen, as she sat at her throne.

"I see you three have brought fresh bread. How thoughtful of you," she said.

Rosa curtsied to the floor. "Please sample it."

The queen's servant brought a sliced loaf on a gold platter and served it. The queen smiled.

"How splendid this is. You are excellent bakers." Sasha smiled at the queen while he bowed to the floor. The queen glanced at Amoli. "Who is this moor you have with you?"

Amoli continued to curtsy. "I am an Indian princess."

"Don't speak!" the queen shouted. She looked at Sasha. "Who is this moor?"

"She is Indian princess," Sasha said.

"You are foreign?"

"Russian royalty."

"How interesting it is that you both are royalty, and I the queen of England, did not even know. You and you," said the queen, pointing at Rosa and Sasha, "will be my personal bakers. As for the moor?"

Amoli gazed at the queen. "I am an Indian princess."

The queen examined her. "Perhaps you do come from royalty. Maybe yes, maybe not."

Amoli was so nervous she urinated on the floor. Rosa noticed the puddle flowing from under her dress.

"You two will be my bakers, and the moor can be placed in the dungeon for now. Put her in the cell Sir Limmerick was in!" the queen demanded.

Rosa lifted her eyebrows. "Excuse me, yer majesty, you are placing the Indian princess in a cell where someone once was?"

"My fallen knight has mysteriously escaped. My guards are out looking for him." Rosa glanced at Sasha. "Take my new bakers to the kitchen and the moor to the dungeon," the queen ordered.

Rosa and Sasha were led to the kitchen. One of the guards looked at them.

"The queen and the king will expect fresh bread by morning. You will be expected to also feed the king's court as well," the guard instilled and he made his exit.

Rosa stood by the wood table. "Oh, God, what are we going to do? Colin isn't even in the castle. Amoli is in the dungeon, and we're expected to bake bread. I haven't a clue how to do this. I've never baked in my life. Do you know anything about this?"

"Nyet. I not know. I only know how to use sword. There is wheat here. What we do with it?"

"Wheat? Don't you make flour from wheat?"

"Sasha picked up a strand of wheat and held it to his mouth.

"I think we grind it up with something and make flour, da?"

"I don't know. I've lived most of my life in cities. Is there some kind of a wheat grinder around?"

"This is fifteenth century. I not know if they know this in this time."

Rosa bent over the wood table and took a deep breath. "Sasha, we're not going to get out of this alive."

"You shut up, da? We be okay with this."

She rubbed her hands over her face. "Colin is mysteriously missing? Amoli peed her pants and now she's in the dungeon. We've been hired as the king's personal bakers. I never baked anything in my life. I spent time sewing and reading, but never in the kitchen."

"How you expect to get husband if you not in kitchen?"

She flicked her hair back. "I don't really care if I ever marry. I don't need a man."

Sasha cackled. "You want Mr. Limmerick or nothing, da?"

"That's not true. I'm over Colin now."

"You never over Mr. Limmerick. You love him so much, I know."

"Yes, I do love Colin, but I accept he will marry Amoli."

Sasha stepped closer. "Why you love him so much? I never understand."

Rosa grinned at the thought of Colin. "He's smart, loving, considerate, and loyal. He's a good man. Who wouldn't fall in love with him?"

"Me." Sasha stepped very close to her. He brought his hand to her cheek. "Why you not love me like you love him?"

His hand caressed her face. She looked at him.

"Because you're married, for one thing."

"Am I not as beautiful as him?"

She chuckled. "Do you think I only judge a man on his outer beauty, Sasha?"

"Da, you are shallow lady, I know." Sasha brought his lips to hers and locked them with hers. He pushed his tongue into her mouth and continued to kiss her.

"Beautiful lady, I mean what I say. I love you. I love you day I first saw you. I take you away from Mr. Limmerick, because I want you."

She slid her arms around his neck. They kissed until Sir Williams walked in.

"Excuse me. I hope I'm not interrupting anything."

Rosa jolted back. "Oh! The bread isn't ready yet!"

"I came to tell you we are expecting guests from France in the morning. You must bake more bread. "

Sasha's eyes wandered the room. "How much more?"

"At least ten more loaves."

Rosa stepped close to the knight. "Excuse me, do you know anything about the knight who escaped the castle dungeon? Has he been found?"

"No, not at all. We're searching for him."

The knight made his exit. Rosa glared at Sasha with panic in her eyes.

"What are we going to do?"

Sasha leaned against the pillar. "Do? We bake bread, da?"

"There's no flour!"

"We must find grinder for wheat."

Rosa searched the pantry. "I don't see a wheat grinder anywhere."

"No wheat grinder? These are primitive people. I hate them."

"I hate them, too. Now we're separated from Colin and Amoli. This is getting worse."

"Okay, we try this." Sasha grabbed a mallet. "We crush wheat with this. We must mill wheat into flour, da? We do this, or we try to escape."

"If we get caught, they'll kill us."

"Da."

133

# Chapter Seventeen

The priest led Colin to a village cottage.

"Peg, hello!" the priest said, to his sister as he pushed opened the door.

She stopped sweeping the floor.

"Nice surprise," a stocky, somewhat masculine-looking woman said, as she embraced her brother. "Who is with you?"

"This is Colin. He comes from Ireland. He's one of the king's knights. He, unfortunately, has had a falling out with the queen, and he needs a place to stay."

"Is the queen after you?" she asked.

"Aye."

"Well, it would be my pleasure," she said, with a toothless smile. She walked to Colin and took his hand. "It would be my pleasure." Colin felt awkward. "By the way, my daughter knows of some festivities tonight if you're interested, Colin?"

Colin glanced at the priest. "Festivities? Exhausted is how I'm feelin'. I'd much rather catch a few winks, if ye know what I mean."

The priest smiled. "Of course. That niece of mine always has something planned."

"Come, sit at the table and I'll fix us all something to eat, ah?"

Colin sat down with the priest. "Where is your husband?" he asked the woman.

"He died in a brothel. What a cad he was. Don't miss him at all. Someone slipped him some poison," she said, with a giggle. She brought a huge jug of wine to the table and poured Colin a glass. "Drink up; it's good for you."

The door swung opened and a girl of sixteen walked in.

"Greetings, everyone," she said. "How now, uncle?"

"Ah, yes, my beautiful niece, Catherine. She spends most of her time at the monastery. She is preparing to be a nun."

Colin smiled at her. "Hello, Catherine."

She leaned against her mother. "Who is he? He's splendid!" she said, giggling with her mother.

Colin guzzled his wine. Peg filled his flask again.

"Drink up. It's what we like to see around here," she said, with laughter.

Colin rubbed his tired eyes. "Forgive me, just so knackered, so I am."

Catherine stood behind Colin and massaged his shoulders.

"Such a strong man," she commented, kneading his shoulder muscles.

He continued to guzzle the wine. "So, yer gonna be a nun, are yez?"

"Yes, I will as soon as I can. I want to follow my uncle's path to God."

Her hands moved to his shoulder blades and lower to his waist. Her mother placed a platter of fruit on the table and giggled when she noticed her daughter's wandering hands. Her hands moved along his inner thighs, back and forth. Colin's eyes wandered the room. Just as her hands rubbed over the sides of his testicles, he took hold of her hands and clutched them in his.

"I thank ye for the massage, but it's best ye stop, don't ye think?" Catherine grinned at her mother. "Oh, feck, I'm payin' the price, so I am."

"Are you alright, Colin?" the priest asked.

Colin took an apple and chomped on it.

"Just dany, so I am. I'm appreciatin' the hospitality of yer family, Father."

"So, Peg, where will Colin sleep tonight?"

"He'll have to share Catherine's room, if that's fine with you?" she said, wiggling her eyebrows at Colin.

"It don't bother me at all to sleep on the floor right here," Colin suggested.

"Absolutely not. Catherine has the warmest bed in the house. You can sleep there."

"Where will Catherine sleep?" Colin asked with a partial smile.

"In her bed, of course." Peg continued to sweep the floor. Colin glanced at the priest. "In fact, Catherine's bed is the only bed in the house."

She placed the broom by the wall and stood beside Colin. Her fingers spooled through his long hair. He glanced at her as he peered at her startling toothless smile.

She bent over the table to fill his flask with wine. "Drink up, you're our guest."

Colin gulped the wine without taking a breath.

\*\*\*

Amoli sat in the corner of a damp dungeon cell. She whimpered with tears. The dungeon guard stopped by with a tray.

"Here is your food. I took a slice of cake from the pantry. I thought it would be nice for you," the guard said. Our royals got themselves new bakers; they don't seem to know what they're doing. I took the cake and they didn't seem to notice."

"There's no reason to put me in this awful place," Amoli said, sobbing.

"The queen doesn't need a reason, you should know that by now."

He turned away toward the exit.

"Please!" He turned to her. "Could you stay here a bit? I'm very lonely in this very terrible cell."

He smiled at her and sat. "I think you're very pretty, even though you come from such a far away land."

Amoli smiled as she gazed at the tray of food. He tried to take Amoli's hand, but she contracted it away from

136

him. "Tell me about the new bakers the queen hired. Are they baking delicious bread?"

"It's now late morning, the king and queen have guests from France, and they still don't have fresh bread."

"Really? You know, I am a very good baker. Maybe the two hired bakers aren't used to baking for the king and queen."

"There seems to be a lot of smoke coming from the kitchen. I think they're fools."

"Maybe I can teach them how to bake bread."

"No, I don't think the king and queen would appreciate a moor baking their bread." He stood up and walked toward the exit. "They were hired because they are supposed to be expert bakers."

Amoli smiled, but remained silent. He left.

\*\*\*

"Just a bit longer. The house is somewhere down the hill, isn't it, Catherine?" The priest asked his niece.

They walked down a winding dirt road that led to a much larger cottage. Catherine didn't bother to knock; her mother followed with the priest and Colin trailing behind. They entered to find several people dancing, eating, drinking wine, and even having sex. The flutist danced around serenading everyone, while a young man sat in the corner playing his lute.

Colin tried to smile at everyone, but his exhaustion got the best of him. Catherine took Colin's hand and licked each finger. He let her do it, because he didn't know what else to do. She pulled the collar of her dress down to show off her slight cleavage.

"Well? What do you think?" she asked him. "Are my breasts alluring you?"

He sighed. "They're not," he said, and buttoned her blouse.

137

Peg sat with her girlfriends. "Look what I brought to the party!"

"Who's he?" her girlfriend asked, pouring Peg a large flask of something.

"My brother found him. I don't know. I find him rather interesting, though."

"He has handsome features, I must say," her girlfriend commented.

"This drink tastes different," Peg said, as she placed her hand over top of her flask. "Don't give me anymore. Is there opium in it?"

"Of course. Drinking opium gives fast effects."

"Offer it to my visitor over there. He needs to relax, I think."

Colin sat on the floor with his back against the wall. Catherine placed herself in his lap. She turned toward him and slid her arms around his neck. He closed his eyes and chuckled.

"There's plenty of lads yer own age. Ye should be with them, don't ye think?"

She placed her lips against his. "Kiss me!"

He pushed her off of him. "Maybe the cell was a better place for me, eh?"

Peg came along and placed a huge flask of the spiked opium wine in his hand.

"Drink this, handsome. You look like you need it."

"Thank-ye, so I will," he said, and he guzzled the drink.

Catherine rested her head on his lap. He finished his drink. He glared at the festivities in the room, and laughed while he stroked Catherine's head still, resting on his lap. He leaned his head against the wall where the room started to pull away and change into different shapes and colors. The music seemed to rise in volume. Peg sat beside him.

"Well, handsome, you seem to be more relaxed, I must say."

"Relaxed? So, I am, dearest Christ, so I am."

"I must say you look special in the hose you're wearing. Would you mind dancing with me?" Peg asked.

Catherine lifted her head. "Mother? He's only going to dance with me."

Colin had difficulty standing up. "Don't know if I can dance with yez, 'cause I'm just not standin' on me feet, so I'm not."

Peg got hold of his arm and Catherine took his other arm.

"Come on, we can only guide you on your feet. Stand up!" ordered Peg.

He finally stood, but leaned most of his body against the wall.

"What's wrong with me?" he asked Peg.

She took his arm. "We need to dance."

"Don't know if I can."

He staggered to the dance floor. He sloppily danced with Peg, where he tripped over his own feet. She fell into his arms and he lifted her off the floor and swirled her around the floor. She giggled and laughed, and he kissed her on the lips a few times. The song ended and he flopped back on the floor beside Catherine. She fell into his arms. He kissed her on the lips and plunged his tongue into her mouth. The fiddler stopped playing. He looked at Colin.

"Can you sing us something, newcomer?"

"Ah, so I wish I was in Dublin," Colin blurted.

Everyone chanted and clapped their hands. The fiddler started to play. Colin stood up with most of his weight leaning against the wall.

"Yez wouldn't know *Rocky Road to Dublin* yet, I know yez wouldn't, but follow me if ye can," Colin slurred to the fiddler, and then began to sing.

*In the merry month of June from me home I started,*
*Left the girls of Tuam so sad and broken hearted,*
*Saluted father dear, kissed me darlin' mother!*

139

*Then drank a pint of beer, tears and grief to smother*
*Then off to reap the corn, leave where I was born,*
*Cut a stout black thorn to banish ghosts and goblins!*
*Bought a pair of brogues rattling o'er the bogs*
*And fright'ning all the dogs on the rocky road to*
Dublin!
(Chorus):

*One two three four five,*
*Hunt the hare and turn her down the rocky road*
*And all the way to Dublin, whack follol de rah!*
*In Mullingar that night I rested limbs so weary*
*Started by daylight next morning bright and early*
*Took a drop of the pure to keep me heart from sinking;*
*That's a Paddy's cure whenever he's on drinking*
*See the lassies smile, laughing all the while*
*At me darlin' style, 'twould set your heart a bubblin'*
*Asked me was I hired, wages I required*
*Till I was almost tired of the rocky road to Dublin,*
(Chorus)

*In Dublin next arrived, I thought it'd be a pity*
*To be soon deprived a view of that fine city.*
*So then I took a stroll, all among the quality;*
*Me bundle it was stole, all in a neat locality.*
*Something crossed me mind, when I looked behind,*
*No bundle could I find upon me stick a wobblin'*
*Enquiring for the rogue, they said me Connaught*
brogue
*Wasn't much in vogue on the rocky road to Dublin,*
(Chorus)

*From there I got away, me spirits never failing,*
*Landed on the quay, just as the ship was sailing.*
*The captain at me roared, said that no room had he;*
*When I jumped aboard, a cabin found for Paddy.*
*Down among the pigs, played some hearty rigs,*
*Danced some hearty jigs, the water round me*
bubblin';
*When off Holyhead wished meself was dead,*

140

*Or better for instead on the rocky road to Dublin,*
(Chorus)
*The boys of Liverpool, when we safely landed,*
   *Called meself a fool, I could no longer stand it.*
   *Blood began to boil, temper I was losing;*
   *Poor old Erin's Isle they began abusing.*
   *"Hurrah me soul!" says I, shillelagh I let fly.*
   *Some Galway boys were nigh and saw I was a*
*hobblin',*
   *With a loud "hurray!" joined in the affray.*
   *We quickly cleared the way for the rocky road to*
*Dublin.*
(Chorus)

The crowd cheered and chanted, banging their hands on the wood tables and stomping their feet. Catherine hung onto him as if they were lovers. His eyes widened with surprise at the response he got from the song.

"So, you can sing?" Catherine said, as she untied his blousy shirt strings.

"So people tell me," he said. "Don't know, really. Not a professional, so I'm not."

"I think you I should be with you tonight."

She giggled in his arms. Colin clutched her and kissed her several times on the mouth. He pressed her body against his. She fell to the floor where he pushed himself on top of her. He sloppily untied his shirt and tried desperately to untie the pouch of his hose. His penis protruded outside his hose while Catherine lay on the floor with her legs spread opened. Peg noticed, but continued to drink. The priest laughed and pranced with some of the young women while he helped himself to some wine.

The music continued to play, with the high pitch sound of the flute and the on-going melody of the lute. Colin thrust himself in and out of Catherine. She screamed with pleasure-pain. He penetrated her and kept thrusting

141

inside her. She screamed and yelled. The musicians paused a bit, but then continued to play.

*** 

Rosa tied her hair back with a ribbon. Sasha found a hammer.

"We use this, da?"

Rosa leaned against the wall. "For what, Sasha?"

"We must convert wheat to flour. Why you act so terrible?"

"Because you're terrible. We've been up all night. I'm exhausted. I need to rest. We've looked for a grinder of some kind; nothing seems to be here. I don't know what these people did in this time. We already destroyed the pre-made dough that we found in the bin. The king will find out that we aren't bakers, and they will probably kill us."

"Rosa, stop! You too negative. We will bake good bread, I know."

"We don't know how to use that hearth thing. It looks nothing like what we're used to in our time," she said, and began to cry.

Sasha took her into his arms. "You must not cry. Do not let them see you cry. French people must be here by now."

"Of course they're here."

"You know, I worry about Miss Amoli. She is in dungeon cell by herself."

"For all we know she could be dead. How about Colin?"

"He escapes. I not worry for him." Sasha's eyes widened when tears streamed from Rosa's eyes. "You cry?"

"Of course I'm crying. The biggest mistake is that we have split up. I don't know where Colin is, and I can't even imagine how Amoli is doing."

"See, you care about Miss Amoli. She is little sister to you, da?"

Rosa lifted her head to look at him. "Little sister? Definitely not."

\*\*\*

It was early dawn when Colin opened one eye to notice a young woman in his arms and her mother flopped over him, both asleep. There were several people asleep scattered about the floor. The priest snored away in the corner of the room. Colin lifted his head sickened by the stench of stale ale, wine, as well as puddles of urine.

"Ah, feck, what's this, eh?" he whispered.

He tried to pry the two women off his body. They both flopped on the floor like dead weight. He stood up to notice several people including the musicians trying to sleep off their opium consumption mixed with alcohol. He felt so ill he bent over with the urge to vomit. He shook, with sweat dripping off his body. Peg woke when she heard Colin yelp from upchucking.

"Here you are a complete stranger and now you're messing up my floor."

Colin turned to her, where his long forelock hung in front of his face.

"I tried to aim on the piss puddles from yer enchantin' guests, truly I did."

She grinned at him. "I must say, you can really sing." She paused to think. "You took my darling daughter and then you took me, you cad." She paused again. "Oh, yes, you can sing."

He was hunched on all fours hovering over his pile of bile. "Well, yer a mighty fine mother, so I must say."

"Cover up. You're hanging to the floor. You're not a decent man, I can tell."

143

Colin fiddled with his tights to try to fasten them. "A proper woman like yerself is no match for a peasant like me," he said with a sarcastic chuckle.

She didn't notice, as she helped herself up. She primped herself and placed one of her breasts back inside her blouse.

He heard the hard sound of heavy horse hooves outside the house. His eyes shifted a bit. "What's that?"

"Probably the king's men, I don't know. Sounds like knights."

"Feck!" he gasped. "They've come for me!"

She leaned her body against the door. "Try to look respectable, if you can do that?"

He stood up with vigil. The knights pushed opened the door. Peg flung into Colin's arms. Three knights entered.

"We have come for Sir Limmerick. I see that he is here!" one of the king's men shouted.

Colin let go of Peg and she fell to the floor. "Aye, so I am."

Peg squirmed on the floor. "Why do you want this man?"

The head knight glanced at her. "He escaped his time in the dungeon. The queen wants to see him at once."

"Oh, feck, what does she want with me? Does she want to send me to France?"

One of the knights pulled out his dagger and shook it at Colin. "You speak again, and you will die right here." He glided his dagger along Colin's throat. "You will come to the dungeon at the castle without a fight, or you won't be spared."

Peg was distraught. She leaped into Colin's arms.

"He's my husband! You can't!"

Colin's eyes widened. The knight stood behind Colin and pressed the sharp point of the dagger into the middle of his back.

"We must get you to the queen's quarters at once."

The king and queen sat at their thrones. The servants brought out trays of freshly baked goods, and Rosa and Sasha followed from behind. Everyone bowed to the floor to honor his/her majesty. The pastry chefs were at the very back. Their French guests arrived as the servants and royal subjects continued to bow. A musician stood at the side to play his lute.

Freshly baked bread was passed to the royals and then to the guests. The king sipped wine from his flask and then he took a bite from the bread roll that Rosa and Sasha had baked. The French guests did the same. Rosa looked at Sasha. She trembled uncontrollably. Sasha appeared fidgety.

The king chewed the bread slowly. He paused for a second and continued to chew. The royal subjects lifted their heads slightly to see if the king approved. He spat it out.

"This isn't bread!" he shouted.

The queen spat hers out as well. Their French guests continued to chew with dissatisfied faces. Rosa stared at the floor and tried to sink as low as she could behind the crowd. The king's royal advisor stood before the crowd of subjects.

"Who is responsible for this?"

The crowd remained silent, still in a low bow position. One of the knights noticed Sasha at the back. He pointed.

"He is!"

The crowd lifted their heads. Sasha forced a partial smile.

"Step forward," the king's advisor demanded.

Rosa looked at Sasha as she was still in a bowing position.

"Oh, my God. Sasha, they're calling you."

Sasha slowly stood up looking disinterested. The advisor gestured for Sasha to come to the front. Sasha straightened his hose and primped his fluffy shirt. He walked to the front and looked at the king. He bowed to the floor before the king and queen. The king stared directly at Sasha.

"Are you responsible for this horrible mess?"

Sasha lifted his head to look at the king. *"Da."*

The king glanced at his advisor. "Da? What is that?"

Sasha forced a smile. "It is Russian for *yes."*

"You are foreign?" the king asked.

"Russian," Sasha bowed his head lower to the floor. "I am Russian."

The king was confused. "Well, you certainly cannot bake bread."

*"aSTAF tye miNYA f paKOye."* Sasha responded softly, but rudely in Russian.

The king stood up. "Who are you?"

"I say you I am Russian. I am Sasha, son of great king."

The king glanced at his queen. "I have never heard of you. Did you bake this bread with someone else?"

Sasha's eyes shifted. *"Nyet."*

The king hit his scepter against the floor. "Is that a *yes* or a *no?"*

Rosa stood up. "Yes!"

The king said, "I see. Step forward." Rosa walked to the front to stand beside Sasha. The king looked at his guards. "Take these two to the dungeon at once. They are frauds."

The king's guards dumped the bread into the moat. The French guests sipped on wine and pretended that all was well, when suddenly four of the king's guards brought Colin before the king and queen. The guards and Colin bowed to the floor. Colin was tied tightly with rope but he managed to bow to the floor in discomfort. The queen grinned when she saw Colin.

146

"Well, well, my favorite knight had escaped the castle dungeon. What do you have to say for yourself?"

Colin lifted his head. "I've done nothin' wrong."

She glanced at the king. "Oh, yes, you definitely have. You have broken the laws of chivalry, and therefore your knighthood should be revoked."

Colin kept his head low.

"I think you need to return to the dungeon where you will undergo hard labor by early tomorrow. If you fail to do so you will be put to death at once. Do you understand?"

Colin lifted his head to look at her. "Aye."

The guards tugged on the rope that was tied to Colin and brought him to the dungeon. Amoli lifted her head and smiled when she saw the guards place Colin in the same cell as her. She ran into his arms.

"Colin! I've missed you."

He held her in his arms. "Lass," he tried to clear his hoarse throat. "Can ye manage to untie this rope? Rather bothersome, so it is."

"I've managed to obtain a small dagger from one of the guards," she whispered, as she cut away at the rope.

He smiled. "Good work, lass."

"It's been very lonely and frightening spending long days and nights in this very horrible place." He ran his hand along her cheek. "Dr. Dimitrikov and Miss Emanuel are in the cell across from this one. They pretended to bake bread, and I'm afraid they didn't pass the test."

"Really. I've been in this cell before. I know there's some loose blocks in the wall. We can't stay in here, so we can't. I'm sentenced to hard labor apparently."

"That's good. I'm surprised they're not going to torture you."

"Lass, this is one method of torture, I'm supposin'. Likely no food or water. We gotta stay together all four of us, 'n get to the time machine. We can't stay here. I'm no longer a knight, so the queen says. I didn't pass her test."

147

Amoli nestled in his lap as he sat on the damp floor of the cell.

"Why wouldn't you pass her test?"

"I told her off, so I did." Amoli laughed. He placed his fingers over her lips. "Yer not gonna care for what I'm about to say to ye. Ye won't be laughin', so ye won't." She grew concerned as she noticed the creases around his eyes. "I slept with the queen, lass."

Her eyes widened and her lips parted.

"Surely, I didn't want to. She forced it along, so she did. I don't find her appealin' in the least. She's a broodin' bitch of the fifteenth century, so she is." Amoli remained on his lap, but kept her face at a distance from his. "I also slept with a peasant woman named Peg. Didn't want to, but she slipped me somethin' strong, so she did."

Amoli sprung up from his lap. "Why are you telling me this, Colin?"

"'Cause, ye need to know the truth before we marry."

"What did this woman slip you?"

"Spiked me drink, so she did."

She began to pace. "Spiked your drink? What does that mean?"

"She put somethin' in it, I don't know what."

He remained on the floor with his back against the block wall. Amoli continued to pace. "Before we marry, yes, I see. This is important for me to know, yes, it is."

"Also, lass."

She stopped pacing and spun to face him.

"I think I slept with the peasant woman's daughter. I think, not sure, we did anythin', but I was badly pissed up."

"Yes, of course, your drink was spiked." She paced with her arms in the air. "What am I doing here?"

He slowly stood up. "Lass, you're the wench I wish to marry."

148

"How can you say this to me? You're no longer promised to me. You're always sleeping with other girls. What's wrong with you? Are you over-sexed?"

"I'm confessin' this to ye, 'cause I can't live with the untruth."

"Well, I can't live with the facts."

"Lass, we's in a dungeon cell in the fifteenth century. This isn't the time or place, don't ye think?"

"Yes, why am I in a dungeon cell in the fifteenth century? I fell in love with a man who is obsessed with time travel. What kind of life is this? We could all be killed. My father wouldn't like any of this, even though he's interested in time travel. You drag me through the past centuries to tell me about all the women you're having sex with?"

"I cautioned ye not to come on me travels. Ye was insistin' on comin' along."

"Oh, the hell with you. All you do is disappoint me. I don't want to marry you. You're probably crawling with syphilis, for all I know. You're just like your uncle Kevin."

Colin stared at the dingy floor. "Don't say that, lass. Me uncle died of that."

"Of course he did. It runs in the family." She sat in the opposite corner of the cell from him and slid down to the floor and began to cry.

"Colin!" Rosa called, from the other cell. "What's going on? Are you two having a fight?"

Colin walked to the tiny window near the top of the door and peered through it.

"Aye, are we that loud?"

"I don't think they thought about acoustics in the fifteenth century," Rosa responded.

"Is Sasha there with ye?"

"Yes! We're doing fine, but we really need to get out of here."

"Couldn't agree with yez more."

149

# Chapter Eighteen

Some light peered through the tiny window. Amoli had slept at the far end of the cell from Colin. She opened her eyes as she tried to take in the slight glimmer of sunlight. The king's guards recklessly entered the cell. Colin lifted his head.

"His majesty has ordered us to enter. You will be given nothing to eat or drink, for you are to begin the construction of the castle's extension. You will be working with the king's enslaved prisoners."

Colin stood up. One of the guards pulled out his whip and lashed it at Colin. Colin got hold of it and yanked it, which caused the guard to crash forward. The other guard pulled out his sword and pointed it at Colin's groin.

"You try that again and you will have your favorite body part chopped off at once."

Colin stood still as he noticed a few droplets of blood from his inner thigh beside his groine. Amoli sat in the corner of the cell and whimpered. The guard kept the sword pointed at Colin as he gestured for him to follow them outside the cell. Amoli cried.

"Amoli!" Rosa called, from the neighboring cell. "What happened?"

Amoli stood by the door but was too short to face the small window at the top.

"The guards took Colin away. They had weapons!"

"Of course they had weapons. We're in a dungeon cell!" shouted Rosa.

Sasha glanced at Rosa. "Mr. Limmerick will survive. I not worry for him."

Rosa had an angry expression on her face. "I'm terrified for him."

"He is three times size of them. He can crush them with one blow, and they know this."

150

"They still have swords and daggers. They have headsmen, Sasha."

"Queen will not allow Mr. Limmerick to lose head."

Rosa's facial expression changed. "Why on earth would you say that?"

"Because she most likely want him, not for love, but for sex." Sasha threw his hands up in the air. "All women want Mr. Limmerick for sex, I not know why."

"You're ridiculous."

Amoli sat by her cell door. "What are you two saying?"

"Miss Amoli! You not worry. Mr. Limmerick is big strong bull. He will crush them."

"Even though Colin and I are no longer a couple, I still love him. I always will," she said, with a few stifles.

Rosa's eyes widened as she glanced at Sasha. His eyebrows lowered.

Colin was brought to a large pit that was filled with stone and granite.

"You will work here until further notice from the queen," the guard said.

Colin glanced at several gaunt-looking men with chains around their ankles.

"I've read 'bout shite like this," Colin said, to the guard.

"Where would you read about this?"

"Never mind. Tell me somethin': why don't the queen just kill me?"

"She says your strength and power will come in handy," the guard responded. "You will work with these other men, who are also his/her majesty's prisoners. They have not committed crimes where they need to be burned to a stake, but they are of great use. They are building an extension to the castle."

"Ye want me to help them with it, do yez?"

"Get to work!" the guard ordered, as he lashed his whip at Colin's shoulder.

Colin took the pain without retaliation. He made his way to the other prisoners and lifted a heavy stone up the slope.

\*\*\*

"I've got to get out of here!" Amoli shouted.

She noticed the loose stone in the cell that Colin had pointed out to her. *How could she move this? She thought to herself.* She glanced at the cell door, which did not appear to be completely shut. She walked to it and gave a gentle push. The door creaked, as it left a slit open. She pushed it again and it swung open. She nervously poked her head out to notice the adjacent cell, which occupied Sasha and Rosa. She noticed that the key was still poking out of the outside end of the door. She looked down the hall to make sure nobody was coming. She gasped for air from her nerves and took the large key and ran to the other cell door to unlock it.

"Amoli?" Rosa bursted, with surprise.

"I found the key. The foolish guard must have left it in the door."

Sasha grinned. "Now we run."

The three of them ran to what looked like an exit from the dungeon. Amoli took a deep breath when they found themselves in the midst of the town's people. Rosa stepped closer to her.

"You and Colin are no more?"

Amoli turned away from her. "I don't want to tell you my personal business."

Sasha placed his arms around both women. "No time for cat fight. Now we find Mr. Limmerick, da?"

\*\*\*

Colin lifted one heavy boulder after another. He noticed how torn up his hands were, where blood dripped from his thumbs. An elderly man with a long beard noticed him.

"We are lucky to get this. Otherwise we'd be burned to death."

"Don't mind the hard work, so I don't. Just used to usin' gloves, if ye know what I mean."

"Gloves? You won't find anything like that here. We're his majesties' prisoners." Colin smiled at the man and continued to work. "I wouldn't mind a decent meal and some water to drink," the old man commented.

"Guess I shouldn't complain. When they knighted me, I ate like a king."

"You were knighted and now you're here?"

"I'm not their idea of chivalry, I suppose."

"What did you do?"

"Nothin'."

The elderly man chuckled. "How I loath that king of ours."

"Ye think this bloke is bad, wait 'till ye see what's next in line."

The elderly man stepped closer. "How do you know what's next in line? Are you a witch?"

"I'm no witch, nor I believe that shite. Just smart, so I am. If this king has a son, 'n I think he will, he'll be the next heir to the throne, don't ye think?"

"You appear to be a smart man, yes, you do. Most of the king's court is a lot of stupidity, if you ask me."

Colin continued to move chunks of granite. One of the king's guards noticed the elderly man talking to Colin. He pulled out his whip and lashed the man on the back several times. The feeble man fell to the ground. Colin placed the granite on the ground and grabbed the whip. The guard pulled out his sword and waved it at Colin. He pressed the point of his sword into Colin's arm and walked away. Colin helped the elderly man up.

153

"Don't waste your time trying to help me. It's no use. They have us beat," the man said, with a quiver in his voice.

"Can't stand injustice, is all. Won't stand for it, so I won't."

"Well, if that's your feelings, consider yourself a dead man. There is no such thing as justice within this feudal society." The elderly man fell to his knees to help another prisoner pry a large piece of granite from the ground. Colin hauled the large pieces of rock from the pit and onto the level ground where the castle extension was to be built. "You're so big and strong, this should be easy for you."

"Some fluid to drink wouldn't be a bad idea, don't ye think?" Colin commented.

"The king and his court have no logic," the man said.

"Shh, ye know ye shouldn't express yer feelin's 'bout these blokes. Ye could really get yerself hurt, so I'm startin' to gather," Colin cautioned.

"I'm old. I don't care anymore. I've seen too many atrocities in my day."

One of the king's guards lashed his whip at the elderly man.

"You're supposed to be working."

"How about some water to drink?" the old man questioned.

The guard pulled out his sword and thrust it deep into the old man's abdomen. The man fell to the ground. The guard then pointed his sword at Colin. Colin kicked it to the ground, but the blade of the sword gouged Colin's leg. Blood poured onto the ground. Colin lunged for the fallen sword and swung it at the guard with so much force and conviction that he chopped the man's hand off. Colin stood back, amazed at his action.

Several other guards came running vigilantly with their swords. The injured guard shouted in agony as he fell to the ground soaked in his own blood. Colin stood beside

154

the dead elderly man. The armed guards chained Colin's ankles and wrists. They lashed their whips at his back and shoulders and yanked him inside the castle.

The king and the queen sat upon their thrones as Colin was brought before them. Colin bowed to the floor. The queen glanced at her king.

"So, Sir Limmerick is showing us some bad behavior?"

The king leered at Colin. "You badly injured one of our top guards. You're going to have to pay for your sins."

Colin kept his head low. Blood droplets fell to the floor from his lashed back. The queen chuckled.

"Such a strong, handsome knight, yet you refuse to practice the laws of chivalry. What a shame."

The king looked at her. "Since you know him better than I, what should his sentence be?"

"He already has a lady-in-waiting. However, he has caused this kingdom such grief. What do you have to say for yourself?"

Colin slightly lifted his head. "Forgive me, m' queen."

"Take him!" the queen shouted, to the guards. "Return him to the dungeon. He will be burned to a stake by morning."

Just as the guards pointed their swords at him, he sprang up and kicked one of the swords to the floor and took it. He thrust it and swung it. The queen screamed, but the king sat at his throne with a smile on his face. Two guards swung their swords at him and sliced his bicep opened. He struck them hard with his sword, but the other guard managed to slice his thigh with a quick thrust. The remaining guards fell forward to their deaths. Five other guards rushed in and also fell to their death.

Colin stopped thrusting his sword. He scanned the room to notice that all the king's guards were dead and the king was wallowing in laughter. Colin focused on the panic-stricken queen in the background.

"I do my job, Mr. Limmerick and I do it well, da?" Sasha said, as he jumped down from the back seating of the gallery.

Colin smiled as he tried to catch his breath.

"Bravo!" shouted the king, as he applauded the two strangers.

Colin bowed to the king as he pulled Sasha to the floor to do the same.

"You killed the king's guards, mate? I didn't hear a gunshot."

"They have daggers in their backs."

The king stood up. "Who are you two men?"

"We are just simple men, yer majesty. We meant no harm," Colin said, in a deep raspy voice.

The king glanced at Sasha. "You, you're the bread maker, aren't you?"

"Da, I am expert baker."

The king laughed. "Your baked bread is terrible, but you know how to throw a dagger." He looked at Colin. "I want you here with me at all times. You could easily win a war for England. Your size and strength is remarkable."

Colin bowed his head to the king, then he looked at the queen.

"Yer highness, am I chivalric enough for yez?"

She stepped closer to Colin. "Who dares question me?"

The king chuckled as he took his queen's hand and held it tightly in his.

"I don't know who these men are or where they're from, but we could put them to good use for the sake of England."

Colin bowed to the floor. "Forgive me rudeness, yer majesty."

"Kiss my hand," the queen ordered.

Colin took her hand and kissed it. Sasha bowed to both of them, unwillingly. The king looked at his advisor.

156

"Take these two men, and be sure to get them cleaned up and well fed," the king demanded to his servants.

***

Rosa and Amoli walked amongst the busy town, where families were selling fruit, vegetables, and wine in the streets. Rosa glanced at Amoli.

"It's been hours. I don't know where Sasha is, nor do we know where Colin is."

"I'm so worried," Amoli commented. "The four of us are never together at the same time. I'm terrified every time someone stares at me, it's because I look so foreign to these people."

"It's 1487. Don't you think I would be noticeable in the streets of Bombay?"

"I suppose you're right about that, Miss Emanuel."

"Colin doesn't do well with authority figures," Rosa commented. "I'm worried for him."

"Where do we go now? I see no sign of Colin or Dr. Dimitrikov," Amoli asked with dispair in her voice.

"We should retire in that small cottage Sasha built."

"I want to leave this time period so much."

Rosa and Amoli continued to walk. "I agree."

"Not so fast," the king's guard said, as he stood boldly in front of them.

Rosa said, "Pardon me, but I think you're being rather rude."

"You two are prisoners to his majesty, aren't you?"

Amoli trembled as she tried to stand behind Rosa.

"Prisoners?" Rosa acted surprised.

"You have spent some time in the castle dungeon, haven't you?"

"Castle dungeon?" Rosa parroted, with a nervous cackle.

"I must arrest you both and take you to the king at once."

157

"For what reason?" Rosa asked.

The guard took his backhand and smacked Rosa so hard across the face that she fell to the ground. Amoli screamed. Rosa noticed blood coming from her face. She tried to stand up. Amoli helped her with a whimper.

"Who are you? A moor?" the guard asked Amoli, as he noticed her whimpering.

Rosa stood up and tried to act as if nothing happened. The guard ran his finger under Rosa's chin.

"You're a fair maiden, but you should know you haven't the right to ask questions. You're only a wench." Rosa stared at the ground. "I should bring you to the king. I'm sure he would like you very much." Rosa pulled away from him. The guard chained Rosa and Amoli wrists and led them to the castle; to a large room. "I will send some servants in to clean you both up. I don't think the king would want anything to do with a moor. You will be sent to the dungeon until further notice is given." Amoli sighed with frustration. The guard looked at Rosa. "But you're so beautiful the king would like you in his bed, no doubt." Several female servants entered. "Give this maiden some new clothes and fix her hair. She will be before the king soon." The guard shoved Amoli from behind and she fell to the floor. "As for the moor, you'll be spending the night in the dungeon."

The guard led Amoli down the narrow hallways. She noticed Colin and Sasha were walking toward her. Amoli winced when she saw her friends.

"Mr. Limmerick, there is Miss Amoli," Sasha indicated.

Colin looked at the guard. "What ye doin' here with this wench?"

The guard stopped. "She's a moor; she's of no use to you."

Colin lowered his eyebrows. "Where ye takin' her?" The guard scanned Colin and Sasha's attire, where he knew they were part of the nobility. "What has she done? Has the king ordered her to the dungeon?"

"I am acting on behalf of the king."

"But ye haven't a clue what the king would say, ye feck. Release her at once." The guard unlocked the chains around her ankles. Sasha waved his sword. "You will be reported to king, and I will cut yer throat for this."

The guard hurried to release Amoli. Colin took her hand and held it in his. Sasha leered at the guard as he walked away. Amoli tightened her hands around Colin's.

"Thank-you. I don't think I could have bared to spend another minute in that very terrible dungeon, especially by myself."

"You are safe now, Miss Amoli," Sasha assured.

Colin pressed himself against her, but she pulled away.

"No, Colin. Please, don't make this any harder than it already is."

Sasha tried not to notice. Colin stepped away from her. Sasha turned to Colin.

"What you want to do now?"

"For starters we need to find Rosa 'n get to the time machine. Don't fancy the idea of bein' their feckin' idea of chivalry."

"They want us to fight war?"

Colin turned to Amoli. "Where's Rosa at now?"

"The guard decided that Miss Emanuel could, you know, satisfy the king," Amoli responded.

"Satisfy king? What you mean?" Sasha's posture heighted. "You English I never know." Sasha glanced at Amoli. "Sex. You mean sex?"

Amoli whimpered. "Yes, Dr. Dimitrikov you must understand what's happening."

"I will kill king."

"We just gotta fetch her back, is all," Colin said. "The king is usually out 'n about doin' this 'n that, so the queen has told me. He's not often in his chamber."

159

"Is that why you slept with the queen?" Amoli asked, with innocent eyes.

Sasha gazed at Colin. Colin took a step back with embarrassment on his face.

"We's wastin' time 'n the thought of Rosa bein' in that feck's bed makes me ill."

"Da, lets go!" Sasha shouted.

Colin tugged on Sasha's arm. "Wait. We gotta think how to do this. The royals don't act the way we'd expect. They function with lovers on the side, so I've gathered."

The three of them walked toward the nearest exit. Sasha smiled to one side of his face.

"Rosa do not give sex to man."

Amoli's expression changed. "She doesn't?"

Colin shoved Sasha. "Shut up. What ye doin'?"

"I love Rosa," Sasha said.

Amoli's eyes bulged as she looked at Colin.

"Ye do?" Colin asked.

"I want her saved for me. I know she not do anything with you, Mr. Limmerick."

"How ye know this?"

"She say me. I can tell she is virgin, not like Miss Amoli."

Amoli's eyes widened with surprise. Colin shoved Sasha again.

***

The king scanned Rosa as they stood in his bedchamber.

"You are so beautiful," the king said to Rosa.

Rosa took a few steps back. "I think you should save your compliments for the queen. I really need to be going if you would excuse me, your majesty," she said, with a sloppy curtsy.

The king placed his arms around her. "Not so fast, my beautiful one, first we must engage in some love, don't

160

you think?" The king tightened his arms around her. She squirmed. "You are here to make me happy, aren't you?"

"Happy?"

"I need someone like you waiting for me when I return from battle or negotiations with other kings. After a long day at court I need to have you waiting for me in my bed."

"Doesn't the queen wait for you?"

"She's the queen, she has too much to do always." Rosa pulled away from him and wandered to the window. She peered through to notice the king's servants were preparing festivities in the courtyard.

"Why are you so distant from me?" the king asked. "I'm the king, no damsel ever strays from me."

"Pardon? Oh, sorry, forgive me, I didn't hear what you said."

Two men entered the room to help the king undress. The servants stood in the corner. Rosa watched the skinny naked king lay on the bed.

"Come to me, my beautiful one."

Rosa's lips parted. "I don't think this is a good idea. I might have Gonorrhea."

"Gonorrhea?" The king squinted his eyes to get a better look at her. "You don't look ill to me."

She rubbed her hands over her forehead. "I think I have a fever. It's very catchy, you know. If I lay down with you, you could easily get it. I think I should be leaving now."

"Not so fast, my beautiful one." He stood up to face her. "If you are my mistress, you would look very good on me, yes I think so."

Rosa felt her forehead. "Please put your clothes on, your highness," she said, trying to look somewhere else.

He pressed himself against her. She backed up against the wall.

"Am I not attractive to you?"

"No! I mean, well, not if I'm ridden with Gonorrhea."

She slid under his arms and to the other side of him.

"You don't seem to have a fever. I will get my doctor here to see you at once."

"What will the queen say about that?"

"I'm the king of England; she has no right to say anything." Rosa glanced to the back of the room to realize the two male servants were still present. "Come now, I will have you undressed and we will be together."

"I can undress myself." The king sat on the bed and waited for Rosa. She stood there with his eyes fixed on her every move. "Your majesty, I don't think I can do this."

"Are you married?"

"Uh, yes, um, that is correct, I am married."

"That shouldn't stop you. I'm the king."

"Well," she fidgeted with her hair by spooling it around her finger, "You see, your majesty, I'm a virgin."

The king sat up in his bed. "How can you be a virgin if you have Gonorrhea?"

She partially smiled, as she tried to dry her sweaty hands on her dress.

"Maybe the Gonorrhea happened without me knowing."

"How could this be?" The king looked at his two servants. "Come, undress this poor virgin for me."

The servants stood behind her. She knew they were there. She could feel each button become loose along her backside. She pulled back and screamed as loud as she could. The two servants stood before her in shock. The king began to dress himself. The two servants leaped by his side to help him with his attire. The king stood beside the bed with his arms spanned out as his servants worked diligently on dressing him.

"I see that this poor maiden needs to be disposed of. She has the audacity to reject a king? What a foolish girl. Call the guards and have her ceased."

162

The guards stormed in and Colin and Sasha followed. Amoli snuck in and stood behind one of the dressing mirrors. Colin and Sasha pulled out their swords and pointed them at the king. Sasha grabbed Rosa and pulled her away.

"Stop right there, yer majesty. Yer not gettin' yer way anymore, ye feck," Colin ordered, with the point of his sword jabbed deeply into the king's belly.

One of the guards swung his sword at Colin, but Sasha intersected with a swift swing and knocked the sword out of his hand. Rosa hid behind the dressing mirror with Amoli.

"That guard just lost his sword," Rosa whispered. Amoli poked one eye from the mirror to take a look. Rosa pulled her back. "Are you mad? Don't draw any attention to yourself. We need to fetch that sword."

Rosa peeked to see what was happening. Colin and Sasha were engaged in a battle with the king's guards. The hard clanging sound of colliding swords penetrated through the king's chamber. Amoli glanced at Rosa.

"Why do we need that sword?" Amoli asked, in a whisper.

Rosa sighed. "We need to help our loved ones. They're in a bloody battle. Colin is holding his own, but he'd much rather be an archer or a grappler."

"Yes, I suppose."

"One of us has to go out there and fetch that sword," Rosa demanded.

"I'm sure you will be just fine. You always seem to know what you're doing."

Rosa placed her hands on Amoli's arm. "You're going out there on your hands and knees, and you will come back here with that sword. Do it. Now."

Rosa pushed Amoli out from behind the dressing mirror. Amoli fell to the floor on her hands and knees. She tried to ignore the goings on around her. Colin was dueling with one of the king's head guards. The guard

163

sliced Colin's shoulder, where the material from his blousy shirt hung down dripping in blood. Sasha was keen enough to take on two or three opponents at once without a scratch.

Amoli continued to shuffle along the floor, where the king's guards tripped over her and fell backwards. She got to the sword and wore a grin on her face. She snatched it and dragged it along the floor. The king's guards continued to thrust and swing their swords at the two male time travelers. Amoli continued to glide along the floor on all fours, where she made her way behind the dressing mirror where Rosa awaited her.

"You got the sword," Rosa yelped.

Amoli brushed herself off. "Yes, I did. And without a scratch. I did well."

Rosa poked her head from behind the mirror to notice Colin and Sasha were still very much in battle with the king's guards.

"I want to help them," she said, gripping the sword in her delicate hands.

"Do you know how to use a sword?" Amoli asked, wide-eyed.

"Not really, but I can mimic quite well."

"You could get hurt," Amoli cautioned.

"I suppose, but I think all those guards who have lived and breathed by their swords are just too much for Colin and Sasha."

"What should I do to help?" Amoli asked, with her innocent eyes.

"Do what you do best," Rosa said, as she stepped outside the dressing mirror and began to swing the sword.

Colin struggled to keep several of the king's guards from slicing him. He noticed Rosa in the corner of his eye. Beads of sweat poured down his face.

"Rosa? What ye doin'? Get outta sight," Colin demanded.

She swung the sword at one of Colin's opponents by slamming him on the head enough to knock him out.

"Not bad for a first try," she yelped.

"Rosa! Please! I don't want ye here!" Colin shouted.

He tried to keep his focus on his several opponents. His thigh was sliced and blood drenched. Rosa screamed. Sasha was trying to keep the opponents off Colin when he noticed Rosa was present with a sword.

"Foolish lady, go! You distract Mr. Limmerick. Now he is hurt."

The king's guards took a step forward. The hard clanging of the swords stopped. Rosa turned her head to see why they were so mesmerized. Amoli stood before the king and his guards topless. Colin's eyes widened.

"Lass! Cover up!"

"I don't mind doing this; really I don't," Amoli blurted.

Sasha managed to catch two of his opponents off guard and sliced both of them along their middle. Another guard swung his sword at Sasha, but Colin intersected with his sword. Amoli ran behind the dressing mirror and the battle continued. Rosa followed her and took a breath.

"Tell me something: are you planning on marrying Colin?"

"I suppose after this he wouldn't want to marry me."

"So, you showed off your enormous breasts to a bunch of dirty-minded fifteenth-century fools. Colin has done a lot worse than that."

Amoli hung her head toward the floor. A few tears fell from Amoli's eyes.

"I love him so much. I'll always love him. I just can't imagine myself with a man who has so many bad habits. I don't think I can live with that."

"Bad habits?"

"You must know what I mean, Miss Emanuel."

Colin swung his sword at his opponent and sliced the man's arm. Colin and Sasha continued to duel as they

165

walked toward the dressing mirror. Colin took hold of Rosa, and Sasha took hold of Amoli.

"Yes, there are definitely some drawbacks when it comes to Colin."

"Were you ever intimate with him?"

"I'm not like you, Amoli Sharma. I'm a proper woman. I'm a product of the Victorian era."

"Oh, I see. Then, I suppose your answer is *no.*"

Rosa took a step back and pretended not to hear Amoli's last statement. She poked her face from behind the mirror where she noticed the king had remained on his bed while he watched the men fight around him.

"What a coward," said Rosa. "The king is afraid of Colin and Sasha."

"Run!" shouted Sasha.

The four time travelers ran down the narrow halls of the stone castle where they arrived at the turret with a tight circular staircase. The king's uninjured guards chased after them. Colin's immense size made traveling down the staircase difficult. The damp stonewalls encased it, where he found his body scraping against every stone. Rosa managed to complete the staircase first, then Amoli. Sasha was just behind them, but Colin struggled. Rosa, Amoli, and Sasha stood at the bottom of the stairs as they watched Colin struggle his way down.

"Don't wait for me! Just run!" Colin shouted.

Sasha shrugged. "Fine, we will go now."

Rosa grabbed Sasha's arm. "We will most definitely wait for Colin. We're not going to even budge until he's here safely with the rest of us."

Amoli nodded in full agreement with Rosa. They could hear the running guards chanting and shouting. Their voices became louder until they also made their way to the turret. They cackled when they saw Colin making his way down the stairs. When Colin completed his journey the four of them ran off. The king's guards flew down the winding staircase with ease.

Sasha noticed a door. The four of them made their exit. They were out of the castle. They ran in the pouring rain without taking a breath to the nearby brush. The guards followed.

Rosa stopped. "Wait!" she said, trying to catch her breath. "We have to hide. They will definitely catch us if we continue this way."

"Da, you are right."

Colin looked up. "We can climb this tree. It's rather plushy. They won't think to look up here, don't ye think?"

Amoli trembled. "I don't like this."

"Just latch onto me back. Don't let go," Colin said.

"We have to hurry," Rosa cautioned.

Sasha leaped onto a branch with Rosa behind him. He helped her up onto the branch. Colin grabbed hold of the same branch with Amoli on his back. He pulled himself up the tree with every bit of force he had. Sasha and Rosa were already as high as they could go. The band of guards infiltrated the area. Amoli gasped when she saw them. Colin placed his hand over her mouth.

"How could we have lost them?" the head guard grumbled.

As they investigated the area they decided to look elsewhere. One of the youngest-looking guards let his bow and arrow fall from his back sack. It fell to the ground without him knowing. Colin slid down the tree with Amoli on his back. He let her down and picked up the bow and arrow.

"We'll surely need this," Colin said, as Sasha helped Rosa down the tree.

"Where's the time machine?" Rosa asked.

"No good. It is in direction king's guards just went," Sasha said.

"It's too risky. We'll have to try for it tomorrow. In the meantime we need rest 'n I know a place we can go," Colin said. "There's this priest, whose sister 'n niece have a small cottage in the opposite direction from here. They helped me when I escaped the castle dungeon."

"Do you think they would accommodate all four of us?" Rosa asked.

"Likely, I'm sure."

Colin, Sasha and Amoli began their journey to the cottage.

Rosa stopped. "Colin!" she called.

Colin turned to her.

"You're badly wounded. Can these people help you with this?"

Rosa stroked Colin's forceps. Amoli glanced over at them while Sasha tried to look somewhere else. Colin sighed.

"Rosa, I know it that I need a doctor, but what am I to do?"

"We're in the fifteenth century. What did they know of medicine in this turbulent time?" Rosa asked, as she turned to Sasha. "It's your ridiculous time machine that put us here in the first place."

# Chapter Nineteen

There was a swift knock at the door. Peg staggered across the room to answer it. Her eyes lit up when she saw Colin standing before her with three of his cohorts.

"Well, well!" She expressed with a smile.

"Hello again, Colin."

"Good to see ye lookin' so well, Peg. Hope yez don't mind me callin' upon ye with some friends of mine."

She clasped both her hand over his and tried to yank him in the house.

"You're looking as handsome as ever, I must say."

Amoli and Rosa followed in as Sasha took his time entering. Peg peered at Sasha. "You're not so bad to look at, either, I must say." Sasha raised an eyebrow. Rosa grinned at him. "The place is a mess. Sit anywhere you can. Can I fix you something to eat?"

"If ye don't mind. We're bein' chased by the king's guards again, if ye can believe it," Colin said.

Peg worked anxiously in the pantry. "Who is everyone I see here?"

Colin stood up. "Forgive me. This is Rosa, Amoli, 'n Sasha; friends of mine."

Peg gave a slight bow. "Pleasant to meet all of you. Tell me, why the king's guards are constantly after you?"

"I'm supposed to be knighted 'n practice the king's ideas of chivalry. Just don't think his idea of chivalry is me own idea of chivalry."

"You don't?" Peg asked, as she pulled out a large platter and sliced a variety of fine cheeses. "We are living in the age of chivalry. I don't understand how you can go against that."

"Easy," Colin responded, as he walked toward her and snatched a grape or two. "The king treats the people of

England with little dignity, don't ye think? Would ye say, he's actin' upon chivalry?"

She gave a masculine chuckle. "We live in a feudal society. You appear as if you are not familiar with this lifestyle."

Rosa glanced at Sasha. Peg pulled out five flasks and filled them to the brim with red wine. Colin took a gulp. Peg whisked past him and sat on his lap. Amoli noticed. Sasha sipped on his wine. He moved close to Rosa.

"I would like to smoke now," he whispered, in her ear.

"Don't you dare,"

Peg looked at Rosa. "So, how do you know my good friend?"

"Good friend? Who do you mean?" Rosa asked.

"Yes, my good friend, Colin," Peg responded, as she lit a candle.

Rosa glanced at Colin. "Good friend?"

Colin grinned at her. Amoli leaned over toward Rosa.

"I think she's one of the women he did it with," she said, in a whisper.

Rosa glanced back at Colin. Peg placed a large platter of fruit and bread on the large wooden table.

"Please, eat. I have to go outside and fetch some fresh eggs."

Rosa watched Peg leave. "Colin how could you? She's just awful. Are you that desperate?"

Sasha appeared nervous. "I must smoke."

Rosa smacked him on the arm. "You better not."

"Rather awful? Look who's callin' a rather kind wench awful? How could ye be so thoughtless?" Colin said, as he paced the room holding his glass of wine.

"Forgive me. I understand her hospitality is all we have right now. But it's unnerving to know that it's likely that you have slept with that woman."

Rosa stood up to get closer to the table. Amoli stood and helped herself to some fruit. Sasha remained sitting at the far end of the room and sipped his wine.

"Mr. Limmerick, she is nice lady, but you now must say truth, da?"

Colin grabbed a handful of grapes. "Why is it so unnervin' to yez who I sleep with? Amoli 'n I are no more, so me own business is mine, is it not?"

"Well, that tells it all. You have obviously slept with that woman," Rosa said.

Catherine danced into the room. She was wearing fine linens draped over her petite teenage physique.

"Oh, my, Sir Limmerick. You have returned," she said, as she danced into his arms. "You had to see me again, didn't you?"

"Catherine, how grand it is to see ye," Colin said, as he kissed her on the cheek.

"My uncle is at the monastery. We have you all to ourselves," she said, and grinned. She paused while she stared deeply at him. "I carry your child, Sir Limmerick."

Amoli choked on a piece of fruit. Rosa leered at Colin. His eyes shifted, as he forced a smile.

"Catherine, is it possible to leave me here with these fine friends of mine? We's was just in the middle of a deep discussion."

She took his hand and kissed it. "I will be back." She made her exit.

Colin glared at Rosa. "I didn't sleep with that young lass, so I didn't. So, I think, I didn't."

"She must be younger than me," Amoli grumbled. "Am I too old for you? You're already 21 years older than me."

Colin took a deep breath. "Sasha, can ye just get us outta here? Where's the time machine at?"

"You say yourself it is at the far end from here; where king's guards are looking for us, da?"

Colin sighed. "Perhaps we should take our chances."

"You know that's not what the four of us want to do. You're just feeling embarrassed by your disgraceful actions. If you don't recall sleeping with these women, it is likely you were drinking. I know you," Rosa commented.

Amoli turned away. "This is why I can't marry you, Colin." She started to cry.

"You two ladies say your opinions. You should stop now, da? We are in dangerous time period, and must not get captured by king's guards. They will torture us before they kill us, da?" Sasha said while he managed to find a piece of straw. He slid it into his mouth.

Rosa stepped close to Colin, who stood in the corner drinking wine. "Colin, forgive me. I don't know what got into me."

"Yer forgiven. We need to get back to our time. Don't wanna be a knight 'n I don't want to fight their wars. Never wanted to be a warrior, let alone a soldier. We need to get back to the time machine. Hopefully, it's still there," Colin said.

"Are you insinuating that the king's guards may have moved it?" Rosa asked.

"How should I know? Anythin' can happen."

"If they move it we must find it, that is all. Not big problem," Sasha reassured.

Amoli turned to him. "Everything about this time period is a big problem."

Colin shut his eyes as he tried to collect himself.

"Look, we's all in a panic just now. I know it. If we stay here it can only be for a short time. Don't wanna be lurin' the king's guards to Peg's home. Don't think it would be fair, that's all. We stay the night 'n we push off in the mornin'."

Colin peered at his three friends. They looked back at him. Peg entered the room. She grinned at Colin.

"I think I'll prepare a plump pheasant for all of us tonight. Would you all like that?"

Colin smiled at her. "Please, no need to go outta yer way."

"My brother will be joining us tonight. I would have prepared it anyway. Please, relax, you're my guests."

"Can we help yez in some way?" Colin asked. "I'd like to repay ye, if I can."

"You don't need to repay me. Just having you here is a gift." Peg nudged herself beside Colin. "My lovely daughter is very fond of you."

Colin forced a smile. "She says she's carrying your child now."

Colin lifted one eyebrow. "Really? Everyone seems to be, so it must be the fashion 'round here."

Peg looked somewhat confused. "You had a wonderful time on that opium the other night, Colin."

Rosa lifted her eyebrows. "You took opium?"

"I did?"

Peg chuckled. "Oh, yes, you most certainly did. You were with me mostly. I didn't see any flames between you and my daughter. It was more with you and me," she said, with a girlish giggle. "Who knows? I could be carrying your child, also."

Colin grinned. "Why not."

Rosa and Amoli sat quietly as they nursed their wine. Amoli had one ear perked.

*"What are they saying?"* Rosa whispered to Amoli.

*"I don't really wish to know,"* Amoli responded in a whisper.

Sasha sat back and sipped on his wine. Some hours passed. Peg set the table with her daughter. A large pheasant was on a platter in the center of the table. Catherine brought a bouquet of flowers and set it beside the roasted fowl.

Father Abbott stepped in. He hurried over to Colin, who was sitting at the table and took his hand.

"So good it is to see you, my son."

Colin stood up and clutched the priest's hand and gave a slight bow. "Glad to see ye again, Father."

Rosa and Amoli sat at the table. Sasha appeared disinterested.

"I see you're not rested. Are you still on the run?" the priest asked, as he sat at the table.

Catherine dragged a chair and sat beside Colin. Peg carved large slabs of meat and placed it on everyone's plate.

"First, my brother must say a few words before we start, hmm?"

"Oh, course," Rosa said.

Everyone bowed their heads as Father Abbot began his sermon. Rosa perked her ears when she realized he was reciting his prayer in Latin. The prayer was long. Sasha sighed out of boredom. Amoli watched how Catherine carefully moved her chair closer to Colin.

"Amen," the priest said and smiled at everyone at the table. Rosa smiled at the priest. The priest smiled back. "Well, well, what a pretty wench you are." Amoli started to eat. "And who is this? A beautiful moor is sitting before us?"

Amoli glanced at Colin. "Why does everyone keep calling me that?"

Colin cleared his throat. "Well, lass, it's because everyone in this century knew very little 'bout other cultures."

Peg burst into laughter. "You speak as if you're not from this time period."

The priest smiled. Colin glanced back at Amoli, then at Peg. Catherine slid her leg over Colin's lap. Colin grinned.

"Oh, forgive me. What would ye do if I said we wasn't from this century?"

Peg laughed so hard her large breasts jiggled as they hung past her waistline. Colin grabbed the jug of wine and re-filled his glass. Sasha sipped on his wine and bent over to speak to Colin. "Shut up your mouth. I am not interested in becoming great friends with these people. Shut up, eat, let's get some rest, and tomorrow we go, da?"

Rosa overheard as she sat back in her chair and peered at Colin. Peg fluttered around her guests.

"Shall I fetch you an ale from the buttery?" she asked, peering at Colin.

"The wine suits me just fine, thanks," he responded.

The priest looked at Colin. "You're part of the king's nobility, so why are you running from his guards?"

"Don't feel our king or our queen have a good handle of what chivalry should mean, if ye follow me?"

"Who's going to question that in this day and age?" the priest responded.

"Precisely." As the evening ripened, Colin consumed several bottles of wine. He stood up from the table. "Peg, you've once again been so hospitable. I'm wishin' I could take ye back with me. Yer so kind, so ye are."

"Take me back? To the castle?"

Rosa and Amoli helped Catherine clear the table. Sasha sat in a chair and tried to smoke a long piece of straw.

"The thought of takin' ye to the castle isn't a kind gesture, so it isn't."

Sasha forced a smile. "I feel so tired. Can we sleep now?"

"Oh, yes, just climb the ladder and you'll find some straw beds, if that's suitable?" Peg stepped close to Colin. "Would you like to share my bed?"

"Haven't I told ye? I'm soon to marry this beautiful lass," he said, as he slid his arm around Amoli.

Peg's lips parted. Amoli glanced at Colin. Peg stepped toward her.

"You're going to marry a moor?"

"She's not a moor, but an enchantin' lass, so she is. Isn't she lovely?"

Amoli took a breath as she noticed Colin tighten his grip around her shoulders. Peg dragged her hands through her long stringy hair.

"Oh, well, I didn't know you were planning to wed." Peg looked at her brother. "She's a moor. Why would Colin want her?"

The priest smiled. "She is beautiful, that's why, Peggy."

"How unusual. So be it," Peg said.

Sasha helped Amoli up the ladder and Colin helped Rosa. Amoli fell onto the bed of straw. Sasha slid his back against the wall to sit on the floor. He continued to light a piece of straw.

"Sasha, would you please stop that?" said Rosa. "You will burn this place down."

"I must smoke."

"You're ridiculous." Rosa stepped toward Colin. "So, tell me, why did Peg act so surprised? You must have had something with her."

Colin glanced at Amoli, who had already fallen asleep.

"Look," he sighed. "It shouldn't matter to yez who I sleep with. Both yez wenches kicked me to the road, eh?"

Sasha laid down in the straw. "I not interested in Mr. Limmerick's love life."

Rosa kneeled into the bed of straw. "It looks dreadful. I don't know how I'm going to get comfortable in this."

Colin watched Peg from the upper loft. He made his way down the ladder. Rosa grimaced as she laid her head beside Sasha. Peg gleamed when she saw Colin climb down to her.

"I think you might love me," Peg said, while she straightened things up.

"I wanted to apologize to yez. I failed to tell ye that I'm promised to someone else. Forgive me."

"I must say, I have developed feelings for you." Colin took her hands and held them tightly.

176

"Tell me something. Where are you from?" She asked gleaming at him.

"Ye wouldn't believe me if I told ye."

"Try me. I trust what you say. You seem very different than any man I've ever seen."

"Lets just leave it at that, then. Uh?"

Upstairs in the loft Amoli awoke. She sat up panting in a cold sweat. Sasha opened one eye.

"Sleep, Miss Amoli, you are having bad dream."

"I was dreaming about Colin. Where is he?" Amoli slowly stood up. She looked around the loft. "Where is he?"

Rosa awoke. "If you are sure you want to break up with him, then you have to completely detach yourself. Let him go, Amoli."

"Miss Amoli, do not do this," Sasha instilled.

"Dr. Dimitrikov, could you hold me until I go to sleep?" Amoli asked, with a few sniffles.

Sasha placed his arm around her. "Sleep, Miss Amoli."

Colin made his way back to the loft. He noticed Amoli asleep in Sasha's arms. He looked at Rosa asleep at the other end of the bed of straw. He removed most of his clothes and situated himself beside Rosa.

"Are you alright?" Rosa asked, half asleep.

"Looks like Sasha took another one of me loves."

"No. Amoli is feeling confused right now and Sasha is just being a friend."

"Friend. He don't even know the meanin' of the word."

"Put your mind to rest. Lets just sleep," Rosa said, as she stroked his face.

# Chapter Twenty

Some hours had passed in the middle of night. The air was damp and foggy when Peg's door was busted down. The loud crashing woke Peg and her guests. Catherine ran to her mother with a look of terror on her face. Peg sprung up from her bed with Catherine by her side. Father Abbott was asleep in the corner of the room.

He sat up. "What is the meaning of this?"

The king's guards ransacked through everything they could get their hands on.

"We know Sir Limmerick is here! Where is he?" asked the head knight.

Peg gave a nervous grin. "Who?"

"Sir Limmerick, you know of him. Where is he?"

Father Abbott stood up. "We don't know of this man. Just let us be. I spend much of my time at the monastery. This is my sister and niece. They are poor peasants who struggle to keep their small farm abreast upon this fief. I will notify the king about your behavior."

Colin, Sasha, Rosa, and Amoli watched from above. Rosa whispered to Colin. "Peg and the priest have done well for us."

"Shh, we'll chat later," Colin responded.

The head knight asked, "What lies beyond this ladder?"

Peg looked at the knight. "My farm supplies and preserves. Do not waste your time."

The priest stood in front of her. "The king will have you and your men punished."

The king's guards stared at Peg and her brother, and left. Colin took a deep breath and Rosa fell into his arms.

"We can't stay here," Colin said.

"On contrary. King's goons already here. They go somewhere else now."

"Don't wanna hold Peg 'n her family liable because of us, if ye know what I mean?"

"Colin, please. Peg appears to be madly in love with you. She marvels at the idea of having you stay with her," Rosa said.

"I wonder what Peg does on the side," Amoli said, scratching her head.

"How about her daughter?" Rosa commented. "What a floozy."

"Would ye just stop right there? Don't be unfair to a woman whose risked her life for us. She's a fine wench, so she is."

"Colin, she doesn't have any teeth and she carries a terrible stench. I find her repulsive," Rosa said.

"Mr. Limmerick is correct. She nice lady, I think. We go in morning. Priest help us. He good man," Sasha commented.

"I think that Peg could be a prostitute," Amoli whispered.

"Don't know how ye got that idea. If she was, why should it matter any way?"

"I guess because you have a long history with women like that," Amoli said.

"Enough of this!" Sasha shouted. "King's guards leave. In morning we gather our things and go down to see Peg and daughter. We say her, *da sviDAniya* and we go to time machine without capture, da?"

"Of course, Sasha. I think we should stop picking on Colin, don't you think, Amoli?" Rosa suggested.

Amoli slid her back against the wall to curl up on the straw bed. She whimpered, but tried not to cry.

"Lass, don't know why ye do this to yerself," Colin called to her.

Sasha laid down on the straw. "Sleep. We all must sleep."

"I just hope, after we push off tomorrow, we can reach the time machine without a problem," Rosa said and curled up beside Colin.

***

Striking rays of sunlight peered through the cottage. Colin turned over to open his eyes. He slid his hand along Rosa's face.

"Love, we bes' be leavin', don't ye think?"

"Oh, Colin, I feel so sleep deprived. I just want to get back to the time machine," she said, with a yawn.

Colin made his way to the ladder. Peg had placed plates of food on the table.

"Did you sleep well, Colin?" Peg asked, with a smile.

Colin got dressed. He bent toward Peg and kissed her lips.

"Wasn't expectin' ye to be doin' so much for us. Yer a wonderful wench. Breakfast as well, how lovely it all is."

He stepped out the door to avail himself of nature to urinate. Peg watched from behind. He gave his penis a shake and placed it back into his uncomfortable hose. He stepped back into Peg who was standing behind him. She scanned him with her eyes.

"Oh, didn't notice ye was standin' there. I suppose I was too busy pissin', so I was."

She smiled at him. "You don't have to leave."

"So, I do. I don't want the king's guards raidin' yer home anymore. I feel responsible for all this. "

"I suppose they woke you and your friends?"

"Aye. Ye 'n yer brother put yer lives in danger. You've done too much for us. Me 'n me friends need to leave your home as soon as we can. I'm sorry. Wouldn't mind stayin' a bit longer, but I have to think of ye, yer fine brother, 'n yer daughter."

She watched him climb the up the ladder.

180

Catherine placed a basket of fruit on the table. "Are we in danger, mother?"

Peg snickered. "Danger? Not at all. Go tell our guests breakfast is waiting for them." Amoli and Rosa climbed down. Sasha glanced at Peg and tried to smile at her. Peg stepped toward Sasha. "Did you sleep well?"

"Not bad. I thank you for all," Sasha responded.

Peg took hold of Sasha's hand. "You don't have to leave after breakfast. Why don't you stay? You seem like a nice man. Where are you from?"

Sasha retracted his hand. "I am from other place. You give very nice hospitality. That is all." Sasha faced her with his eyes. "We have bad guys after us. Mr. Limmerick say me he not want you in danger."

She leaned her square body against him. "I'm not afraid of the king's guards."

He gently pushed her off him. "You should be. That is all. I will sit now."

"I like the way you speak. You are foreign, I can tell."

"Not important."

He sat at the table beside Rosa. She grinned at him. "She marvels over every man who steps in this house, doesn't she?"

"I must eat," Sasha said, ignoring Rosa's comment.

Catherine sat beside Colin. "I don't want you to leave us. I'm afraid of the king and his guards."

Colin broke some bread. "I'm very sorry the king's knights paid an obnoxious visit last night. Don't try to protect us anymore. We have to take care of ourselves. It's not worth it for yez."

He stroked the back of her head. She nestled in his arms. Amoli concentrated on the food she was eating.

"Will we ever see you again?" Peg asked, with deepness in her eyes.

Colin shifted his eyes to Rosa and Sasha. "Don't know. Just don't want yez to put yerselves at risk, is all."

181

"I have horses," Peg said. "You can have as many as you wish."

Sasha grinned. "Give us four."

"I think yer bein' a bit over indulgent, don't ye think?" Colin commented and nudged Sasha.

Peg stood up from her chair. "Do you need four? Yes, you can have four."

"Two will do us just fine. Thank-ye," Colin said, as he continued to eat his breakfast.

"I hate riding on a horse. In India we always rode in a rickshaw," Amoli said.

Peg's eyes widened. "India?"

Colin smiled at Amoli. "Too much information, lass. Surely, you'll love the horse ride. Ye've done it before."

"I suppose I haven't the choice," Amoli said, with a sigh.

Sasha chuckled. "So many kind ladies give us horses on these expeditions," he said, stuffing his mouth with food.

Peg's eyes widened. She walked behind Sasha and massaged his back. "I can be even kinder than this, if you wish?"

Sasha continued to eat as Rosa glanced at him. "Not massage for me. Give to Mr. Limmerick; he like it very much."

Colin stood up. "It's gettin' on 'n we best be off. Peg, hope to see ye again."

Catherine nestled up to Colin. "Tell us where you're going?"

"Other side of castle. Our chariot awaits us, da," Sasha interrupted.

"Chariot?" Peg asked, with wide eyes.

182

# Chapter Twenty-One

Colin rode the horse with Rosa behind him as Sasha and Amoli rode alongside. The terrain was wild and untouched with the strong aroma of lavender in the air. Sasha scanned the terrain.

"Mr. Limmerick, king's guards could be anywhere here."

"Colin, I think we should park the horses here in this dense forest and do the rest on foot," Rosa suggested.

"Agreed, love."

They stopped and slid off the horses. The brush was moist with perfume. Amoli wandered off into the thorny brush, where she was captured by the fragrance. Colin had one eye on her at all times.

"Should we rest here?" Rosa asked.

"Brilliant idea, but I would hesitate at the actual act of restin'," Colin responded, with worry in his eyes.

"I think king's guards could be close," Sasha cautioned.

Amoli bent over to bring her nose to a wild rose bush.

"Do you like this fine flower, maiden? Or should I say 'moor'," an unfamiliar male voice said, as he helped her to straighten up.

Amoli gasped. "I don't know you," she squealed.

"I should say not," the well-dressed stranger responded.

Amoli's eyes widened with fear. "Are you the king?"

"I should say not. I am the viscount of this kingdom."

"Viscount? What's that?"

He snorted in his own stench. "One could say I'm like a king, but not quite." Amoli casually looked behind her to see if her friends took notice of the stranger. "Ah, I see you're not alone."

"I'm here with two great warriors. If I were you I'd run for my life."

"How dare a mere moor speak to me in such a tone."

"I'm not a moor. I'm an Indian princess."

"Don't even try to complicate England's trading relationship with India."

Colin noticed Amoli speaking to the stranger. He pulled his bow and arrow from his knapsack and held it in front of him as he approached the man.

"Can I help yez in any way?" Colin called out.

The stranger glared at Colin. "What do we have here? A true giant ogre?"

"Call me what ye want, who are ye?"

"Lovell. I am the viscount to the throne." Colin lowered his bow and yanked Amoli close to him. "Are you part of the nobility?"

Colin hesitated. "I am."

"Perhaps a man of your size can help me with my upcoming plan."

"Don't even know ye. Be gone before I jam me arrow up yer bleedin' asrse."

"I'll just call for my partners, the Stafford brothers," he emphasized, as if Colin would know of whom he was speaking.

Colin pulled Amoli along as he walked away from the man.

"Not interested in yer plan, mate. Just bugger off now."

"Perhaps, I'll have you killed right here and now."

Sasha and Rosa perked their eyebrows with distaste. Sasha stood beside Colin.

"Maybe we will kill you right now." Sasha said, drawing his sword.

Rosa sighed. "Oh, God."

Two men on horses rode to the viscount.

"Problems, Lovell?" one of the men asked.

"Yes, we should cease these people. They claim they are nobility and show no signs of chivalry to the throne. I am disgusted by their behavior."

The two men drew their swords, but remained on their horses. Colin pulled Sasha toward him.

"They's not gonna get their arses off their horses. They'll surely cut our throats this way."

"Da, we go on our horses. We take girls with us, da?"

Sasha charged with his horse toward one of the horsemen. He swung his sword and thrust it. The tip of his blade sliced the man's arm. Sasha continued to ride with conviction as he watched the man's arm bleed. The viscount stood beside his horse and quickly jumped on.

"We will leave these fools. They show to be strong warriors, though." Rosa sat behind Colin on the horse where Amoli sat behind Sasha. The viscount lowered his sword as his horse trotted to Colin. "I think you and I can work together."

"Work together?" Colin glanced at Rosa.

*"Colin, we should leave now,"* Rosa whispered to him.

"We should discuss things over some ale, don't you agree?" Lovell suggested.

"Like the sound of that, but what's there to discuss?" Colin responded.

The Stafford brothers moved closer behind the viscount.

"We're planning on overthrowing the king. Help us do it."

Colin stared at his horse's mane and fondled with it.

Sasha glared at the viscount, and then shifted his eyes to Colin. "This is nonsense. We have no interest in this," Sasha responded.

"He's an ineffective king. Most of the nobles, guild workers, and merchants have great distaste of him."

Colin turned his head to Rosa. "What happened here, love? Did they actually overthrow the king?"

*"No,"* she whispered to him. *"Don't even consider it. We need to find Sasha's time machine and go to our time."*

Amoli rested her head on Sasha's back. "Dr. Dimitrikov, I want to leave this time period. It's so very awful."

"All times in history are not pleasant places, I assure you," Sasha responded.

The viscount and his two cohorts began to trot away.

"Will you meet us for some ale? We'll be on the other side of the castle at the alehouse. Do join us."

Rosa squeezed Colin's arm. "That's where the time machine is."

"Don't I know it, love."

Sasha grimaced. "Do we join them?"

"Ah, this is gettin' dicey. Sure, we'll join 'im for just a pint or two."

The time travelers followed the viscount and the Stafford brothers to the other side of the king's castle. They parked their horses outside the alehouse. Rosa approached Colin.

"I suppose Amoli and I will blend in with the crowd."

"Just don't get yourselves into any trouble," cautioned Colin.

Rosa stood on her tiptoes to kiss Colin on the cheek. Amoli pretended she didn't notice. Sasha was already in the alehouse. Colin walked in to see barmaids laughing with knights and guild workers. A young squire stood in the corner playing his flute. Some dancing was in going on in the corner. The viscount was sitting at a table with the Stafford brothers. He noticed Colin and gestured for him to join him. Sasha appeared disinterested in his surroundings.

"Hope we's doin' the right thin', mate," Colin said, as he brushed past Sasha amongst the crowd.

Sasha followed. The two time travelers sat at the table. The viscount poured two large flasks of ale for Colin and Sasha.

"There's some pieces of swine over there, if you're interested," the viscount said.

"Thanks," Colin said, while he tried to adjust his tight-fitting hose.

Sasha picked at a scab on his wrist. "Okay, why we here?"

The viscount grinned. "We're planning an uprising against the king. We need your help."

Colin asked, "Why our help? Of all the young healthy gents ye got runnin' about the land, surely you could choose them to help yez."

"Your size is immense with muscle. You would scare off any opponent. Your partner handles a sword quite well."

Colin gulped his ale. "Or, is it 'cause we's strangers to yez?"

"I can recruit any stranger in our fine lands," said the viscount.

Sasha grimaced when he sipped on his ale.

"I'd rather ask both of you fine gentlemen." The viscount took a deep breath and sat back on his chair. "I could remind you two lords that I am the viscount of the castle. I can have you killed."

Sasha sat on the edge of his chair. "If we don't kill you first."

The viscount looked at his two cohorts. They drank up their ale.

"Now that I have told you this, you will inform the king, no?"

Colin peered at the viscount. "This is the king's battle, not ours."

"If we win this battle, you have a strong possibility of becoming king."

Colin crossed his arms. "Wrong. Ye have the strong possibility of becomin' king."

The viscount and the Stafford brothers rose from their chairs and vanished in the crowd. Sasha looked at Colin.

"Maybe we should help him take over kingdom? We hate this king, do we not?"

"Aye, we do. But Rosa's right, we's aren't here to change history."

"Who cares?" A barmaid approached the two time travelers to refill their mugs with more ale. "I not want more of this terrible drink. It tastes like hell," Sasha complained, with a sour expression. "How you drink this stuff?"

Colin smiled at the barmaid. "Then, don't feckin' drink it."

# Chapter Twenty-Two

The two male time travelers made their exit from the alehouse. They walked amongst the crowd in search of Rosa and Amoli. Colin scanned the busy crowds of people with his eyes.

"Mate? Do ye see our wenches anywhere?"

Sasha stood on his tiptoes. "Nyet. I not see them. We lose them, da?"

"Oh, feck, don't say that. Ye think they's at the time machine, already?"

"You ask me to predict these two ladies' thoughts?"

"Should we get ourselves to the time machine, is what I'm askin' ye, man."

Sasha stopped walking, as several peasants passed by him in the crowd.

"We go to time machine now and our ladies not there, you will attract attention because you are size of bull. It is risk if our ladies not there. We could lose time machine. Then what?"

"We's in no position to lose anythin'. I don't think Rosa 'n Amoli would go to the time machine without us. It would be pointless. They too have 'n will continue to attract attention because of their beauty."

"You are right. Women in this fifteenth century are ugly. I not know why, but our ladies do have so much more beauty."

"Don't know what it is really. That queen certainly don't wet me fancy with her appearance. She only married the king a year ago, so I think. Maybe he hesitated to marry such a homely wench. Who knows?"

"King is no beauty man, either," Sasha grumbled. "Newlyweds?"

"Surely don't act like it. Don't think the king wants his queen to have any rights to the throne as well," Colin added. "Do ye think it's 'cause she isn't a fine beauty?"

"Who cares?"

"Mate, I think ye best need to care as long as we's in this feckin' century. It's yer time machine that put us here. It's best ye care."

"Why we stand here and talk about so boring topic? We will be found by king's guards, da?"

"Lets keep movin'. Hopefully we'll find our wenches."

They rummaged through the crowds of peasants, merchants, and guild workers. A young boy played the flute in the distance, while a young girl danced. Colin and Sasha looked everywhere for Rosa and Amoli. Colin tripped over a female merchant's basket of fruit. He fell to the ground. The merchant cackled at his fall.

"Shite!" Colin expressed, as he helped himself up.

He was brushing himself off, when he noticed Sir Williams standing before him.

"Sir Limmerick? So, it's you making much noise? There's a search for you." Sasha shrugged his shoulders as if it were the first time he'd heard this information. "The queen needs to see you at the castle at once."

"Why?"

"You're the kingdom's first knight. There could be a political revolt." Colin's eyes widened. "A revolt could mean the overthrow of this kingdom."

Sasha stepped closer to the knight. "Who plans this revolt?"

"It is Viscount Lovell. This is dreadful news. You must see the queen at once."

"What am I to do with this, I don't know," Colin said, shaking his head.

"The king is consumed with his Tudor victory and only is vigilant against the Yorkists."

"Still not understandin' what this has to do with me," Colin responded.

"The king doesn't listen to his queen, where he has given her little power. She would like to see you, because she knows about the viscount's plan. You are the head knight; this has everything to do with you."

Colin gave a slight bow where he and Sasha followed Sir Williams on horses to the see the queen. Colin and Sasha were led to the castle. They came to the tight staircase in the front turret that led to the queen. Colin and Sasha stopped before the staircase.

"Sir Limmerick, you are to follow me to see the queen," Sir Williams said, as he began to climb the twisted staircase.

Colin sighed. "So, I hate to climb these stairs, so I do."

"What's the delay, knight?" Sir Williams asked, as he reached halfway up.

"Whoever built this castle did not build it to accommodate a man of me size, for sure."

Colin grudgingly climbed the stairs. His body scraped against the winding stone walls that encased the stairs. Two guards opened the double wood door and escorted Colin and Sasha in. The queen stood up from her throne. She gleamed when she cast her eyes on Colin. Colin and Sasha, took a few steps forward and bowed to the floor.

"Where have you been hiding, Sir Limmerick?" she asked.

"Forgive me, yer majesty."

"Stand up, both of you." She peered at Sasha. "Well, well, isn't it my fine bread baker?" Sasha smiled. "Well, we should get down to business. There is a possible uprising against this kingdom." Colin bowed his head to the floor. "Since you left this kingdom, you may have had your rights as a knight revoked, therefore, you and your cohort here will be knighted this afternoon at the courtyard."

191

"I'll be re-knighted, yer majesty?"

"Yes, of course. You need to lead the other knights, and you must cease the viscount at once. He will be captured by you and executed." The queen gestured to Sir Williams. "Take Sir Limmerick and his friend to the chamber he was given before. His friend will be knighted as well, because this kingdom is in crisis."

Sir Williams led Colin and Sasha to their chamber.

"This should be suitable for you both," Sir Williams said, and left.

"Much better than the roundhouses in 840 AD, eh?" Colin commented.

Sasha scanned the room. "Small windows, with so little light."

"Aye. We's in the fifteenth century, what ye expect?" Colin sighed. "What ye after, a view? Just wishin' Rosa 'n Amoli could be with us."

"They strong ladies. I not worry for them."

"So, we's to capture that chap we met 'n watch 'im get executed, eh?" Colin paced a bit. "I don't fancy the idea of execution."

"How this different than dying Vikings?"

"Don't fancy any of this, so I don't."

"How this different than pub brawls in your Dublin?"

Colin continued to pace. "Feck off."

"You so rude all the time."

"Don't think we can leave this room just yet. As soon as we's knighted, it will be me second time. We've gotta find our wenches. I'm worried."

"You worry too much. You must be missing your booze."

"That too."

There was a knock at the door. Two guards entered with Colin's lady-in-waiting.

"Where did you run off to? The queen was concerned," Beatrice said, as she pranced inside the room.

She noticed Sasha and gave him a direct stare. "Who is he?"

"He's me partner, I suppose," Colin responded.

"You have a partner? How interesting." She smiled and then frowned. "Why do you run from me, Sir Limmerick?"

"Run from yez? Surely, I'm not doin' such a thing."

"Then tell me my name. Do you even remember my name?"

"What is this? A quiz? Why ye doin' this?"

Sasha brushed by Colin. "In Russia, man would beat her for this."

Colin grinned. "*Beat? Beat. B-Beatrice?*"

She smiled and slid into Colin's arms. Colin made a fake grin. She pulled out a small lace fan to cool herself, and left. Sasha chuckled.

"I wouldn't laugh if I was ye, 'cause the next of kin to Beatrice will likely be yer lady-in-waitin'."

"I not worry about this, because we are not from this time. We must get our ladies and go to time machine and go, da?"

"The four of us keep splitin' up, that's what's wrong here."

"Circumstances have changed. We now in alleged more civilized time."

"Dungeons, be-headin', 'n torture methods is not me idea of civilized."

"You think your British and Dutch Boer War is – was – will be civilized?"

"Aye, cannons. I evaded it for a good reason, mate."

"Now, you are soldier, warrior – same thing. Now, you pay for your sins."

\*\*\*

Rosa and Amoli rummaged around the outdoor markets.

"Should I buy gifts for my family members, Miss Emanuel? Indian tradition is to buy gifts for family when one is on vacation," Amoli said, holding up a beaded necklace.

"Are you mad? This is no vacation. It's a science experiment, you idiot," Rosa blurted, as she shoved Amoli. Rosa slapped the necklace out of Amoli's hand. "Put that down. We should look for the time machine."

Amoli sniffled, but agreed. They left the crowded markets and ventured to the other end of the castle wall, where they last saw the time machine. The brush was dense and the tree-cover blocked out all sunlight. Amoli felt nervous.

"I don't like doing this without Colin and Dr. Dimitrikov," Amoli said.

"I just want to make sure it hasn't been moved. If it has, then we really have a problem." They struggled to walk in the tall wet grass with their long gowns. Rosa pulled some of the bushes back. "There it is."

"I don't think anyone even knows its here."

Rosa glared at her. "Of course these people know. They took pieces of it and used it as jewelry, did they not?"

"I wish Colin and Dr. Dimitrikov were here, then we could all go home," Amoli whimpered, with lament in her voice.

"Well, we can't. I just don't know what happened in that pub with those strange men. Do you think they're still there?" Rosa sighed. "I can't believe the four of us are separated again.

\*\*\*

Colin and Sasha had been knighted. They were brought to the chamber to rest before court. There was a knock on the chamber door. Sasha opened it. It was Sir

194

Williams. Sasha backed away. Colin was sitting on the bed.

"What now?" Colin asked.

"The queen wishes to see you."

"Can she see me later? Just exhausted, so I am."

"You can't act this way. You are her favorite. You must go to her now."

Colin grudgingly laced his shoes around his calves.

"Why would I be her favorite? I don't practice chivalry in her favor."

Sir Williams chuckled. "Perhaps, she fancies the way you wear your hose."

Sasha chuckled as well. Colin stood up to examine his hoses to make sure they fit on his body correctly.

"Fine, take me to her. Where's the king at?"

"He will not be near her bedchamber. Do not worry."

When they entered the queen's chamber she was laying in her bed naked. Sir Williams bowed and announced Colin to her. He left. Colin bowed.

"Rise, my royal subject, my noble knight." Colin stood up. She stared at him profusely. "Come to me."

"M' queen, forgive me for askin', but are ye ill?"

"Yes. I have been yearning for your return. Come here, sit beside me on the bed. How I long for your touch."

"Why, yer majesty? Surely, the king's touch is more suitable for yez?"

"Not at all. He doesn't give me the respect that you give."

"Respect? Ye sentenced me to death for the way I spoke to yez, yer majesty."

She stared at him. "I never had an execution planned for you."

Colin rolled his eyes back. "Well, that's just dany of ye."

"Tell me, do you know anything about the viscount?"

195

"Aye. Had ale with 'im, so I did." She sat up in the bed. "Didn't particularly fancy the bloke. He told me what his plans are for this kingdom. He needs to be stopped."

"By who, my knight?"

Colin took a few steps closer to her on the bed. "By me, yer majesty. I'll stop 'im. Since you've made me yer lead knight. I won't disappoint ye or the king. I promise."

The smile on her face intensified. "Come to me. I want to kiss your handsome face." He kneeled beside the bed, and took both her hands and kissed them. "I see how loyal you are. You do practice my idea of chivalry."

"Perhaps ye don't fancy the way I talk, or maybe ye don't care for the way I fit into me hose. But, definitely, I'll be loyal to yez." Her eyes widened. He kissed her on the lips. "Don't worry, I'll keep this kingdom safe. I'll begin to plan immediately."

He stood up. She smiled at him. He kissed her again and left. Colin returned to his chamber. Sasha was sitting at the table with a large tray of food before him.

"You not with queen so long as other times. You not have sex with her?"

"Thankfully, we didn't do anythin'."

"Why not?"

"The king could be near, perhaps, who knows? Mate, we need to do some plannin'. That viscount bloke wants to overthrow this kingdom. I promised the queen that I'll make sure it doesn't happen."

Sasha sipped some hot tea. "Have fun."

"Yer doin' it with me, ye feck."

"Do what? I hate king and queen. They not like my bread."

"We, first, need to find our wenches. Then we need to gather the knights 'n make sure all weapons are in workin' order, what ye think?"

Sasha finished his tea. "I need Vodka now."

"Look, it's fifteenth-century England. Ye won't be seein' any Vodka. Can ye get up off yer Russian arse? We need to fetch our wenches."

"It is more peaceful without them, da?"

"Let's get on with things. We need our wenches."

Sasha stood up. "You offer to fight this battle with viscount? Let's just get our ladies and go to time machine. You offer to do such stupid things. Why you do this?"

"I'm the queen's head knight. I can't let her down."

"Why you can't? I would."

"'Cause this is me way of showin' chivalric tactics, ye see?"

"Our ladies will shout at you for this."

"Gotta do it, is all. Can't let the viscount get his way with this kingdom. The history books say that King Henry VII didn't let it happen."

"History books do not say Captain Limmerick save kingdom, do they?"

"Yer helpin' me win this battle, ye shite. It was yer bloody time travel device that brought us here, 'n therefore, we've already mucked up a part of history."

Sasha stopped eating. He stood up and bowed his head toward Colin.

"Fine, we do it your way. You always get your way, Mr. Limmerick."

"We need to fetch our wenches first."

They made their exit down the narrow hallways, and out of the castle to the busy market square. Colin towered over the town's people, where it made it easy for him to spot their women.

"Don't see them. Don't even smell their perfume."

"Where would they go? Would they wait for us at time machine? It is located at other end of castle, da?"

Colin shrugged his shoulders.

# Chapter Twenty-Three

Rosa and Amoli both lay on the grass exhausted.

"What could be taking them so long?" Rosa asked.

Viscount Lovell was riding on his horse, when he noticed the two women beside the time machine. He stopped and got off his horse.

"Well, well, what do we have here? Two pretty maidens without their men? And, what is this you both seem to be tying to protect?"

He walked to the time machine and brushed his hands along the outer rails.

Rosa stood up. "We didn't even notice this contraption. We were just so fatigued, this looked like a perfect place to rest."

Amoli stepped closer to her. "Yes, what is this thing? *Hmm.*"

"You're telling me that you didn't even know this object was here? My, my, what keen liars you both are. Pretty, yes, very pretty, but very unthinking as well."

"We're expecting our men any second now. I suggest you get back on that horse and ride off," Rosa suggested.

He grabbed Rosa's arms. "Such a beauty you are. I'd like you to tell me the truth, or you will suffer for your misbehavior."

She pulled away. "I don't know what this is. Your guess is as good as mine."

"So defiant. Which one of your men are you promised to?"

Rosa's eyes widened. "Both."

Amoli looked at her, but was silent. He looked at Amoli.

"What is such a beautiful moor doing in this part of the world? Are you from India?"

"Yes, and I'm not a moor. I'm an Indian princess."

He cackled. "Really?"

He stepped closer to Amoli and grabbed her. He rubbed his hands along her buttocks. She squirmed, kicked, and tried to pull away from him. Rosa jumped on his back and punched him several times. He grabbed Rosa and Amoli by their arms and pulled them to the ground. He tore part of Amoli's dress and tried to press himself on top of her. Rosa found a rock on the ground and smashed in the back of his head. He fell on top of Amoli.

"Get him off of me." Amoli squirmed.

Rosa tried to pull him off. "Do you think I killed him?" she asked, trying to catch her breath.

"Who cares if he's dead? He tried to do sorry things to me," Amoli squealed.

"If he isn't dead Colin will make sure of it when he finds out." They heard hooves rustle through the trees. "Colin? Sasha? Is that you?"

The Stafford brothers approached the women on their horses. They stopped when they noticed the viscount laying on the ground out cold.

"What did you do to him?" One of the brothers called out. "You both will be executed for this."

Rosa kept her distance from them. "What gives you the right to make such decisions?"

"We are part of the king's hierarchy." The brothers got off their horses to attend to their partner. "He's still breathing."

The viscount slowly opened his eyes. "Cease. Cease those women," he ordered with a faint voice.

"Run!" Rosa shouted, as she grabbed Amoli's arm and they got lost in the brush.

The brothers left their horses beside the viscount and chased after the time travelers. Amoli's dress was torn, parts of it lagged on the ground, which slowed her pace. One of the brothers got hold of her sash and pulled her to him. He threw her to the ground. She screamed. Rosa

199

turned back, and she also screamed. The two brothers took the women and shook them hard.

"You'll be put in the castle dungeon until your execution."

The viscount walked to the Stafford brothers and the two female time travelers.

"These two women carry on as if they are knights. Who do they think they are? It's as if they are from another century," the viscount said, in a weak voice.

"Should they be executed at once?" one of the brothers said, as he had a firm grip on Amoli's arm.

The viscount grinned. "Of course they should. They haven't learned their place in the world. How dare she strike me?" he said, pointing at Rosa.

The brother who had a firm grip on Amoli's arm pushed her to the ground and tore off more of her dress. She screamed and kicked. Colin and Sasha were on the other side of the castle wall.

"Did ye hear a scream, mate? Was that Amoli?" Colin asked. He shoved Sasha aside. "I know I heard Amoli scream. We bes' get to the other side of the castle."

They made their way to the time machine. Colin jolted with surprise when he noticed two unfamiliar horses beside the time machine.

"I see blood spattered on grass," Sasha said, kneeling to the ground.

"I smell Amoli's perfume," Colin said, as he walked around searching. "Somethin' happened here, mate."

The brother pressed himself on top of Amoli. He pulled down his hose. The viscount had a hold of Rosa. She kicked him and screamed. When he wasn't looking, she thrust her foot directly into his groin. He yelped and fell to the ground. The other Stafford brother grabbed Rosa and pushed her to the ground. She kicked him in the teeth, where his two front teeth chipped off.

"You menacing wench. I'm going to make sure you never forget what you just did," the Stafford brother shouted.

He slapped her across the face several times and gave her a bloody nose. The other brother pulled out his penis, but Amoli gripped it with both her tiny hands and squeezed as hard as she could. Amoli and Rosa continued to call for Colin and Sasha. Despite Rosa's bloody nose, she plunged her foot into the Stafford brother's gut. He couldn't get closer to her. Amoli rolled over onto her hands and knees. The other brother chased after her, but she grabbed hold of his leg and bit his calf until she saw blood. He shouted with pain and kicked her in the face. He toppled over her. She stood up and saw Rosa on the ground kicking the other Stafford brother in the stomach. She kicked him so hard he lost his wind and doubled over. Amoli grabbed Rosa's arm and they fled through the forest. They ran without looking back. Amoli's dress was practically no more, where she was half nude. She ran into Colin's stomach.

"Lass!" Colin shouted.

Sasha stopped Rosa. "Who give you bloody nose? Who do this to you?"

"The viscount and his two cohorts are over there," Rosa answered, trying to catch her breath.

"Amoli, yer dress? What the feck happened? Did the viscount try to rape ye?"

She trembled and cried in his arms.

"Oh, Colin it was just awful. They tried to have their way with us."

"Yes, Amoli, but we didn't let them. They were so surprised to see two beautiful women like us fight them to no end," Rosa added.

"Where are these fecks? Show me 'n they'll be sorry they was ever born," Colin demanded.

"They're over there somewhere," Amoli said, pointing to the dense brush.

The four time travelers walked into the deep forest to find the viscount and the Stafford brothers lying on the ground drenched in their own blood. Sasha knelt beside the viscount.

"He not dead. Too bad, da? It would save many headaches."

"Looks like he got slammed with a rock, eh?" Colin said. "Looks like all three of these blokes are doin' fine, but I must say wenches, ye did good."

A man they didn't recogize rode up to them on a horse. He scanned the situation with his eyes and slid off his horse.

"What is this? These men are part of the king's court. Did you know that?"

Rosa glanced at him. "So what?"

"Look what they did to my dress?" Amoli indicated.

"You two ladies speak to me without being spoken to? How dare you!"

Colin took Amoli and Rosa into his arms.

"They's me wenches, 'n I'm the king's lead knight," Colin said.

"I don't care who you are. I haven't seen you at court. Who are you, I don't know. I want to know who did this damage to the viscount and the Stafford brothers?"

Amoli stepped toward him. "Us women did, because they are bad people."

Colin pulled Amoli back. "Lass."

"Who are you to speak to me? You are just a moor. You will come back with me to the castle dungeon where you will learn to honor royalty. It is likely you both will be sentenced to hard labor. If a high end to the throne wishes to have his way with you, then he will do so. You haven't the right either way."

Two other unfamiliar men on horses appeared. They took Rosa and Amoli and chained their wrists. Colin stepped closer to the men.

"What ye doin'? I'm the king's head knight. Ye don't have the authority to do anythin' to these wenches."

"I work under the viscount, who works under the throne. You are only a knight. I have more authority than you."

"You have title?" Sasha asked.

"Who are you? A foreigner? You must be English. I will take no commands from a man like you," the man said.

Rosa shoved the man, who had chained her wrists, and Amoli kicked the man, who also chained her wrists. They both ran into the forest. Colin grabbed the man and lifted him by his collar.

"I catch ye again, ye'll be a dead man."

Rosa and Amoli ran as fast as they could, but the chains around their wrists weighed them down. They pushed through the dense forest where two more guards heard the sound of dragging chains. Two guards approached Rosa and Amoli and smacked both of them so hard across the face they knocked them out.

***

Amoli paced around the tiny cell.

"This horrible place is starting to become a second home to me."

"You know, I really hope those pigs didn't make any deals with Colin and Sasha. Only God knows what was discussed in that pub. My nose is finally starting to clot."

"Pigs, that they are. Disgusting. They wanted their way with us. I barely have a dress. I look dreadful."

Rosa slid her back against the stone wall of the dungeon cell so she could sit.

"You couldn't look dreadful if you tried."

"Thanks, Miss Emanuel, that's the nicest thing you ever said to me."

"We have got to get out of here. Do you think they'll execute us just because we fought for our rights?"

"I don't know. I know that I'm very terrified. I don't know what they will do to us."

"The important thing is that we didn't let them get their way with us, because we're smarter than them," Rosa said, pacing. "We're twientieth-century women. We know our rights. We are law-abiding citizens and we also have the right to vote."

"Vote? Well, I'm not British. I don't think I have that right."

"This time period seems like there were no rights at all in this feudal society."

"I don't really care. I just need better clothes so I can cover up, and I would really like to return to our time period."

Colin and Sasha searched around the time machine. The Stafford brothers' two horses remained.

"I found one of Rosa's blue hair ribbons," Colin said, with tears forming in his eyes. He held the ribbon close. "Do ye think our wenches got away safely?"

"Oh, don't start. I have no doubt they are safe now, da? Do not forget our ladies, how they are. They will fight. They want to be man. I not know why."

Colin's head hung low to hide the worry on his face. "Somethin' happened, I'm afraid. They may've been caught. We could've done more, mate."

"More? Like what?" Sasha found an embroidered viscount crest in one of the sacks that hung over the one of the horse's sadles. "Is this Lovell's horse? I wonder, or is it those other two goons? I should have used gun and viscount would be no more, and the same goes for his stupid followers."

"Perhaps, aye. I donno. Just want our wenches safe."

"Come, we must go back to castle."

"Can't, man. We've gotta search more for our loves."

"We look everywhere in forest. We not see them. Time machine seems okay; few minor parts missing, but okay."

Colin threw his arms in the air. " Oh, God! This bloody time machine put us here in this time period. Where's our wenches at?"

"Relax, Mr. Limmerick. I not worry for our ladies. They can take care of themselves. You think all woman cannot survive without your huge muscles." They returned to the castle to sit in a very long-winded court session with the king. Sasha glanced at Colin. "This so boring. I must smoke."

"Well, ye can't. Yer now part of the king's court."

The king continued to drone on about Viscount Lovell's planned uprising.

"I am pleased to say our head knight, Sir Limmerick, has a plan on how to capture Viscount Lovell and the Stafford brothers, and will bring them to their execution." The king rose from his throne and the nobility applauded. "Please, Sir Limmerick, stand up and tell our nobility how you plan to stop these diabolical thieves."

Colin stood up and was gestured to stand before the king.

"First, we need to examine our weapons. Me friend here, uses gunpowder quite well."

The nobility expressed their surprise. They sat up straight in their chairs and were very attentive. Colin watched the nobility talk amongst themselves about gunpowder.

"It's like yez all never seen it before," Colin commented, as he glanced at the king. "I know it's less familiar to yez, but it may be the only last resort."

The king interjected, "Most of my nobility may not have ever seen gunpowder. You say you're from Ireland, but you appear to have a broad range of experience. You discuss gunpowder as if we keep it in our houses. What world do you come from?"

The nobility exchanged words with one another.

"I, meself, don't know as much as me fellow cohort here. He comes from Russia where gunpowder is more readily used," Colin said, feeling his nerves act up.

"I see," said the king, as he repositioned himself in his throne. "I know very little about the kingdom of Russia. It is a country that is much too far for us to reach."

"Ah, but India is a tradin' partner?" Colin said, wiping the sweat from his hands onto his shirt.

The king cleared his throat. "Yes, India is our new trading partner. They have tea and spices, amongst other things."

The nobles chattered to themselves.

"What I was tryin' to convey to yez all is gunpowder could win our war over any traitors. I, however, prefer a fair fight usin' our skills of archery, daggers, 'n swords."

Colin immediately sat down beside Sasha. The court stood up with applause.

"Mr. Limmerick, you speak like great warrior. You are now soldier boy."

"The last thing I want is combat, especially on a time travel expedition. Don't wanna encourage war 'n killin', so I don't. Look what time period we's in, 'cause yer time machine is so faulty."

"For that, I will smoke."

Colin crushed Sasha's hand in his. "Ye try it, 'n don't expect me to bail yez out."

"I not twist your arm to come on my time machine, da? You do it because you choose. Your stupid academic advisor make you do this like you cross street, da?"

Colin pretended to be interested in what the king was saying at court. He sat with a straight back and puffed his chest out to take a deep breath. He chuckled and turned his head toward Sasha.

"You know, this is silliness. We's livin' in a dangerous time period. We all need to work together, be friends, 'n watch out for each other.

"You are one who poke fun at my great achievement."

"I'm sorry for that, mate."

The king looked at Colin. "Should all my nobles try to use gunpowder?"

Colin stood up. "We should only use it if and when all else fails." The nobility chanted a bit. "We need to test our archery equipment, 'n make sure our swords 'n daggers are ready."

The king chanted along with the rest of the nobility. The queen stood up to applaud Colin. The nobility cheered. The king gleamed at Colin.

"Do you have anything to add to that, knight?"

"Lets get started. No time to waste, yer majesty."

"Sir Williams, take Sir Limmerick and his foreign friend to the dungeon courtyard. They can choose their new slaves there."

Colin and Sasha followed Sir Williams.

"All the slaves have been sentenced to hard labor outside right now. Choose your slaves," Sir Williams said.

Colin and Sasha looked at the prisoners at work.

"I did this," Colin said, to Sasha.

"I not want to do such primitive labor. These people so dumb. They not know anything."

"How would ye have thought in the fifteenth century?"

Amoli and Rosa were at the opposite end of the courtyard pruning rose bushes.

"Ouch! I stabbed my thumb again," Amoli yelped.

"It's as if you never did any form of physical labor in your life," Rosa commented.

"What was that?" Colin turned his head. "Shite! Look. Our wenches. They's in prison again. Thank Christ, they's still alive."

Amoli noticed Colin and Sasha. "Look, Miss Emanuel. Our wonderful men are here to save us."

"I must say, they took their sweet time," Rosa said, as she watched them walk toward them.

Amoli looked at Rosa. "I'm getting used to this. Colin usually takes forever to save me. It's his way, I suppose."

"He's not God," Rosa responded. "He has been rather busy with battles with swordsman and jousting tournaments. He is a twentieth-century man, you know.

Colin took Rosa in his arms and kissed her several times on the head.

"Worried is what I was. So happy to see yez, love."

Sasha embraced Amoli.

"I'm glad you're here, Dr. Dimitrikov," Amoli said, with a smile.

Sasha kissed her on the head. Colin looked at Amoli and awkwardly embraced her as Sasha held Rosa in his arms.

"I love you, my Rosa," Sasha said, and he kissed Rosa's lips.

Rosa pulled away. "I t hink I'll take what you said with a grain of sault."

Colin tightened his arms around Amoli and lifted her in the air. He kissed her several times on the lips.

"I love ye so much, lass. Just never stopped."

"I love you too, but please try to understand we are no longer a couple."

He stood straight. "Lass, why ye doin' this? Ye know we's meant to be."

"No, Colin. I've thought about this all those long days and nights in those dungeon cells. I came to realize that you and I are not meant to be."

A tear trickled down her face.

"What ye sayin'? Of course we's meant to be. We love each other, 'n that's all that matters."

"This is almost impossible for me to do, but I cannot accept the fact that you have been with so many different women, even women from past centuries. You sleep with everyone. Am I not beautiful enough for you?"

208

"Lass, please, the only woman I wish to marry is ye. Yer so beautiful."

"Yes, but you have broken my heart in two. I don't know if we could have a healthy marriage."

His smile dissipated. "Lass, we're made to be together. Why ye doin' this?"

"I also learned that you fathered a child when you were a teen. Is that true?" He was silent. "I just can't stand the fact that you have been with so many women even when you were in your teens. It bothers me. If I married a man from India he would be a virgin, but now I am no longer a virgin, because I've been with you. I don't think any man from India would take a chance with me," she said, with a whimpering sob. "Where is your child now?"

"Lass, why ye bringin' this up on our time travel expedition? I was forbidden to come close to that child or her mother. They were put in a convent somewhere south of Dublin. Never heard a thing again. I was sixteen."

"How sad."

"Very sad. I cried for months, so I did. Me parents didn't try to make me feel any better about it, either. They just damned me for it. Ye know, I went against God's wishes, 'cause we was only kids 'n weren't married. Ye know what I mean?"

"How awful. I feel very sorry, Colin."

"All I know is I have a daughter somewhere in Ireland."

Colin embraced Amoli. Sasha pulled away from Rosa.

"We better not act so different here. Guards watch all move we make, da? We are here to pick our slaves."

"Aye, mate. Supposin' our slaves are Rosa 'n Amoli," Colin said.

"Da, it sounds good to me. Come, we take our slaves and begin our fight."

Rosa pulled at Sasha's arm. "Fight?"

"Da, we fight viscount, now."

"Has the king ordered you to fight him?" Rosa asked.

209

"He's plannin' on ursurpin' the kingdom. He's a shite, that's for sure," Colin answered.

"You don't have to convince me," Rosa said.

"Did you know Miss Emanuel bashed his head in with a rock? If she hit him a little harder maybe he would be dead by now," Amoli added.

Colin and Sasha looked at each other with lifted eyebrows. Colin took Rosa's hand.

"Colin, I don't really know what you two discussed with that viscount in the pub, but he isn't worth it. He tried to have his way with Amoli, so I had to do something," Rosa explained. "You know I don't agree to violence as a solution."

Colin pulled Amoli against him. "He'll pay for that one, that's for sure. What an ogre, I must say. Love, ye did good. Ye stopped 'im 'n that's all that really matters." Colin bent over to kiss Rosa on the lips. "Yer a heroin; ye saved Amoli."

"So, now we have our slaves we are ready to execute viscount," Sasha said.

"Colin, you're going to kill him?" Rosa asked.

"He wanted me 'n Sasha to help him overthrow this kingdom. I told the king that I won't let it happen. I just wanna kick the shite outta 'im."

"If we are to do this with boring nobility, we must go now," Sasha said.

"Where do we go, since we are your slaves?" Amoli asked Colin.

"I suppose ye just wait for us in our chamber." Colin tightened his arms around Amoli and kissed her on the lips. "Glad ye got yerself covered up, lass. Don't want these creepy fifteenth-century blokes lookin' at ye."

She backed away. "I know you love me. I don't think we can do this any more. You remind me of a pot that bubbles over," she said, while he caressed her shoulders.

Rosa chuckled. "That's Colin."

Sir Williams noticed Colin and Sasha in the courtyard.

"I see you have chosen your slaves."

"Aye. Get the knights gathered at the bailey of the castle with every weapon they know of," Colin ordered. Sir Williams gave a slight bow. "Sasha, bring our wenches to our chamber. I'm needed at the castle bailey."

He kissed Amoli on the cheek and he kissed Rosa's hand.

"I must say, you are quite the chivalric knight, aren't you?" Rosa said, with a girlish giggle. "Lets see, you've grown back that beard. Your hair is long as always and you're wearing tights. I think knighthood fits you," Rosa said, creating a square frame with both her hands.

He chuckled. "At least somethin' fits me."

Sasha took Amoli and Rosa's hands and they walked off to the knight chamber. Colin pulled a rose from the prison courtyard, and rushed to appear at the castle bailey. The king was brought in; he kept his distance and stood amongst the knights. The queen then appeared. She caught Colin's eye and waved at him. Colin pushed through the gathered nobles and bowed to the queen. She gleamed at him. He handed her the rose, which caught her off guard.

"I will win this battle for the kingdom, yer majesty," he said, and bowed.

"I know you will, knight," she responded, with lusting eyes.

He bowed to the ground and then stood up. He gazed at her and she at him for a few seconds. The nobles sat on their horses with their bow and arrows in hand, and their swords beside them. Sir Williams glanced at Colin as they both climbed upon their horses.

"Where are we going?"

"We sit and wait for their attack. When they do, we'll be ready," Colin said.

"I haven't seen Lovell within the castle walls in days," said Sir Williams. "I asked the barons and they also said they have not seen him."

"Then he's likely not within the castle, but could be plannin' his attack from outside," Colin said. "I know he has those brothers behind 'im, but who else? If he's plannin' on usurpin' the king he's likely got others behind him."

Sasha waved his gun. "I will blow their heads off."

Sir Williams stepped his horse closer to Sasha.

"Where did you get such gunpowder?"

"I make it."

"You made this gun? May I see it?"

Colin peered at Sasha with a sight nod against it.

"I not think it is good idea, because only I can make it work because I build it myself."

"Nobody else would know how to operate it?"

"Da, you not know. Only I know because I am creator."

The other nobles listened with intrigue. Just as the nobles positioned themselves on their horses and Sasha and Colin did the same on their horses, there was a hard thud against the main wood door at the front of the castle. The hinges of the door started to bend. The crashing of a large object was trying to force the door to collapse.

Colin positioned his bow and arrow, the door busted opened, and enemy attackers raided the castle bailey. Colin directed his horse toward Viscount Lovell and his followers, who showed himself with a thrashing sword in his hands. Colin shot his arrows. Lovell and his men were surprised at the retaliation from the king's knights. Lovell indicated to his men that they needed to vacate immediately.

Arrows flung through the battle along with thrashing swords. Several knights were knocked off their horses. Several of Lovell's attackers lay dead. Lovell rode his horse away from the caste. Colin's horse increased its

212

speed. He was not going to allow him to escape. He pushed his way through the dense cluster of knights. His horse picked up more speed. Lovell rushed over the hill past a cluster of trees.

The moon was bright, which gave Colin some light to see where the viscount was. Colin followed;  his horse was keen in keeping up with Lovell's horse's pace. The rest of the knights, including Sasha, followed behind. Arrows were flying, while everyone followed over the hill and past the trees.

Lovell came to a cave by a steep cliff. He entered with his horse. Colin pulled out his battleaxe and entered. Colin's horse stepped over a flowing stream. The cave's ceilings and walls were cluttered with stalagtites, as moisture dripped from them onto Colin's armor. Colin removed his helmet, so he could understand the layout of the cave. He could hear Lovell's horse step through the rugged wet ground of the cave.

He could also hear his knights outside the cave. He took a deep breath relieved to know that they were following him. His vision couldn't cut through the darkness, but he continued to venture deeper into the cave. Colin removed his armored gloves so he could feel around. He felt the cave walls as his horse took short steps.

His horse yelped and stepped backward. Colin could feel that there was a drop in elevation. He slid off his horse and gestured for it to return outside. He had his bow and sack full of arrows, his battleaxe, dagger, and sword. He continued on foot. He knelt to the ground and felt that there was a definite drop in elevation. Like a blind man he slowly positioned himself on his hands and knees. His dagger fell from his belt and dropped a great depth with a splash into another flowing stream.

"Go knight! Leave me! You cannot find me in here!" Lovell shouted to him.

"Where are yez?" Colin called out.

"I'm riding my horse along the cave ridge!" Lovell responded, with a diabolic cackle.

"Yer wacked, man! If yer horse makes one wrong move, yer done for!"

"I will conquer the kingdom! My uprising will take over the kingdom and England will be mine!"

Colin grimaced. "Got news for yez: ye won't be takin' the kingdom. The king's gonna continue to reign over England, 'n he's gonna have a son, who's gonna leave a legacy for his acts of tyranny, but also his greateness."

"Wishful thinking, or you're crazy!" Lovell shouted, as he scraped along the cave ridge.

"Neither! I'm not from this time. I'm from the future! Don't really care if I spill me guts to yez, 'cause I'm gonna kick yer bleedin' arse anyways!"

"How I hate the Irish."

The cave rumbled and shook. Some of the stalagtites broke off from the dripping ceiling. Lovell tried to climb back up the ridge. The cave shook again, and Lovell's horse panicked. He slid off his horse and tried to walk it up the ridge to the higher elevation. Loud thundering of an animal echoed through the cave. Lovell's horse jumped and fell off the ridge to its death. Lovell yelped with horror in his voice. Colin could hear the loud splash of the horse when it fell to the bottom of the cave.

Colin was on his hands and knees, which was a challenge to do in armor. He tried to stand up by leaning his body against the rough walls of the cave. He glided his body against the wall and finally stood. He moved toward the opening of the cave. The moonlight was all he had to see with. Another loud grunt from some kind of animal shook the cave. Colin was more concerned with falling stalagtites. He finally saw the exit of the cave.

Sasha and the other knights awaited his return with their weapons in position. Sasha smiled when he saw Colin exit the cave holding his armored helmet in hand.

The knights slid off their horses to welcome him back. His horse stood beside Sasha's.

"Did you see the viscount?" Sir Williams asked.

"Didn't see 'im, so I didn't, but exchanged some words, so I did."

The viscount crept along the cave's ridge where he heard another loud animal sound roar throughout the cave walls. Debris shook from the ceiling and walls; pieces of the narrow ridge also crumbled beneath his feet. He clung with his back to the wall as he edged back to the higher elevation until he saw what was behind the echoing animal sounds. It was standing below him on the much lower elevation, where his horse had fallen. Its long neck raised its face to stare at the viscount. It grumbled and moaned. Lovell pressed his back into the cave wall. He shouted with horror at the sight of this animal.

"The mythical dragon has come to life!" he shouted.

The large mammal stomped its feet on the wet cave floor splashing about. It used its strength to bust the cave walls to make its exit. The viscount was close enough to the higher elevation. He clutched onto an intact stalagtite and hoisted himself up and away from the beast.

Colin, Sasha, and the knights waited for the viscount's exit from the cave. The viscount finally made his appearance. He took a few breaths when he noticed a line of the king's knights on their horses, poised with their bows and arrows in their hands. The viscount appeared disheveled and confused.

"What's wrong, Lovell?" Colin called out, as he sat tall on his horse.

"I've seen it." The viscount glared at Colin. "The mythical dragon awaits us in the cave. I saw it with my eyes. I felt its hot breath. I felt the cave move. A dragon is there."

Colin glanced at Sasha, then at the rest of the knights.

215

"Dragons, man? It's all folklore, so it is. No dragons in England, or anywhere else, so there isn't. Not even Nessy. It's a myth."

"You should know, giant knight. You claim to be from our future. You know the future of the king? You know all," Lovell grunted, as he fell to his knees. "I witnessed the most feared beast of all: the mighty dragon."

Colin glanced at Sasha. "What ye think he's goin' on about, mate?"

"I not know. All people are stupid in this century."

The cave crashed and exploded as the knights and Lovell watched it crumble before their eyes. Sasha looked at Colin.

"Earthquake in England?" Sasha expressed.

"Never. Just not an earthquake zone, mate; Italy maybe."

"Italy not that far. It is closer than my Russia. Tremor, maybe?"

"Possible. If it's a tremor, why's it so localized? Just the cave, mate, don't make any sense."

"You think viscount see dragon?"

Colin laughed. "I think Lovell's a feckin' idiot, is what I think."

"Da, they all are."

"Shh, mate. Look, the cave's got somethin' up with it."

The knights appeared terrified when Colin glanced at them.

"Our men wish to leave, Sir Limmerick," Sir Williams said.

"Leave? Don't they wanna see why the cave is destroyin' itself?"

"You're very brave, but we all fear a dragon could be doing this."

"Just curious to know why the cave is doin' what it's doin', is all."

"Curious? We're not curious. Yes, you are a very brave knight, indeed."

Colin chuckled as he rolled his eyes back when he looked at Sasha. The cave continued to crumble and rumble. The sound of the animal's groaning grew louder as the cave collapsed. A long neck appeared with a much smaller head appeared as debris tore off the creature. The viscount was on his knees with exhaustion. He was so terrified that he could no longer move.

"The dragon will breathe fire," he warned.

Colin looked at Sasha and chuckled at Lovell's fear. The rest of the knights got their terrified horses moving and off they went.

"So stupid, these people. That is no dragon. We see this thing before. What is it?"

Colin examined the enormous creature and grinned.

"That there, mate, is *Indicrithirium*. Aye, mate, ye was right when ye said ye saw it before. Love 'im, so I do."

"I not want to end your love affair with beast, but we have same problem again. We did not close pathway through time. I hear Rosa's voice say me that I am idiot, da?"

"Kinda think we did close it, mate. I was wonderin', though, some species, could've been misplaced, 'cause not all of 'em most likely, made it through the pathway. I'd have to discuss this with Rosa. She'd probably figure it out better than me."

"Oh, well, you not worry about this large mammal?"

"Love to take it back with us, but don't think it would fit on the time machine."

"You want it in 1910? How it survive?"

"It wouldn't. It would also die here in the fifteenth-century with all these ridiculous beliefs of dragons. Shite, it don't even resemble their idea of what a dragon is supposed to look like. Don't know what to do really. I'd like to discuss this with Rosa."

The two male time travelers watched *Indricotherium* break out of the cave and flick off the debris left on its head. It noticed Colin and Sasha sitting on their horses. The king's knights had gone and Lovell remained on the ground with a white complexion of terror.

"The dragon has come to take us!" he shouted.

"Giant knight, you show no fear of this beast? You must be a sorcerer. A relative of Lucifer himself."

Colin glared him. "Sorcerer? Don't even know what the hell that is."

"You are a man of magic. You're from my future. You're the devil," Lovell cried, as he placed himself on the ground on all fours and pounded his fist on the ground.

Sasha grinned. "I need to smoke."

"Aye, 'n I certainly need a shot of whiskey, or two, or three."

"Soon the dragon will breathe fire on us. Oh, what shall our lord do to help us?" he continued to cry, and pound his fists.

"*Indricotherium* don't breathe fire? He's misplaced, poor thing," Colin said. "How in the hell did he get inside that cave, I donno?"

Colin scratched his bearded chin. *Indricotherium* got closer to Colin and Sasha. He lowered his long neck to bring his face closer to them. He expanded his large nostrils to sniff at them. Colin leaned forward on his horse and touched the large mammal's head to give him a friendly pat. Sasha smiled.

"Lets go back to castle. I am tired and I want Rosa to give me love."

Colin glared at him. "What ye doin'? Ye got yerself a wife in Russia."

"I love her now."

*Indricotherium* expected more attention. Colin took a deep breath as he pushed *Indricotherium's* huge head away.

"Poppycock, man. Ye got a strange way of showin' a wench ye love her."

"You have Miss Amoli, why you care?"

"Amoli don't want me anymore. She thinks I'll give her a terrible life," he said, with his head hung low. "She's likely right."

"So, now you want my Rosa?"

*Indricotherium* lifted its head and made a few grunts. It noticed the viscount squirm on the ground. The huge mammal lowered its head close to the viscount. It sniffed at him and watched the viscount yell and scream with terror. Colin and Sasha sat on their horses and watched.

*"Indricotherium's* not doin' anythin' to get Lovell in such a huff, don't ye think? Why is he actin' like such a bleedin' arse? Rather embarrassed of him, so I am."

"He acts this way, because he is product of his own time. I hate all people in this fifteenth-century time."

Colin chuckled as he watched the giant mammal's amusement over the viscount's behavior. Lovell continued to yell and scream as the giant mammal brought its face closer to him. Then *Indricotherium* brought its long neck up again and stood straight. The Viscount continued to wail and screech, where *Indricotherium* moved his enormous leg forward and unknowingly stepped on top of the Viscount. Colin's eyes widened and his brows lifted. Sasha stared in silence.

"Oh, feck, what just happened?" Colin expressed. The large mammal lifted its leg. He tried to scrape Lovell of his foot. Colin closed his eyes. "Can't look, it's just too heinous, I'd say."

Sasha shrugged. "Oh, well, now you tell king no more uprising and king keeps throne, da?"

"I suppose so, mate." *Indricotherium* stared at the two time travelers. It slowly turned its enormous body and stomped off. Colin took a deep breath. "Could sure use a shot of somethin' just now."

"Lets get our ladies and go to time machine."

219

They rode to the castle.

# Chapter Twenty-Four

Colin and Sasha opened the door to their chamber. Rosa smiled when she saw them.

"I am so very glad to see both of you in one piece," Amoli expressed.

"Well? Did you cease the viscount?" Rosa asked. "You're both here, so I'm assuming you defeated him with a victory."

Colin smiled as he tried to remove his own armor. "Ye could say that. He's not gonna bother the king, or anyone else ever again."

"Was it an easy fight?" Rosa asked.

Sasha smiled. "Too easy." Rosa batted her eyelashes and took Sasha's hand in hers.

Colin appeared a bit disinterested as he continued to wear a smile on his face and struggled to remove his armor. Rosa stepped close to Colin and helped him remove his breastplate. Sasha immediately took it from her because of its weight.

"Mr. Limmerick do good deed in 1487; we must go back to 1910, da?"

Amoli handed Colin a cloth; he took it from her and wiped the dripping sweat from his face.

The door swung opened. Sir Williams entered. "You are both expected at the king's celebration of victory held in the main square of the castle. Your slaves are expected to serve you both accordingly. Please, change your clothes for the occasion."

Sir Williams gave a slight bow and left.

"That was a quick appearance by the Royal's mate, wouldn't yez say?" Colin commented as he took a few deep breaths. He closed his eyes and extended his hand to the wall for balance.

221

Rosa appeared concerned and she stepped closer to him. "Colin?"

He paused before answering her. "Aye?"

"Colin, if you're not up to attending the victory celebration, are you allowed to decline?"

Colin found a chair and slowly sat in it. "Likely, not."

Sasha leaned against the wall and stared at the floor.

"Colin? Are you alright?" Amoli asked in a soft voice.

Colin tried to catch his breath a few times. "Just exhausted, so I am. Never been so exhausted in me whole life. Just not used to bein' a chivalric knight, I suppose."

"Of course not, Colin, maybe because you're not even from this century. We're all misplaced and it's been a trying experience for all of us, however, you're the instant warrior," Rosa commented.

Colin's head suddenly drooped forward. Amoli stepped

closer to him. His head drooped even more forward and he fell to the floor.

"Oh! My God!" Rosa squealed. "Check if he's still breathing!"

Sasha turned his head to glance at Colin lying on the floor.

"Sasha! Do something!" Rosa shouted.

"Do what? I need smoke. Let Mr. Limmerick sleep."

Amoli looked terrified. "Oh, my, maybe he doesn't want to be a knight, Miss Emanuel."

"Maybe? Of course, he doesn't want to be a knight!" Rosa lashed out. "Amoli Sharma, you are so ridiculous at times!"

Sasha glanced at the ceiling, then at the floor. "None of you two ladies feel sorry for me, I not know why."

Rosa chuckled. "Sasha, tell us why we're supposed to feel sorry for you?"

"I not have smoke and I must."

Amoli glanced at Rosa, then at Sasha. She was silent.

"I not want to go to celebration. I hate these terrible people."

"Fine, Sasha, you don't want to play this game? Do what you want," Rosa bruted. "What do you want to do, just sneak out of the castle when they're about to reward you with medals of bravery?"

"I want smoke. I don't care about stupid medals from so many centuries in past. I am physcist. I not care for this history."

Colin began to snore loudly.

"Mr. Limmerick is big bull. He even snores like bull. How you ladies like him so much? I not know this. He have big pet with him to fight viscount. Even prehistoric pet is size like him."

Rosa's eyebrows lowered. "Big prehistoric pet?"

"You know it with long neck. It eats plants, but no dinosaur, it come later than that."

Rosa's eyes widened. *"Indricotherium?"*

Sasha grinned. "Da! That is it!"

"Sasha, did we not close the passage through time correctly? This is horrible!"

"It is good. Big pet help Mr. Limmerick. It save us."

"Mr. Limmerick say maybe not all prehistoric species slipped back to their time period. Some will be misplaced, he say."

Rosa stared at Sasha with her lips parted.

"Ask Mr. Limmerick."

"Oh, yes, that is very likely. However, it's very unfortunate," Rosa responded.

"I don't like this one bit. I can't really imagine all the prehistoric beasts getting back to their appropriate time, however."

"Big pet show up; viscount think it is dragon."

Rosa's eyes widened. "Dragon? How did he arrive at that? How absurd."

"You see? It was easy battle," Sasha said, as he chose his new attire from the wardrobe room.

223

# Chapter Twenty-Five

The celebration began at the castle. The trumpets sounded as the king and queen entered. All the nobles, and subjects bowed to the floor to show their respect. Colin and Sasha with their two slaves sat at the side of the main square. Horses were aligned and dressed accordingly. The king and queen sat at their thrones.

"All my subjects, please hear what I have to say. There is no more word of an uprising to this throne." The king's royal subjects and nobility applauded. "Our lead knight, Sir Limmerick, and his cohort have successfully ceased the traitor," the king said. The nobles and subjects applauded along with the queen. "Lead knight Limmerick, please rise. I want the court to see who you are. You are the finest knight I have ever witnessed. I want to honor you with a special token of royalty."

Sir Williams stood beside Colin and gestured for him to follow him to the king. Colin bowed to the floor as the king stood up and held a gold necklace in his hand. As Colin continued to bow, the king placed the gold necklace around Colin's neck. The court applauded, the lute and harp played; servants walked out in a line and brought trays of fresh food. Beatrice, the lady-in-waiting, was escorted to Colin. The middle part of the floor cleared, as the dancing began. Flutes began to play. Rosa slowly approached Colin.

"So that's your lady-in-waiting?"

Colin grimaced. "I suppose."

Beatrice gleamed at Colin. "You are the kingdom's hero, Sir Limmerick."

He smiled and took her hand as he continued to look at Rosa.

"Would you care for a dance?"

Sasha, Rosa, and Amoli sat back and enjoyed the festivities.

"Sasha, why don't you ask someone to dance?" Rosa asked, as the crowd paired up for a dance.

"Okay, so I do. I want to dance with you, beautiful lady."

"I'm a slave, remember? Ask one of these fine women to dance. That's what you're supposed to do, since you have now practiced the ediquette of chivalry."

"I not care."

Colin danced with Beatrice.

"I'm grateful you will soon be my husband. I feel very safe with you," she said.

"Glad to hear it, Beatrice."

"Do you wish to continue dancing, or do you wish to be in your chamber with me, m' lord?"

Colin tugged at his snug hose. "Oh, I um, see what yer askin', so I do."

"What's the matter, m' lord?" she asked.

" Me testicles are about to burst."

She stared at him and paused. She didn't know how to respond to his comment. "Shall we leave here, m' lord?"

"Leave? Oh, aye, I see."

"We will wed soon enough, won't we?"

Sir Williams approached Colin and Beatrice.

"Sir Limmerick, the queen needs to see you right away at her throne."

"So, she does, eh?" Colin held Beatrice's hands in his. "Forgive me, I must go to the queen."

"I understand you are a man of great importance within this kingdom. Please, adhere to our queen's wishes."

"Ah, aye, great importance is what I bring to yez all," Colin snorted, and left with the other knight.

"The queen is thrilled with your accomplishment. She wants to thank you, personally," Sir Williams said.

225

Colin looked at Sir Williams. "Me accomplishments? Aye, so I slayed the viscount. I didn't really do anythin', Sir Williams except lure the viscount to his demise. He had it comin', wouldn't ye think?"

"Stop this chatter, knight and adhere to the queen."

Colin bowed to the floor. The queen stood up and gleamed at the handsome time traveler.

"Sir Limmerick, please rise. You achieved our goal in so little time. Tell me, how did you cease the viscount?"

Colin's smile was frozen. "How?"

"Yes, tell me what your measures were to achieve our kingdom's goal?"

"Well, um, me cohort 'n meself are fine archers 'n swordsmen, surely, ye know it already." His eyes bounced around the room. "Um, lets just leave it at that, shall we?"

"Well, alright, then. Knight, the king will soon rush off to the stables. I will soon rush off to my chamber. Are you interested in joining me?"

He took a deep breath and his eyes opened wide with suprise. "Don't think I can do that, yer majesty. I am loyal to the king, as I should be. Forgive me. So sorry, so I am."

"Well, I demand to see you in my bed chamber in a short while. You must do this or you will pay a high price. I have never shared my bed with such a handsome hero before."

He lifted one eyebrow. "High price, yer majesty?"

"Yes, you will undergo a series of tortures and it would commence immediately. Stand up, knight. You're to do what I tell you. You're not in any position to do as you wish." He stood up. "Go to my chamber. I will be there, shortly. Go, now, knight."

Colin bowed to her and left. He walked through the crowd of festivities and met up with Rosa.

"Colin? What's wrong?" Rosa asked. "You look like you have seen a ghost."

"Do ye know if the time machine is ready, love? I'd say we've overstayed our welcome, wouldn't ye say?"

"I thought you wanted to engage in your knighthood experience, so you can display to the world your conduct of chivalry?" she said, with a slight snicker.

"The queen threatened to torture me if I don't agree to be her bed mate. If the king ever catches me in their bed I'd surely be killed. Just don't wanna do this, so I don't."

"Oh, Colin, I feel so bad for you. Look at Sasha over there with Amoli, stuffing his face. Lets get the both of them and get to that time machine right now," Rosa instilled, as she took Colin's hand and pulled him through the crowd.

Sasha was eating a huge piece of cheese with red wine to wash it down. Amoli smiled when she saw Colin approach them. Rosa pulled the cheese chunk out of Sasha's mouth.

"Alright, Sasha, over-indulgence time is over. It's time to go to the time machine," Rosa shouted in his ear.

"I just sit and relax and now you say me this?"

"Get off your tuft and lets go," Rosa demanded.

Amoli clapped her hands. "Finally. We get to leave this horrible time period."

The four time travelers plowed through the crowd of festivities. They ran through the narrow stone corridors of the castle, where they tried not to be noticed. Sir Williams noticed Colin outside the castle with his cohort and two slaves.

"Sir Limmerick! Where are you off? The queen is requesting your presence."

Sir Williams trailed them from behind. Colin ignored the confused knight. They ran to the other side of the castle with Sir Williams still trailing behind them.

"Sir Limmerick, you are going in the incorrect direction. Her majesty is requesting you. Where are you going?"

Sasha pointed to the time machine. The four time travelers were out of breath, but did not even stop to swallow. They placed themselves onto the time machine and held onto the handles. Sasha set the large clock dial at the top to the year 1910 AD.

"Sir Limmerick! What is that contraption? I was meaning to dispose of it. Where are you going? The queen will be very dissatisfied."

The dial began to spin. Their hair blew in the draft of the dial. It made a spinning sound that was too loud to bear. The time machine rattled with a generating motor belt that flapped so loud the machine started to lift from the ground. Just as the machine stirred a puff of smoke, and dust festered, Colin noticed in the corner of his eye a large animal. He took notice of the animal's over-sized antlers. The animal reacted to the loud spinning dial and motor-generating belt. Colin glanced at Rosa and smiled.

"Love, look, there, *Megaloceros giganteous.* Poor thing is misplaced."

Rosa turned her head. "Oh, my. Poor thing is right."

Colin could still hear Sir Williams shouting at him in the midst of the dust and smoke and discoloration.

"Sir Limmerick! Come back here at once!"

"Sir Williams, it was brilliant knowin' yez, but I'm not from yer time. I'm from yer future! Give the queen me best!" Colin shouted, and the time machine spun through the vortex of time.

228

# Chapter Twenty-Six

The time machine hit ground. Rosa was bent forward over the wrought iron rail of the machine. Her hair was disheveled and her dress was torn. She lifted her head to glance at their new surroundings. Amoli had fallen to the floor of the machine. Sasha was also bent over the rail.

"Sasha, are you alright?" Rosa called to him.

Sasha lifted his head. "I am fine." He stood straight and looked up at the large dial above their heads. He sighed. "Dial not say 1910. I am sorry."

Rosa's eyes widened. "It doesn't? I should hope we are no longer in 1487?"

"Fine, I will tell you what you wish to hear. We no longer in 1487."

"The landscape looks different. It looks like we did time travel," Rosa commented.

"Da, we time travel."

"But not to 1910? Alright, then? I know we're not in 840, or 1857, so what time period are we in, Sasha?"

"Past our time 1910. To our future."

"Future?" Her hands rubbed her face. "Oh, my. How far in the future are we? What does the dial say?"

Sasha strained his neck to try and read the huge dial above him.

"It say 1970. Is that okay time for us? I not know. We are sixty years in future."

Amoli opened her eyes. "Are we home?"

"Miss Amoli, I am so sorry to say you we are not home. We are in future. This is very modern time. I not know this time."

Rosa crossed her arms. "The future sounds scary to me. I wonder what life is like in 1970?"

"Well, you will soon find out."

Amoli yelped. "We don't have any idea of the future? What are we going to do? I'm so exhausted from the past, I don't know if I can bear the future."

Colin's torso hung over the wrought iron rails. He flinched a few times as he opened his eyes. He slowly stood straight and looked around. "Well, mate, it looks like we's not in 1487 anymore. I can tell just by lookin' around, thankfully."

"Mr. Limmerick, you not sick. You have comfortable ride, da?"

"Better than other times, I'd say."

Rosa stepped beside Colin. "Maybe you should sit down for what I'm about to tell you." She rubbed his arm. "We're not in 1910." Colin glanced at Amoli sitting on the grass sobbing. "We're in 1970. I've never studied the future. I'm an archeologist. Do you know anything about how things would be sixty years in our future?"

"Sixty years, eh?" He grinned. "Well, don't worry, 'cause I'm assumin' plate tectonics is likely a course offered at the university, wouldn't ye think? Cushing called me a lair. Surely, evolution would also be an offered course as well, wouldn't ye think?"

"Who cares? We're not from 1970. I think its best we get back onto that time machine and find our year?" Rosa instilled.

"Future? How 'bout that? Well, anyone who studies the future would just be basin' things on assumptions, wouldn't ye think? I wonder if Ireland ever separated from England?"

"We're not in our own time. That concerns me," Rosa said. "We haven't had a lot of luck with the past. You were almost killed. How has society changed, I wonder?" Rosa scratched her head.

Colin chuckled as his eyes were focused on Amoli.

"We must try not to stay in this time," Sasha said.

"That all depends, mate," Colin said. "We might find a cure for infections or somethin'. Wouldn't ye as a scientist wanna see what the future holds, so we can bring back some solutions to our time?"

Sasha chuckled. "Mr. Limmerick cannot help himself. He must play God, always."

"Colin, change your major and go into medicine if that's what you want," Rosa commented.

"Mediciine? I'm already over forty. It's too late for me, but maybe we can take a shortcut by observin' the future."

"Fine. We'll stay for a short time, but then we must return to our time. I'm not interested in getting tangled up with polticial upheaveals or executions," Rosa said.

Amoli sniffled and looked up at Colin who stood beside her on the grass.

"Colin, look at this grass. It's so short. The flowers look very nice. This is not usual for us," Amoli said, with a whimper.

"It's usual for 1910, but not for 1487," Rosa said. She looked around. "There's music coming from that direction. I see a crowd sitting on the grass."

"Aye, a concert, no doubt."

"Yes, a concert," Rosa smiled.

"I wonder if I'd be a grandmother in this time?" Amoli wondered.

An airplane flew overhead. They all looked up.

Colin's eyes widened. "Dirigibles have definitely changed. Appear to be motorized. They got wings, so I see."

Rosa kept staring at the aircraft overhead. "That's no dirigible. That's something completely different, I think."

"What else could it be, love?"

"This is future. It is more scary than 1487, I think," Sasha commented. "Maybe time machines are mastered in this time? Or maybe Mr. Limmerick would like university course on how to make them, da?"

Colin chuckled. "Likely so, mate, likely so."

231

"I not know why my dial in time machine want to always go to 1970. It makes me angry. Why it do this?"

Rosa stared at him. "Because you have no business building time machines."

"I am curious about this time period. I bet time machines are perfected, da?" He said as he walked toward the concert.

"Sasha, what are you doing?" Rosa asked.

"I want to explore. We are scientists. Don't we want to know about future?"

"We should return to our time period," Rosa cautioned. "Haven't we learned enough by trying to intervene in past time periods?"

Amoli looked at Colin. "Do we follow Dr. Dimitrikov?"

"Surley, we should. The year 1970 must be highly civilized, unlike the past, eh?"

Sasha walked on the manicured lawn. He stopped when he saw a large crowd of people sitting on the grass. He heard the gentle picking of an acoustic guitar. Colin, Rosa, and Amoli followed.

"Is it a concert!" Rosa blurted with a grin.

"Donno, love. I hear singin' 'n such."

The four time travelers walked to the end of the sitting crowd. They slowly kneeled onto the grass.

*Oh, baby, baby, it's a wild world*
*It's hard to get by just upon a smile*
*Oh, baby, baby, it's a wild world*
*I'll always remember you like a child, girl*
*You know I've seen a lot of what the world can do*
*And it's breakin' my heart in two*
*Because I never wanna see you a sad girl*
*Don't be a bad girl*
*But if you wanna leave, take good care*
*I hope you make a lot of nice friends out there*
*But just remember there's a lot of bad and beware*

232

Two young women sat on the grass in front of the time travelers. One woman with short black hair, in particular, took notice of Colin. She kept twisting her body back to catch another glimpse of the handsome stranger. Colin noticed her staring at him. He felt slightly awkward, so he tilted his head forward and smiled at her as a gesture for *hello*. She nudged her friend, who also looked behind them and and took notice of him. Colin's awkwardness intensified. He tried to push his long, unkept hair behind his ears and buttoned his fifteenth century doublet jacket. He tried to look at himself to see if everything was in place and that he wasn't looking upscene. Then, he realized he was wearing fifteenth century hoes in the latter part of the twentieth century. *'Good God'*, he said to himself. *'I must look upscene.'*

She turned her body to face him. "Hi!" She called to him. Rosa and Amoli tried not to notice.

Colin smiled at her.

"You look lost!"

He chuckled with nervousness. "Do I? Perhaps that's 'cause I am lost."

The two women stood up and walked to Colin. The woman with short black hair sat beside him. "Are you enjoying the concert?"

"Just got here, so we did, but, so far, I'm enjoyin' it, aye, so I am."

"You're not from England, are you?" She asked. She sat closer to him.

"Irish, I'm Irish."

"Crazy," the young woman commented.

Amoli pretended not to notice.

The young woman ran her fingers through his hair. "You look like Sir Lancelot."

He tried to gaze at the perfomer. "Do I?"

Sasha looked at the two women. "Do you lovely ladies know any man who would have cigarette?"

233

The friend of the woman pulled out a pack of cigarettes. "Help yourself."

Sasha's eyebrows lifted with surprise. "Woman carry cigarette?"

"So?" The friend, with the long straight hair said.

Sasha sighed with relief. *"Spasiba."*

The two women looked at each other and giggled at Sasha.

Sasha grinned at them. "What I say, so funny to you? What I do?"

"What did you just say?" The friend asked with a burst of laughter.

*"Thank you* in Russian. Why I say so funny words to you?"

"Wow, you have a smashing accent. Where are you from?"

Rosa leaned to Sasha and whispered. *"Be careful what you say, we really need to leave this time period."*

"These two lovely ladies of 1970 are interested in me, why you want to leave so fast, da?"

Rosa nudged Sasha. "What's got into you? You're just as crazy as Colin when it comes to these women from different time periods."

Sasha pulled away from Rosa and tried to focus on the two women. "You say I have accent?"

The two women continued to giggle. "Yeah, you sound like you're from the USSR."

Sasha's eyes widened and he hesitated to respond. "Um, what you say? What is USSR? I am Russian."

"Yeah, Russian, that's what you are, same thing."

"I think you're smashing. Never met anyone from behind the *Iron Curtain* before," the friend said.

Sasha glanced at Colin and lit his cigaratte. "What they say me? I not understand."

"It's likely, mate, Russia underwent a name change, so it seems so to me," Colin tried to explain.

234

Sasha gazed at the two women: he tried to clear his throat as he hacked on his cigarette. "What does USSR mean?"

The two women laughed. "I donno, maybe something like *Union*..."

The friend continued. *"Soviet Socialist?"*

"Oh, yeah, and maybe *R* is for *Republic."*

The woman with the short black hair to the liberty to place her hand on Colin's lap. "That's it!"

Colin looked at her. "What's it?"

*"Union of Soviet Socialist Republic,* that's it! The USSR!"

Colin grimaced as he glanced at Sasha. "Oh, really? It's gotta rather awful ring to it, don't ye think, mate?"

Sasha appeared upset. "Why did name change?"

"I donno, I think it was this power-hungry bloke in 1917, who killed the Czar, don't quote me. I think he wanted to control all those surrounding countries around Russia, like Latvia, the Ukraine, I think."

"Ukraine! Why you put article? Ukraine! Ukraine!"

"Okay, whatever."

Sasha's eyebrows lifted, and his eyes bulged. "What? Nicolas ll gets killed? By who?"

Colin placed his hand on Sasha's shoulder. "Mate, ye need to calm yerself. We's in 1970, there's nothin' ye can do."

The young woman with the short black hair appeared concerned for Sasha. "Sorry, thought you would have already known this, since you're a Soviet bloke."

"Do not call me that! I am Russian not Soviet!"

Rosa took Sasha's hand. "Sasha, you need to get us back to our time. It isn't working out well here for us."

"My name is Trish, what's your name? Wait! Don't tell me! I bet your name Sir Lancelot."

"This is Sasha, Rosa, 'n Amoli. I'm Colin, not Sir Lancelot."

Trish giggled. She ran her fingers through Colin's beard. "I think I could really dig you. Do you wanna fuck?"

Colin's eyes widened. Rosa glanced at Colin with an expression of disgust on her face.

"Pardon? Trish?" Colin tried to get her to clairify.

"Yeah, would you like to fuck? Oh, maybe she's your old lady and she's not crazy for that idea," Trish said pointing at Rosa.

Colin took a few deep breaths. "I think I'm gettin' too old for this."

Trish stood up and took Colin's hand. "You're as old as you feel, *Big Daddy!*"

Colin smiled at her as he tried to stand up.

"What's wrong, Sir Lancelot? Did you hurt yourself in a jousting tournament?"

Colin struggled to stand but somehow managed with some winching and pain. "Jousting tournament, ye say? Aye, lets leave at that."

Rosa nudged herself up to Colin. "I don't like her. Can't we leave this place?"

Colin looked at her. "Well, I must say I'm not feelin' me very best, physically 'n emotionally. Amoli wants nothin' to do with me 'n I just don't think I can bear another time period that isn't civilzed. Thankfully, 1970 is."

"You know what this woman wants, don't you? She's no lady in my books, Colin. She's definitely not civilized. If women are allowed to run about acting like sailors, then this time period is definitely not civilized."

"Definitely not, love, but perhaps in 1970 she is considered civilized. Perhaps, it's likely the *norm* for women to ask men for sex?"

Trish ran her hands along Colin's lower half. "I really dig your tights."

Colin felt uncomfortable and stepped back a bit from Trish. "Um, Trish," he took time to clear his throat. "Do yez always go about askin' men ye just met for sex?"

"Sure! Why not?"

Rosa glared at Colin. "I think she's out of her mind."

"Likely, love," he responded to Rosa.

"Well, ye see, ye just met me 'n ye don't know me 'n ye keep touchin' me."

"So?"

Colin felt awkward and glanced at Rosa. "Shite, I donno, love."

"Well, ye see, yer a wench, 'n I never really met a wench who would do such a thing unless she was a whore."

The two young women looked at each other and giggled.

Trish stepped closer to Colin and continued to stroke his body. "Whore? I'm not a whore. I work. I have a normal job and I receive a respectable pay cheque."

Colin wore a blank expression on his face. "Aye, but yer a wench, a woman, a lass."

"So?"

"Well, a respectable wench isn't supposed to be touchin' men she don't know."

"I keep touching you because I can't help myself."

"I must say, since I just met yez, that it makes me rather uncomfortable."

"Why?"

He tilted his head toward Rosa. "Love, help me with this."

Rosa stepped in front of Colin. "You don't know him! A respectable lady is not supposed to take liberties with a man and especially with a man she just met!"

"Why?"

"Because it isn't proper!" Rosa shouted at the top of her lungs. "A respectable lady is not supposed to do anything of that nature."

"Says who?"

"It is the unwritten rule!" Rosa shouted back.

Trish stepped face to face with Rosa. "We've come a long way, baby!"

\*\*\*

Colin scanned the park; he noticed the concert had ended and patrons were starting to leave the premises. "Speakin' of Amoli, where is she?"

"Oh, I don't know. Did she get lost in the crowd, I wonder?" Rosa didn't seem to care.

Colin noticed Sasha was still sitting on the grass with Trish's friend. "Mate, did ye see where Amoli buggered off to?"

Sasha looked up at Colin. "Why? She is missing?"

"Aye, so she is. Did ye see where she buggered off to?"

"I not see her leave." Sasha continued his indepth conversation with Trish's friend.

"My name is Jane, but you can call me *Free*. All my friends call me that," the woman said to Sasha.

"Free? What name is that for lady? How stupid, I never hear this before."

Jane ran her fingers along Sasha's face. "Soviet bloke, groovy. I think you're smashing."

Rosa flicked her hair back with disgust. "Good gracious, he has already moved on. I suppose I'm no longer the flavor of the month."

"Love, please stop thinkin' ye 'n Sasha will someday be a perfect couple. It'll never happen, I'm sorry to say."

"You're just jealous."

Colin cracked a slight smile. "Love, I really wish we'd stop this silliness 'n start searchin' for Amoli."

The three time travelers searched the outdoor concert grounds, behind the stage and around it. They came to a concrete wading pool with washrooms, but still no sign of her.

Amoli sat in a bush. Tears fell from her face, where she sniffled and tried to swaddle herself in her fifteenth century shawl. *"I've never felt so alone. I don't really think anyone would miss me if I didn't travel back to 1910 with the others. There's always so many women interested in Colin. I'm very tired of it. I wonder if he's tired of it? I don't think so, he doesn't seem to push any of them away."* Her crying intensified.

She heard leaves crackle, and bushes sway.

"Who's there?" She gasped with fear.

The sound of the crackling leaves intensified.

"Colin? Is that you?"

Branches broke where the sound of cracking bark startled her.

"Colin? Please, show yourself! This is not a game!"

She heard nothing. She waited a few seconds and tried not to make a sound. She heard nothing. She felt swallowed by her thoughts while tears ran down her face. *'I think Colin does push women away. I know he loves me very much, I think.'*

She heard branches break again, but just for a second. She was silent. "Who's there?" She paused. "Colin?"

There was no response and there was silence again. She started to cry. The sound of breaking bark grew louder and closer to her. She trembled and cried and no longer tried to stay silent. Leaves rustled and cracked and the sound of swaying branches intensified. Her breathing was uneasy, she gasped and cried.

"Colin! Colin!" There was no response. She paused. "Colin!"

*** 

Colin briskly stomped through the concert park. He was rattled with angst in search of Amoli. Sasha and Rosa

239

looked around but didn't feel the penetrating fear that Colin felt. Trish trailed behind Colin and Jane kept her eyes on Sasha.

"What does she look like?" Trish asked.

"She's tiny, quite short, with rather long straight black hair. She's from India, so she's got a darker complextion than ye or I," Colin responded with a nervous jitter. "Just can't find her. She's silly sometimes 'n just doesn't understand danger, ye know."

Trish ran her hands along his chest. "You have to calm yourself, Big Daddy, because I think you hurt yourself somewhere and you seem like you're in some kinda pain."

"Aye, so I am, but now me emotions are gettin' the best of me. Just won't rest 'til I find Amoli."

"You love her, don't you?"

"We was to be married," he stared at the ground. "But, she called it off."

Trish grinned. "Why would she do that?"

"She's got her reasons."

***

Amoli found herself dozing off, croutched up in the comfortable bush. Her eyes started to close, where she fell into a light sleep. Hot breath spewed on her face. Her eyes flickered and she awoke. Someone was staring at her. She felt as if she was being watched. Her eyes opened and she realized someone was sitting very close to her. She looked to see a being of some kind. She gasped and sat up immediately. Her eyes were wide and she started to pant with fear.

"Oh, God! Who are you?"

The strange being grunted, and moved closer to her. The smell of its hot breath was repulsive, which made Amoli feel nauseous. It raised its hands to stroke her tear-soaked face. It tried to wipe her tears. It grunted and snorted, but Amoli did not feel threatened.

"Who are you? What are you?" She noticed that it had more body hair than what was common. Its face reminded her of an ape. *'What is this creature?'* She thought to herself.

Colin approached Amoli but he couldn't see her because she was encased in foliage. "Amoli! Amoli! Please lass! Amoli!" He called out.

She gazed at the creature. "Oh, that's Colin calling. He would know what you are." She tried to crawl out of the dense bush. It jolted and grunted at her movements.

"Colin! I'm over here!"

Colin turned his head. "She's here? Amoli, where are yez? Can't see ye, so I can't!"

She ran away from the bush. "Colin! I'm over here!"

Colin turned his head. He immediately noticed her running. "Lass! Thanks to Christ, yer alright!"

She ran toward him and he wrapped his arms around her. He took a deep breath with relief. "Lass, ye had me terrified."

She tugged on his arm. "Colin, come you have to see. Come!" She tried to tug him toward the bush.

"What did ye see, lass?"

"Come! I don't really know what it was, but I think you would know."

"How's that?"

She brought him to the bush she was sitting in. Her facial expression appeared deflated. "Oh?"

"What? What ye wanna show me so desperately, lass?"

"He's gone."

"Who's gone?"

"My new friend. I was crying and he wiped my tears."

Colin's eyes widened. "He? Really? Who was this? Did ye catch his name at all?"

"He grunted but didn't really say anything."

"Grunted?"

"Yes, he didn't really look human."

Colin took hold of her shoulders. "He didn't look human? Then, what did he look like?"

"I don't really know. He had more body hair than you, I think."

"More body hair? What else? How did his face look?"

"He didn't really look all that human to me, I suppose."

"How ye mean, Amoli?"

"He reminded me a bit of an ape, but not really, more like half man, half ape."

Colin tightened his grip on her shoulders. "How was he with yez?"

"What do you mean?"

"Did he try to harm ye in any way?"

She smiled. "Not at all, he was very gentle with me. I liked him."

"Shite!"

"What's the matter, Colin? Is something wrong?"

*"Neanderthal!"*

"Huh?"

"It sounds to me that ye was just in an encounter with a *Neanderthal.*"

Her eyes opened wide. "Oh!"

"Do ye realize that, lass?"

"What is a Neander…?"

Colin smiled at her, where she noticed the dimples in his cheeks and the creases around his eyes meant that he wasn't angry with her.

*"Neanderthals,* lass, was one of the evolutionary links from apes to humans or *Homo sapiens,* should say. They was very similar to us in many ways. Almost the same biological make-up, one could say."

"So, are you saying he was prehistoric?"

"Aye."

"Something prehistoric just sat with me in a bush?"

"Aye."

Amoli placed her hands over her face. "Oh! Oh! No! I could have been killed by that creature!"

Colin embraced her. *"Neanderthals* are close ancesters, lass, he meant no harm to yez. Lets just thank Christ."

Sasha and Rosa approached Colin, where Amoli was still in his arms.

Rosa smiled. "Well, well, I suppose you two love birds are making your wedding plans?"

Amoli pulled away from him. "Not that! We're not making any wedding plans. The wedding is still off!"

Colin stared at an insect on the ground and was silent.

"What just happened here?" Rosa asked.

Colin stood straight and stared at Sasha and Rosa. "Amoli had an encounter with an *Neanderthal,* no doubt."

"Another misplaced prehistoric species? Oh, Colin, this is terrible!" Rosa blurted.

"Aye, so it is. We need to find it 'n we need to bring it with us to 1910."

"Why, Colin? Don't you think 1910 is just as bad as 1970?" Rosa asked.

Sasha smoked a cigarette and leaned against a tree.

"We created the mess, that's why its misplaced, therefore, we need to bring it to our time so we can nurture it before Sasha sends it back twenty-eight thousand years, where it belongs."

Rosa threw her hands in the air. "Colin Limmerick, have you lost your mind? How are you going to take care of a prehistoric primate in our time of 1910? If anything, we should take this misplaced being to the authorities in this time period, they would have better sound technology than our time."

"How ye know its so much more advanced? All we've seen so far is a concert!" Colin blurted.

Sasha took a puff from his cigarette. "They have television in this time, Mr. Limmerick. You not know what that is, da?"

Colin stepped back. "Television? How ye know what that is?"

"Colin, when Sasha and I were helping you search for Amoli, we were with Trish and Jane or *Free,* whatever her name is. They told us about television."

"Ye didn't act like ye never heard of it, did ye?"

"Don't worry, Colin, we acted it out quite well. They didn't detect anything."

"Da, but those two young ladies were on something hallucinogenic. I can tell because they act like crazy ladies, da?"

"Most definitely, what real lady would try to rip off a man's clothes?" Rosa commented with disgust in her voice.

Colin chuckled. "Is that what Free tried on yez, mate?"

"She is not real lady. Very bad."

"Tell me what television is, then?" Colin asked.

"Colin, they watch stories, interviews, newspapers and a variety of music and comedy on a picture tube. Every household has a television or two," Rosa said. "Colin,

automobiles in this time are superior to ours. Nobody uses a crank anymore.

"Da, nobody wears goggles anymore to drive auto," Sasha added.

"Fine, so ye think the *Neanderthal* should be turned to the authorities here? Where? The universities, perhaps?"

"I wonder what it eats?" Amoli asked in a soft voice.

"I just don't know if this is the correct time period for such sophisticated being such as the *Neanderthal.*"

"Colin, you're silly sometimes, 1970 has television and it has air flight at that," Rosa said.

"Hey!" Trish called out. "Hey Sir Lancelot, did you find your pretty mama?"

Colin smiled at Trish and reluctantly knodded *yes* to her.

Trish stood closely against Colin. "Is she yours?"

Colin appeared saddened. "She's not."

Rosa stepped close to Colin. "Colin, there's a prehistoric primate roaming this park. If we don't do something about it, things could get ugly."

"Aye."

Trish took Colin's large hand in hers. "Were you cats on your way to a costume party or something?"

"Colin glanced at his attire. "So we were."

"Anyone can tell you that you're Sir Lancelot. Those tights of yours are driving me wild."

Rosa leaned into Colin. "This woman has definite problems."

Jane buried herself in Sasha's arms. "Hey Soviet man, our friends are having a gathering at their pad. Are you interested in coming along?"

"Will there be food?" Sasha asked. "I must eat, it has been too long since we eat, da?"

"We'll bring a few bags of crisps, I guess," Jane said.

"We need to find another friend, but if we find him soon enough, we'll definitely attend your mate's gathering," Colin said.

Trish and Jane looked at each other and chuckled.

Trish took Colin's hand in hers. "Who did you lose now?"

"He's my friend," Amoli replied.

"Oh, okay, fine, he's yours. Is that why you both broke up? She's got someone else?" Trish asked.

"Colin smiled at the two young women. "Just give us the address 'n surely we'll turn up."

"Crisps?" Sasha questioned with disgust.

Trish wrote it down on a scrap piece of paper.

Rosa looked at Trish and smiled. "I like your writing stick."

"It's not the greatest ball-point pen. It blobs sometimes."

# Chapter Twenty-Seven

The time travelers watched Trish and Jane leave the park. Colin took a deep breath.

"We've gotta find this prehistoric primate. We need to spread out in pairs, likely. We should never be alone."

Amoli stepped beside Sasha. "Dr. Dimitrikov and I will search together."

Colin was silent as he and Rosa faced each other.

Amoli and Sasha walked off. Amoli led him near a cluster of rustically placed shrubs and bushes. "Maybe he's back here. This is where I met him. He could be trying to hide."

"Who cares," Sasha responded. "I need food and smoke."

"Maybe we should sit here and wait for him. What do you think, Dr. Dimitrikov?"

"If that is what you wish. I not care. I am not naturalist, I am physcist."

Colin walked through the park with Rosa.

"Colin, brighten up. Amoli will come around. She's very young."

Colin ignored Rosa's comment and focused on scanning the park for the *Neanderthal*. He noticed something move behind a tree. "Love, do ye see something behind that tree?" He blurted, pointing at the tree.

Rosa squinted her eyes to try and focus for such a distance. "It's really hard to see that far away, Colin. I really can't tell."

I'm gonna get over there at once!"

"Don't run, Colin, you're in a lot of pain, besides, you could startle the poor thing."

"Stay here, I must see, but don't doubt me, love, I'll be very careful with this," he assured and briskly hobbled off.

Rosa remained still and watched Colin hobble to the tree. She kept her eyes on Colin.

Colin gingerly walked to the tree, only to notice a man sitting on the ground with a guitar in his hand. The man had long hair and a bushy beard; he glanced up at Colin and grinned. "Brother? Wanna join me?"

Colin peered at the man. "Forgive me."

The man looked at Colin and continued to play his guitar.

Colin walked slowly back to Rosa. His head stared at the ground, where Rosa couldn't see his face from a distance.

Colin looked at Rosa. "Where would a misplaced ancient primate wander off to?"

"Colin, you're getting yourself too disheveled over this. Try to relax, it's difficult to lose a *Neanderthal* who is twenty-eight thousand years old."

"I feel so responsible, ye know? I just gotta find it, surely I do."

"Colin, please breathe. You will."

Colin wandered around the park aimlessly. His body was hurting from the episodes he had endeavored in the fifteenth century. He hobbled with a limp, until he saw a figure run across the park. He stood still with his lips parted. "Rosa! Look there! Is that him, or do I need to get me specs on?"

"Colin, its hard to tell for sure, but just by looking at the stance of this being, it doesn't resemble *Homo sapiens*. Not at all! We just don't walk like that."

"I'm in agreement with yez. I'm gonna follow it," he said as he hobbled off to follow it.

Colin made his way to a cluster of bushes and trees; he stopped. Rosa stood behind him.

*"There it is,"* Colin whispered to Rosa.

*"It seems to have found some food. What do you think it's eating?"*

*"Flowers, maybe?"*

Rosa smiled. *"I think it's magnificent, don't you?"*

*"I'll be more magnificent when it's placed in its proper time period."*

*"Well, now that we've located it, what do you want to do?"*

*"I think it's imperative that it come back with us on the time machine."*

*"Colin? Really?"*

*"Can't imagine leavin' it here."*

*"Colin, we're in the future. If we leave it with the authorities, I'm sure they will figure something out. Besides, while we're in the future, you should see a modern doctor for all your fifteenth century wounds."*

*"Don't change the subject, love. We don't know what life is like in this future time. What if they simply dispose of Neanderthal, then what?"*

*The Neanderthal* turned its head and looked straight at Colin and Rosa.

"Colin, it spotted us. I suppose we were whispering too loud."

Colin stepped toward the prehistoric primate. "C'mon, mate, ye gotta get yerself up. I'll fetch yez some real food."

"Colin, do you really think it understands you?"

"Not at all, but perhaps it understands intonation 'n gestures. *Neanderthals* was highly intelligent, ye know."

It stood up, where the top of its head reached Colin's chest. Colin tried to appear non-threatening. It appeared somewhat anxious and frightened.

"Now what, Colin?"

"We take him to Trish's gathering."

Rosa's eyes widened. "Why?"

"It needs to get used to us, 'n it needs food 'n water, no doubt."

249

"Crisps are food?"

"We'll have to pick something up along the way. It looks rather undernourished, wouldn't ye say?"

"Colin, you're ridiculous sometimes."

Sasha and Amoli approached them. Amoli wore a smile on her face when she noticed the *Neanderthal*. "I'm so very glad, you found him. I was getting worried."

"It's already been decided, we're taking *the Neanderthal* to Trish's gathering," Colin announced.

Sasha gave Colin a blank stare. "You are nuts! Leave it here and lets go on time machine. Why we go to stupid party of 1970?"

"Cause we need to learn about this time period, perhaps it will help our time period move faster with discoveries."

"Colin, has a point, Sasha," Rosa said.

***

The four time travelers and *the Neanderthal* knocked on the door. A young man with long hair and a beard answered it. He looked at the four time travelers dressed in fifteenth century attire; then, he noticed *the Neanderthal* standing off to the side.

"Crazy," the young man said as he left the door opened and he delved into the festivities of the gathering.

Colin and Sasha walked in to notice several couples having sex on the floor.

The music was loud and coming from some kind of box. There was spilled beer everywhere and bowls of crisps placed on the floor. Several females had very short straight hair, or very long hair. All the men had long hair and out of control beards.

Trish noticed Colin right away and ran to him. "Hey Big Daddy! I didn't think you were going to come."

"I said I would."

"Do you care for a few hits of LSD?" She asked.

250

Sasha glanced at Colin. "What she say?"

"Don't know."

Rosa looked at Colin. "The music is autrocious and much too loud."

Trish smiled. "Led Zepplin is smashing!" Trish took Colin's hand and pulled him from his cohorts.

"Can't really leave me friends, Trish," Colin said.

"That former girlfriend of yours has made it clear that she doesn't want you anymore. I think its time you loosen up and start smelling the roses." She led him to a bedroom; another couple was already having sex in the bed. "When they're done, it'll be our turn."

"Oh, God."

"By the way, who's your hairy friend?"

"Hairy friend?"

"Yeah, what's his name?"

Colin glanced at Trish with angst. "Name?"

"Yeah, he has a name, doesn't he?"

"Call, call, um, call him Neander. Aye, that's his name."

"Groovy, I guess." Trish turned her head and noticed the other couple left the bed and walked out of the room without getting dressed. Colin's eyebrows lowered to his eyes.

"Wow, I'm about to get fucked by Sir Lancelot! Very Smashing!"

Colin slowly lowered himself to sit on the bed. He winched with pain.

"You're pretty banged up aren't you?"

"That I am."

"I know a doctor, not too far from here."

"That would be lovely, thanks."

***

251

The man who had answered the door offered Rosa and Amoli some beer. "Hey, is that cat your man?" He pointed at *the Neanderthal.*

Amoli snickered. Rosa did not even flinch.

Rosa took a sip of the beer. "This tastes awful."

"I made it myself," the young man said.

"Who is that cat? He ate all the crisps and drank all the beer. We're gonna have to go out and get more," the young man said.

Rosa leaned against the wall; she found a table to place her beer on.

"Hey beautiful chick, do you wanna get high with me?"

Rosa turned away from the young man. "This place smells autrocious. I refuse to even sit down on your disgusting chairs. Who lives here?"

"This is my pad."

Rosa noticed Amoli was seated in the corner of the room with *the Neanderthal.* She scanned the room in search of Sasha. She didn't see him.

Rosa slid herself along the wall to Amoli. "Amoli, did you see Sasha anywhere?"

"Dr. Dimitrikov? I haven't seen him since we arrived, sorry."

Rosa walked around the room, she had to step over bodies of people having sex and overdosing on drugs. The music was loud and crass to her ears. People danced in the middle of the room without a partner, some were even naked. She looked behind a beat-up coach and saw Sasha on the floor with Jane.

"Sasha?" Rosa expressed.

Sasha turned his head to face Rosa. Her eyes widened with shock when she saw that he was naked.

She had an expression of disgust on her face. "Sasha! How could you?"

"I am man, what you expect?" He blurted and smoked marijuana.

252

Amoli approached Rosa. "I think I saw Colin leave with that Trish woman. He didn't even tell us he was leaving. I suppose he likes her better than me."

"That's not like Colin. And, I know he doesn't like her better than you."

Rosa turned her head and noticed several people gathered around the *Neanderthal*. "I suppose our new friend has gained some popularity."

\*\*\*

Some hours had passed, Colin and Trish returned to the gathering. Rosa walked to Colin. "So, where did you go?"

"I just saw a 1970s physician. I saw airplanes in the sky, wonderful lookin' roadsters, improved telephones, 'n television, all on the way 'n back form the doctor's office. He put me on penicillin to ward me against infection. I've undergone a fair bit of cuts from swords, daggers 'n such."

"Did the doctor question you on why you had wounds from swords and daggers?"

"Aye."

"What did you tell him?"

"I told him that I'm from Ireland, 'n that it's a way of life there."

"Did he believe you?"

"He did."

"So the doctor gave you Penicillin? What is that? A wonder drug?"

"I suppose so, he said by tomorrow I should be feelin' better. It works fast, apparently."

Colin glanced at Sasha, who was lying naked on the floor and smoking marijuana. "Mate, what ye doin'? I think it's time for us to leave. Our *Neanderthal* appears to be too much of a socialite." *The Neanderthal* was dancing in the middle of the room with some of Trish's girlfriends. Colin appeared concerned. "Should I be grateful that our

253

new friend is so adaptable to the latter part of the twentieth century?"

Colin turned his head to the Neanderthal, where he noticed that their prehistoric primate was also smoking marijuana. "Good God!"

"Colin, this *Neanderthal* ate all the food, drank all the beer and now he's smoking that strange cigarette. How appauling!" Rosa exclaimed.

"What ye expect, love? Biology has made us very similar to each other. His level of intellect is close to ours." Colin glanced at *the Neanderthal* again and noticed him kissing one of Trish's girlfriends.

Amoli looked at Colin. "Is he smootching with her?"

"I suppose."

"Well, the *Neanderthal*, looks similar to some of these men, there really isn't much of a difference," Rosa said.

"Me bushy sideburns didn't fade out of fashion, did they?"

"Mr. Limmerick, if we go now," Sasha said trying put on his pants. "We go without monkey man. It stays here."

"It will not. I couldn't live with meself, with the thought of leavin' it here. Just not right, so it isn't."

Rosa took a long stare at the prehistoric primate. "Colin, I think it's safe to say, our new friend is male. Amoli was correct on that one."

"I told Trish his name is Neander."

Rosa grimaced. "How rediculious."

Sasha continued to smoke marijuana. "This is great. I feel so good!"

Rosa shoved Sasha. "Get us out of this time period."

Colin glanced at *the Neanderthal* to notice that it was making sexual gestures to the young woman it was kissing. "Oh, God," Colin expressed as he made the sign of a crucifix across his chest.

"Colin, I think we better leave, right now!" Rosa urged.

"Fine, we'll leave this gathering 'n leave the *Neanderthal* here?"

"I really don't know what to do. If we take him to 1910, what can we provide for him there? And, how will your life be, if you are trying to keep up with a twenty-eight thousand year old primate?"

"Look, I'm naturalist, I'm willin' to take on that responsibility."

"What would this mean for your ship and your crew?"

"We'll have to take shifts taking care of him, I suppose."

"We?"

"Aye."

Sasha buttoned his shirt. "This is your experiment, Mr. Limmerick. I not want any part of monkey-man."

"Can ye stop with the name callin'? Look, mate it was yer faulty time machine that shot us all the way to 1487, then to 1970. Ye need to do some serious re-adjustin' to this extraordinary work of yers."

Sasha stood directly in front of Colin. "You are nothing without me, da?"

"Sasha! I think you have said enough!" Rosa shouted.

Trish approached Colin and ran her fingers along his groin. "Hey Big Daddy, are you fighting with your brother and sisters?

Rosa glared at Trish. "You're not a lady in the least. How dare you take such sexual liberties with this man? You don't even know him."

"Wow," Trish placed her hands in front of her to block her view of Rosa. "I think you better be cool. I know I just met Sir Lancelot but so far, I really dig what I see."

"Well, I think you need to learn some respect," Rosa said trying to focus on something else.

"Hey, sister, what is up with you? If you're his and he's yours, smashing, but we can all be together and love one another, nothing wrong with that."

"Colin, did you do anything with this woman, yet?" Rosa asked with angst.

"Not yet, love 'n not likely."

Amoli wandered throughout the house and watched *the Neanderthal* dance with the other women.

Sasha sat on the couch with Jane and continued to smoke marijuana.

Trish took Colin's hand. "I think we should split. You look like you need either a stiff drink or a toke."

Colin looked at her. "A stiff drink, that's just lovely. I think I may definitely need one."

Rosa tugged onto Colin's arm. "No, Colin! Don't do it! You'll regreat it!"

Trish shoved Rosa. "What gives? Are you his mother?"

"I'm his friend!" Rosa started to cry. "What has got into everyone? Even the *Neanderthal!* We need to leave this time!"

Rosa saw how Trish lured Colin to the other end of the room. She handed him a bottle of something hard. She noticed Colin drink from the bottle.

"What's wrong, Miss Emanuel? Why are you crying?" Amoli asked.

"Look at Sasha, and look at Colin, and even worse, look at the *Neanderthal.*"

"I'm sorry about Colin, but aren't you glad our *Neanderthal* is making friends so easily? He's having great fun."

"Amoli Sharma, that creature is a *Neanderthal,* he is not supposed to be engaging in human festivities. He's not supposed to have any fun!"

"Oh."

Rosa glanced at Sasha on the couch with Jane. *The Neanderthal* had joined them, where they all smoked marijuana together. Rosa rolled her eyes back. "Oh, my God! This is so surreal! How can this even be happening?"

"I think Colin is getting drunk with that woman over there," Amoli said. "You see, this is why we can't get married."

"Sasha is out of control," Rosa blurted with anger. "Colin is out of control, and even *the Neanderthal*, who isn't even human, is out of control!"

# Chapter Twenty-Eight

It was early morning. Colin opened his eyes to notice Trish lying naked in someone elses' bed with him. He tried to sit up, which woke Trish.

She kissed him on the lips. "You were fantastic."

Colin appeared distressed. "Good God, how I need to stop drinkin'."

"Yeah, you put away a few bottles at least."

Colin tried to locate his clothes with his eyes.

"Are you looking for your Sir Lancelot get-up?"

"Aye."

"Everyone digs your threads, so boss."

He slid out of bed and began his struggle with slipping on his hoes. "As ye can see, this isn't easy."

She snorted with laughter. "Lets do it again!" She fell over the bed, high on a substance.

Colin ran to her and tried to help her onto the bed. "Ye really should be mindful of hurtin' yerself."

"Oh, wow, you even talk like a knight."

"Believe me, I don't."

She lied back in bed, naked, with her legs spread out.

"Do ye live here?"

"A bunch of us live here. It's easier on the rent, you know."

"I see. Do any of ye attend university?"

"We're anti-establishment. That's the last place you would ever see any of us."

"I see."

"Are you free like us?"

"Likely not."

"Join our family and you can be free with us."

"Family?'

"Yeah, we're a family."

He laced up his blousy shirt around his chest. She watched every move he made.

"So tell me, Trish, how would ye describe the year?"

"Huh?"

"Aye, how would ye describe 1970?" he smiled when he finally got his hoes on. Penicillian?"

"It really blows my mind that you're so freaked out over Penicillian. You're acting like you never took it before. Who knows? Maybe you're one of those people who never get sick."

"Believe me, I get sick, too often, really. Must be me line of work."

"Where do you work?"

"I run me own fishin' business 'n I'm currently goin' for a doctrate at the university."

"Where?"

"Here. London."

"A fisherman gone scholar? Cool."

"You look more like a jouster."

"I'm afraid to say there really isn't a need for that anymore."

"Yeah, what a drag everything is now. I wonder what it would be like to live in those days, you know?"

"Which days?"

"Henry the Vlll. He was a cruel shit, don't you think?"

"Believe me, ye wouldn't wanna live in that time period. Definitely not."

"Yeah, I think I would. I'd order all my servants around and make passionate love to the king. It would be so cool."

"Perhaps ye should read about it. You may be surprised."

"So, anyway, tell me how you could live your whole life without penicillian? Crazy."

Colin sat beside her on the bed. "I'll be honest with yez, this was me first time."

259

"Holy shit! Really? Wow! Freak me out!"

"Well, yer actin' as if its been available forever, is that so? Was it around when ye was a kid?"

"Yeah, it was always around. I was born in '52, so yeah, it was always there."

"Not really."

"When were you born?"

"Well, I'm older than ye, see, much older."

"I can tell that you're older, but not that much older."

"Trust me, I'm much older."

"What year were you born? I told you the year I was born."

Colin chuckled. "I think ye'd be surprised how much older I am than yez."

"I don't think so. You look really good to me. I like older men, anyway."

"Likely, not this much older, Trish."

She laughed. "What is this? A man doesn't want to tell his age? Usually blokes don't care."

"If I told ye, lets just say, ye wouldn't fancy me anymore."

She sprung out of bed and pressed her naked body against his. "Lets just say I'll always fancy you."

"Alright, if it makes such a difference to yez, here goes. I was born February 1$^{st}$, 1868."

Her eyes widened. "Huh?"

"Aye, I'm one hundred 'n two years old. I think I'm much too old for yez. Likely, yer parents wouldn't approve."

He gave her a slight bow, kissed her hand and left. She fell to the floor, flat on her face.

He turned to the face the rest of the disheveled house. His eyes widened when he took notice of the shamble. He stepped over sleeping bodies; some dressed, some not. Amoli was sleeping by herself in the corner. He made his way to her, where he tried to avoid stepping on food, spilled beer, and soda pop on the floor. He stood over-

260

looking Amoli. Her eyes opened and she smiled when she saw him.

"Lass, are ye alright?"

"Look at this place. It's disgusting. Of course, I'm not alright," she said.

"Where's Rosa 'n Sasha at?"

She began to cry. He took her in his arms and held her. "Lass, did they leave this house?"

"I don't know. Everybody was dancing and smoking those strange cigarettes. There was a lot of alcohol. You drank a lot, as usual. Then you went off with that girl."

He took her arm. "Walk with me a bit, lass."

They exited the house.

Colin caressed her in his arms. "Where would Rosa be at, I wonder?"

They stood on the sidewalk in front of the house.

"She could have left last night's escapde and maybe she went to the time machine."

"Why would she venture to the time machine without us?" Colin asked.

Amoli continued to cry. "She said something like that. I don't really remember. She was angry."

"Angry?"

"Yes, at Dr. Dimitrikov's behavior. He wasn't himself last night."

Colin held her tighter in his arms. "Aye, he wasn't; surely, he wasn't."

"All I know is these time travel expeditions are taking their toll on me. He had sex with that girl, and then after that, I don't know anymore."

Her crying intensified.

"We're separated again. I don't see *The Neanderthal*, either. He could be runnin' about London. I don't know anymore, lass."

He held her closely. She continued to cry. His head hung down, flustered with frustration.

"What you do here?" Sasha asked, as he appeared. He staggered a bit and held his head. "I sick. Not good. I not know these cigarettes."

"Ye smoked marijuana, ye feckhead. Why'd ye smoke so much?"

"I not smoke so much in fifteenth century. I need it."

"Where's Rosa at?" Colin asked.

Sasha appeared confused. "Rosa? I not know."

Colin took hold of Sasha's arms and violently shook him. "Where's Rosa at?"

Sasha pulled back. "I not know this information. Why you not know? What did you do instead?"

Colin sighed with frustration and stared at the puke-coated porch. "I got drunk – again."

"Hah! You see? You are bad man like I! You no saint, Mr. Limmerick. Far from that, da?"

"Look, nobody's claimin' to be a saint. I just want Rosa with us 'n I feel completely responsible for *the Neanderthal* roamin' about."

"Colin, let me guess, you got drunk and then you slept with that girl, right?" Amoli asked.

Colin's knees were bent, so he could face Amoli. He paused before he answered, with his lips parted. "Aye, lass."

Amoli started to cry again. "I've had it with you! I can never marry you!" She ran back into the house.

Colin continued to stare at the ground.

"I must say, Mr. Limmerick, girls are great fun in 1970. I think I want to stay here."

"I'd stay for the Penicillian. I'm always gettin' sick, workin' on the ship 'n such."

"Don't be so sad, Mr. Limmerick, Rosa is grown up lady and she can take care of herself."

"And what about *the Neanderthal*, hmm?"

"Now, that is other story."

262

# Chapter Twenty-Nine

Rosa walked the streets in a rage and panicked state. She crossed the road and was almost hit by a car. Rosa noticed briefly that the driver was a woman; and blared her horn at Rosa. She was startled, but continued to walk in her flowing fifteenth century dress. She peered at some of the store windows and ogled the women's fashions. She entered one of the stores and enamored herself with sample fragrances, make up, and jewelry.

"Can I help you?" asked a mature saleswoman.

Rosa stared at her. She primped her hair and cleared her throat.

"No, I'm just looking," Rosa appeared as if she was going to walk away, but didn't.

The saleswoman smiled at Rosa. "I must say that I think your dress is beautiful."

"Thank-you," Rosa said with uneasiness in her voice.

"Where did you get it?"

"The fifteenth century."

"Never heard of it. Is it a name of a clothing shop?"

"Shop?"

"Yes, it sounds like it could be, but if you're not sure what I'm talking about, then you obviously made your purchase somewhere else."

The woman giggled. "You appear as if you lost something?"

"I'm actually with three other people, actually four other people, well three other people and um, um, um another being of sort. They seemed to have got out of control at a party."

"Really? Were they doing that dope that young people do today?"

"Dope?"

"Why, yes. It has taken hold of so many young people. The times are changing rapidly, I must say. Who can keep up? Now, everyone owns a color television, can you imagine?"

"N, I can't."

"Everyone seems to have at least two televisions. Many, so I hear, are stashing their black and whites in their basement. Things are moving much too fast."

"Color, huh?"

*\*\**

Colin walked briskly through the streets of London in 1970, dressed in fifteenth century attire. Amoli and Sasha followed also dressed in their five hundred year old fashion. Several people stared at them, but Colin was focused on finding Rosa and the *Neanderthal*.

"Slow down, Mr. Limmerick! You walk too fast!" Sasha requested.

"Concerned is what I damn well am, for the sake of Jesus Christ!"

"Slow down!" Sasha shouted.

"Alright, then. What's wrong with us?" Colin shouted back.

"What you mean?"

"Are we such fools that we can't stay together?"

Amoli had to run in order to keep up with Colin's pace.

"We're not to stray from each other, if we yern to return to 1910, don't ye think?"

"Mr. Limmerick maybe you need whiskey to calm down."

"Everytime I drink, I get meself in trouble. What good is that, eh?"

Amoli hid behind Sasha, she focused on the busy streets and the towering double decker buses. She also noticed the *Neanderthal* crossing at the light, blending in with the crowd. "Oh, my! Stop the bickering, gentlemen! I think I spotted the *Neanderthal!*"

Colin and Sasha immediately turned their heads to where Amoli was pointing.

"Good God!" Colin blurted. Colin and Sasha ran to the street, not realizing how much more dense the traffic was with cars from what they could remember from 1910. Colin and Sasha jumped in front of a double decker bus, the bus stopped immediately, where the driver stepped out to face the two time travelers.

"Look at the way you two are dressed! Do you always run infront of buses?" The driver asked.

Sasha appeared as if he was about to respond, Colin pulled him away and they continued to follow the Neanderthal in the crowd.

"This is no bullshit time, mate. Keep yer wisecrack remarks to yer bleedin' self."

The two time travelers ran through the crowded streets of London, where people would get in their way and gawk over their style of dress. Amoli remained on the sidewalk and decided to wait for their return.

"Hey!" Colin called to the ancient primate, as he was almost out of breath.

"Hey! Monkey man! Turn your head!" Sasha called.

Colin turned to Sasha and tugged on his arm as they continued to run. "If I hear ye say that again, I swear I'll punch the bleedin' lights outta ye!" Colin managed to pull onto *the Neanderthal's* arm. The ancient primate appeared surprised and threatened. It quickly turned to Colin and thrashed him to the pavement. Innocent bystanders quickly sputtered off in a panic with screams of terror. Colin who is tall, robust, and packed with muscle had just been thrashed to the ground.

Sasha stood beside Colin. "Mr. Limmeirck, are you alright?"

Colin felt almost faint. "Mate, help me up."

"Beast run away, now what?"

Colin stood up to realize his back hurt. "Don't think I'll survive this time travel expedition much longer, mate. A man of me own size can't deal with this much physical abuse, wouldn't ye say?"

"I not know how this beast is so much smaller than you and can throw you to ground, da?"

"There's a simple answer to yer question, mate. It's a *Neanderthal* 'n I'm not.*"* Sasha helped Colin up. Colin winched with pain as he stared into the crowd. "He's got away, no doubt."

"So what? It is not worth you getting slammed by monkey man."

Colin sighed with frustration. "Stop callin' im that. It's getting' on me nerves, rather." Colin hobbled to take a step.

"Excuse me, sir, but are you alright?" A middle-aged woman asked. "I just witnessed that you have been badly hurt by that person who just ran off."

Sasha glanced at Colin. "Person? Who? What person?"

"Is this man your friend?" The woman asked.

"Da, he is."

"Shall I notify the police? Do you know the man who just did this to you?"

"Colin chuckled. "Man?"

"Maybe I'll go to that phone booth and ring the authorities."

Colin and Sasha stared at the phone booth.

Colin glanced at Sasha. "I must say our red telephone boxes have changed in their appearance, wouldn't ye say, mate?"

"Nyet. It look the same to me."

Colin took the woman's hand and kissed it. "Yer very kind, but there's no need to trouble yerself."

She giggled like a schoolgirl. "Oh, my, I suppose chivalry still exists."

"Don't most gents act t this way?"

266

"Not at all, it's like you're from a different time. Is that why you're wearing those clothes?"

Colin scanned his own body. "Actors! That's what we are. Actors."

Sasha chuckled. "We are not good actors but it is what we do."

***

Amoli leaned against the wall of a building, waiting for Colin and Sasha's return. She kept her eyes on the crowds of people that passed her by, hoping she would see the *Neanderthal*.

"What are you waiting for?" Rosa asked.

"Oh! Miss Emanuel, Colin and Dr. Dimitrikov are looking for you."

"They were having too much fun with those people. I really don't know why they've suddenly felt that I'm so important?"

"I detect that you are angry with them?'

"Furious is more the word."

"The *Neanderthal* has gone somewhere."

Rosa's eyes widened. "Oh, really?"

"They're not only looking for you but they're also looking for *the Neanderthal*."

"Really?"

Amoli's eyes brows raised. "Miss Emanuel? Don't you care anymore?"

"Care, Amoli? Why no, I think my days of caring for those two men are long over. Actually, I've quite had it with their ridiculous behavior. They act like children."

"You can't mean that, I know that you love them very much."

"Love, Amoli? I'm not quite sure what you're referring to. I don't think those two men are capable much of anything."

267

"I actually stopped at a tiny café and had a bight to eat. It was rather charming, where I noticed some desent orderly people. Not everyone of 1970 is so out of their minds, as those women, Trish and *Free*, and their disgusting gentlemen friends."

"I didn't like them either."

"They smelled."

"Sasha smoked marijuana with *the Neanderthal* and they got high together. Is Sasha a man? Not really, he's more like a fool. He's definitely not a scientist."

"Fool? No, Miss Emanuel, I think you're just very angry."

"No, Amoli Sharma, I'm beyond disgust with those two. And, as for Colin, well, I think I should keep my thoughts to myself on that one."

"If we wait here, they should come back."

Rosa threw her arms in the air. "Fine! We can wait for them."

***

Colin and Sasha noticed a gathered crowd. There was music, which lured people. Colin's height gave him the advantage of seeing over most people's heads. He noticed two young women dressed in t-shirts were dancing. Their long straight hair swayed from side to side. They were also dressed in flared-bottom trousers. Colin was already used to seeing women dressed that way, but then he took a second look to notice that *the Neanderthal* was dancing with them. People were throwing money at them.

"What you see, Mr. Limmerick?" Sasha asked standing on his tiptoes.

"Well, I'm just not surprised at anyhin' anymore, mate."

"What you see?"

" Our beast of ours is dancin' for money, if ye can believe it?"

"Maybe he make great money to do this, da?"

"He's twenty-eight thousand years old, mate. He's not supposed to be dancin' for money in the latter part of the tweintieth century, don't ye think?"

"So? I'm ninety-two years old, am I supposed to be doing this?"

"When we return to our time, you won't be ninety-two years old, ye wanker!"

"So now what we do? What if monkey man not want to come with us? He will smash your face, da?"

"Most definitely."

"Then what? All ladies like your beautiful face, then what?"

"Well, he can't stay here."

"I say, leave him here. Who cares?"

"I've gotta get him to come with us to the time machine 'n we need to get back to our time."

"So, go and disturb him. He is having great time with two ladies dressed like men. Do it, go!"

"We haven't the choice."

"Say good-bye to your beautiful face, Mr. Limmerick."

Colin pushed himself through the crowd. Some of the crowd appeared bothered and offended by Colin's aggressive behavior. Colin lunged at *the Neanderthal's* arm and pulled him away from the spectators. *The Neanderthal* appeared angry; he made certain sounds and gestures. Colin braced himself for a hard blow. *The Neanderthal* grabbed Colin's bulging bicep and shoved him with force, where Colin fell on several people. Colin was a bit stunned but managed to pick himself up. He stood straight and jumped onto *the Neanderthal* and pinned him to the ground. Some of the spectators screamed and ran away. Colin sat on *the Neanderthal* and used every bit of his strength to pin the beast to the ground.

Sasha stood behind Colin and tried to hold the beast's flailing feet, which were almost too powerful for Sasha to grip.

"Sasha, get some rope? We gotta get his hands tied behind his back, or he'll surely kill me! I'm holdin' down with every bit of strength, here!"

"You are beast as well! I must try to get rope! I'll be back!" Sasha ran through the crowd, where he noticed Amoli and Rosa standing on the opposite side of the street. He ran to them almost out of breath.

Rosa's arms were folded in front of her. "Well, well, if it isn't *mister try anything*, why are you in such a fluster?"

"Stop such child behavior!" Sasha panted with exhaustion.

"Huh! Child's behavior? Look who's calling the kettle black?"

"Mr. Limmerick is now sitting on monkey man. Monkey man is too strong. Mr. Limmerick must have rope to tie monkey man hands? Claws? I not know what!"

Rosa appeared concerned. "Oh! Where can we get some rope?"

"A shop!" Amoli blurted.

"Yes, but not all shops sell rope, Amoli!" Rosa responded curtly.

"Go buy rope, or ask policeman! I not know! Mr. Limmerick will be killed by monkey man!"

"Oh! We must get some rope! I'm going to ask that policeman over there!" Amoli screamed with angst.

"Go!" Sasha shouted back.

Amoli ran to the police officer; Rosa watched the officer walk Amoli to his car, open his trunk and hand her some rope.

\*\*\*

270

When Sasha, Rosa, and Amoli ran to Colin, they saw a crowd of people with police cars and swat teams,. The time travelers cut through the crowd to find *the Neanderthal* handcuffed and Colin lying on the sidewalk drenched in blood.

Rosa and Amoli covered their eyes.

"No! Tell me, Sasha! Is he alive or dead?" Rosa squeeled.

Sasha walked up to Colin. He glanced at the police officer. "What happen, here?"

"This *thing*, or *being*, or whatever, may have killed this man. Do you know this man?"

"Da, he is friend. Is he dead?"

The constable kneeled beside Colin to see if he was alive. "Yes, he is still breathing and he has a pulse. I have called for an abulance. He really needs to be sent to Emergency at the hostial."

Sasha glanced at Rosa and Amoli, with a slight grin.

"Mr. Limmerick need this very much," Sasha said. "Where you take monkey man?"

"Jail. Do you know him as well?" The constable asked.

"Not fortunate, but da," Sasha responded.

The time travels watched Colin be carried off on a stretcher and into an ambulance.

*** 

The following morning, Rosa opened her eyes to realize she was in a 1970s hotel room. She noticed Amoli and Sasha were still very much asleep in individual twin beds.

She made her way to the window, which faced the hospital Colin was in.

Sasha lifted his head from the pillow. "Why you up so early? You must sleep."

"I can't sleep knowing Colin is in the hospital and *the Neanderthal* is in jail. Don't get me wrong, Colin needed to be in a hospital long ago."

"Be glad he is in 1970s hospital because technology is better. He will be good as new, da?"

"Hopefully," she continued to gaze out the window. "How can we get the *Neanderthal* out of jail?"

"I think we need to pay bail," Sasha said. "That makes me so angry because I not even like monkey man."

"No matter what, Colin will pay the bail, knowing him."

"He should get his boat fixed instead."

"Maybe you're right, Sasha. When will Colin ever stop playing God?"

"Forget it!" Sasha sat up in bed and lit a cigarette. "This is who Mr. Limmerick is, he must play God."

"Well," she sighed. "We'll see if Colin can leave the hospital and he will definitely pay *the Neanderthal's* bail. Then, we can go to the time machine and venture home."

\*\*\*

Finally, they made it to their time travel exporter. Amoli took *the Neanderthal's* hand and led him to step inside the time machine. She placed its hands on the handles. She remained silent and pleasant at all times. Sasha set the dial to 1910 AD, and it started to spin. *The Neanderthal* shouted and yelped with confusion.

The time machine began to slowly rock from side to side. It shook and spun. Amoli felt uneasy, she glanced at *the Neaderthal* and took its hand for reassurance. Colin had his knees bent and felt the machine rock and spin, which made him dizzy and nauseous. The machine levitated from the ground. The spinning motion grew faster, where it gave a sharp spinning sound. Amoli held *the Neanderthal's* hand and squeezed it tight. The machine spun through time, bumping, shaking, rattling and banging. *The Neaderthal* squealed, but Amoli kept squeezing its hand to reassure it. The machine spun through the vortex of time. It spun like a spool with hard banging sounds that made *the Neanderthal* jolt with fear. Wind and turbulation filtered through the machine, but the time travelers continued to hold on. *The Neanderthal* held on with fear, but Amoli stood by its side. Rosa noticed how Sasha wore a fiendish grin on his face, almost as if he were the doctor Jekyll.

They finally landed. This time the machine toppled over on its side. The four time travelers were awake and aware the moment the machine hit ground. Rosa tried to climb out of the debris. Sasha pulled himself out. He stood beside the machine, curious to get a glimpse of the state of their prehistoric primate. *The Neanderthal* was motionless. Amoli looked at Sasha and put her hand out for him to pull her out of the machine. Colin sat up, and brushed debris off his body.

"Mate, is our speciman doin' well?" Colin asked.

Sasha knelt beside it to listen to its heart. "It is alive, Mr. Limmerick."

Colin crawled to *the Neanderthal*. "Thank God."

Rosa tried to exit the machine without help. "Well, Sasha? What year are we in?"

Sasha looked at the dial. "It is 1910. Can you not see around you? Grass is not lawn, it is grass, da?"

Colin smiled. "I'm supposin' we gotta take our ancient primate to the lab at the university, shouldn't we?"

The four time travelers walked the streets of London in late autumn 1910. Several people gawked at the time traveler's fifteenth century attire. Not one person took notice of the prehistoric beast as it causually stepped into the university lab with them. The four of them sat on the lab stools and watched *the Neanderthal* search the lab for food.

"Sasha, fetch some food for the poor beast," Rosa commanded.

"What do caveman eat?" Sasha asked, shrugging his shoulders.

"Likely, some raw meat, fish, 'n berries, if possible," Colin responded. "Also, bring some water. He's likely parched from such a hard day."

*The Neanderthal* knocked a few beakers on the floor, which made a crashing sound.

"Shh," Colin expressed to the beast, with his finger to his lips.

Timothy Duncan stormed into the lab.

"I heard a noise. Did something break?"

Colin sat on one of the stools and dragged his fingers through his hair. "Aye, aye, so ye did, Timothy," Colin responded, with a sigh of frustration.

"What is that?" Timothy expressed, pointing his finger at the beast.

"What's it look like to yez?"

Timothy took a few steps closer. He noticed Rosa sitting on a stool. He scanned her appearance, and then looked at the beast. He, then, glanced at Colin. "What is this *thing?* And, were you and your friends off to a costume party?"

Colin stared at the floor. "Likely."

Colin took a few steps toward Timothy. "We was just in the middle of somethin', if ye don't mind me sayin'. There are three other labortaries on this floor. Sorry for the inconvenience."

"Did you just time travel?" Timothy asked feeling confused.

"We did."

"Fine, I'll leave, but you can't have that *thing* roaming the campus. You know that, don't you, Limmerick?"

"I'm very well aware of that, Timothy. Please, now, could ye please use another lab?"

Timothy leered at *the Neanderthal*, then he leered at Colin and left.

"He's going to eat you out of house and home, Colin," Rosa mentioned.

Sasha returned with a large paper grocery bag filled with food. He placed it on one of the lab tables and the creature took notice instantly. Sasha looked at the prehistoric beast.

"You want? Come, I buy food for you. Eat."

*The Neanderthal* walked to the bag of groceries. It stared at Sasha and grabbed the bag. It sat on the floor and tore away at the food. Rosa glanced at Colin.

"Hmm, it even ate the wrapping. Interesting."

Amoli sat with the beast and tried to demonstrate how to get at the food without eating the paper wrapping. Colin smiled.

"I was plannin' on venturin' back in time to when *Neanderthals* lived, ye know. I think that would be the right thing to do, so I should."

"So, you would be traveling twenty-eight thousand years ago," Rosa confirmed.

"Aye."

"I need to fix time machine first. It take us to 1487 and then 1970. I must find why it do this, da?"

"It's exhausting me to even think about another time travel expedition," Rosa commented.

Sasha slid his arm around her. "You not have to go."

"I think I must go because who will keep you two on task?"

# Chapter Thirty

The first snow of the new season fell on the busy streets of London. It was December and Colin sat at his typewriter by his apartment window and watched the snow trickle down. There was a faint knock at the door. He swung it opened to find Rosa standing there wearing a fur coat. She entered without asking.

"I must speak with you."

"Where'd ye get the fur?"

"It's from Russia."

"Would ye like to sit a bit, love?"

"Love?" She removed her gloves and threw them on the couch. "You can no longer use that as my nickname. My name is Rosa, not *love.*"

"Is something the matter?" He walked to his liquer cabinet and poured himself a glass of whiskey.

"Colin, first, I want to know if *Neanderthal* is alright?"

"He's in that cage I built for 'im in the laboratory. Why?"

"I want to show you something." She placed her hand in front of him. He was startled to see a diamond ring on her finger. He took her hand.

"Sasha proposed to me."

His lips were parted.

She pulled her hand away from him. "Colin, I think it's the right thing to do. Sasha says he loves me. I suppose I love him."

He slowly sat down. "I see."

"Well? Is it alright with you?"

Colin grimaced. "Yer askin' me permission? I'm not yer bleedin' father. Ye wanna marry a married man, 'n create bigamy, go the feck ahead. It's fine by me."

"Bigamy? Sasha said its over with his wife in Russia."

Colin lifted his eyebrows. "Over? So, he feckin' well says."

"I didn't want to even tell you, because I know what kind of a temper you have, especially when you've been drinking."

He stood up and paced the room. He rubbed his hands over his face. "Yer makin' a serious mistake. Ye know, it's over with me 'n Amoli. She did make up her mind not to pursue our relationship anymore. I kinda thought ye 'n I still had a chance. Ye wanted me back, so ye kept pushin'."

"No, you and I will never be."

He stood straight and placed his hands on his hips.

"You are always sleeping with some ancient woman from past centuries, or somebody from the future."

"Rosa, do as ye wish. I've got me own problems. It's your life."

She picked up her gloves. "Well, I've had enough of you tonight."

He stepped close to grab her. He tore off her fur coat and pressed her body against the wall. He jammed his tongue down her throat and continued to kiss her for a good while. She wrapped her arms around his neck, where her legs lifted and locked around his body. He pulled off her blouse with the buttons flying to the floor. He threw off his shirt and pressed his bare chest against her tiny breasts. Before she knew it, her panties were lying on the floor. She could feel his erect penis enter.

"Colin! Stop! No!"

He pulled away. "What ye mean?

She tried to catch her breath. He stopped what he was doing and pulled out. He took a deep breath and sighed with frustration. She tried to calm herself.

277

"I know that this isn't the right thing for us to do. We've become good friends. If we go through with it," she took another breath, "we'll destroy everything we built."

"Everything', what?"

"Colin, my love for you is too strong to describe. I've never known love like this."

He kissed the side of her long neck. "Then, what's the problem?"

"Amoli."

He pulled back. He stared at the floor in silence. "I know you never stopped loving me. I know you're very attracted to me as well, but Amoli is who you really want." She began to cry. "I can't even hate her, because she's so young and sweet. I've come to know her on these time travel expeditions. I wish I could hate her, because she's the real reason you and I are not together." Her crying intensified.

He took Rosa in his arms. "I'll never stop lovin' ye. I love ye with all me heart. Ye mean a great deal to me, but yer right 'bout Amoli. She doesn't want me anymore, though. What am I to do?"

"Colin, she's an immature, spoiled little girl. She's confused. She doesn't know what she's doing. Give her some time to think things over."

Rosa cried in his arms. He caressed her and kissed her several times.

"Ye know what, love?" He appeared a bit startled by his thoughts. "I was just about to get to the lab to feed *Neanderthal*. Sure hope he's not bustin' the place down."

"Are you late on *Neanderthal's* feeding schedule? Isn't Sasha helping you?"

"He could be in the lab right now workin' on the time machine. Who knows?"

"You better get your trousers on and feed *Neanderthal.*" Colin struggled to dress himself in a matter of seconds. She threw her fur coat over her shoulders. "I'm coming with you."

278

She followed him out the door. They ran across the street, where they tried not to slip on the icy roads. They ran up the stairs in the Natural History building. There were screams, and people running. Several file cabinets went crashing down the staircase. Colin and Rosa looked at each other as they made their way to the lab. *Neanderthal* had torn opened the cage Colin had built. Sasha was encouraging spectators to leave the building. Colin had to dodge flying beakers, test tubes, and filing cabinets.

"Rosa, get outta here. It's too dangerous!" he shouted.

Rosa made her way to the opposite corner of the room.

"I'm not leaving until everything settles down."

Colin confronted *Neanderthal*. "Okay, sorry, mate. Brought ye some food, so I did."

He placed the bag of groceries on the floor. His arms were ready for any kind of attack. Neanderthal calmed down when he took notice of the food. He tore the bag of groceries to shreds and began his feast. Colin glanced at Rosa and took a deep breath. Sasha managed to get university students and professors to leave the building. He had returned to the laboratory. He walked to Rosa and placed his arm around her. He kissed her lips. Colin was more focused on *Neanderthal*. Sasha and Rosa watched him eat his breakfast.

"*Neanderthal* must be on a strict feeding schedule," Rosa instilled.

Colin caught a glimpse of Sasha kissing Rosa.

"No doubt, but it's not as if we's experts at somethin' like this. We's gonna have to adjust our lives maybe."

"Mr. Limmerick I will be on shiftwork for this thing some days, but not always. Weekends you are on your ship. You cannot expect me to mind this thing always on weekends."

"Fine, I'll very well bring *Neanderthal* on me bleedin' ship, so be it."

Rosa stepped close to Colin. "You can't be serious? You can't bring this creature on your trawler. That would be utter chaos."

"It's all I can do."

"Think of your crew. Your first mate, Eddy. You can't expect them to understand all of this," Rosa pleaded.

"You make big mistake taking this thing to 1910. You should have left it in 1970 to die," Sasha commented, while lighting a cigarette.

Colin turned to him with an expression of anger on his face. "What ye sayin', man? What was I to do? I couldn't leave this primitive primate in 1970. Are you mad?"

"I am man of logic. You, Mr. Limmerick, are not."

Colin stepped toward Sasha and stared at him.

"Ye got yerself a wife in Russia. What ye doin' proposin' marriage to Rosa? Ye must be fecked in the head. Whose got the logic?"

"I not want my wife. I hate her. I want Rosa."

Colin took a deep breath. "What ye sayin'? Ye don't even know what yer sayin'. If ye truly love Rosa, ye'd keep her as a friend. Besides, ye smoke too many fags."

"Rosa, she want me, I know. We will marry and have babies. She will take care of them and I will be university researcher, da?"

Colin shoved Sasha. "Yer such a feckhead! How do ye live with yerself?"

"I live with myself fine. It is you who cannot."

Colin glanced at the calandar on the wall. "Feck, it's Thursday. I've got to get meself to me ship at the harbor. I'll be takin' *Neanderthal* with me. I'll be back Monday mornin' at the latest, so I will."

*Neanderthal* had just finished eating.

\*\*\*

The Atlantic Mermaid docked at Fishgaurd Harbor. The first mate waved at Colin as he lowered the gangway. Colin and *Neanderthal* stepped onto the ship. Eddy smiled at his captain. His smile dissipated when he noticed the *Neanderthal* follow Colin onto the gangway.

"Well, what do we have here, Captain?" Eddy expressed, as he watched the prehistoric creature follow Colin onto the ship.

Colin stopped in front of Eddy. "Mate, do me a favor, don't want ye or any of the crew to even ask me 'bout the mate who just walked upon the ship, is that clear?"

"Captain, but can you just tell me what it is?"

"I won't do that, Ed."

THE END

THE END.